Broken Dreams

Book Eight of the Barrington Family Series

Chris Taylor

LCT Productions Pty Limited

Other books by Chris Taylor

The Munro Family Series
(in order)

The Profiler
The Investigator
The Predator
The Betrayal
The Deception
The Negotiator
The Christmas Vigil (A novella)
The Ransom
The Defendant
The Shooting
The Maker

CHRIS TAYLOR

The Sydney Harbour Hospital Series (in order)

The Perfect Husband
The Body Thief
The Baby Snatchers
The Final Bullet
The Debt Collector
The Lab Test
The Stolen Identity
The Cliff-top Killer
The Likeable Fraudster

The Sydney Legal Series (in order)

An Accidental Murderer
At the Hand of her Father
A Woman Scorned
Lies and Deception
Ordinary Evil
The Ties that Bind
The Perfect Crime
A Toxic Inheritance
Malicious Love

The Craigdon Family Series
(in order)

Callum
Joel

Isabella
Nicholas
Sophia
Flynn
Noah
Logan
Elizabeth

The Barrington Family Series
(in order)

Broken Lives
Broken Promises
Broken Bonds
Broken Spirits
Broken Minds
Broken Vows
Broken Hearts
Broken Dreams
Broken Homes

The Fairfax Family Series (in order)

A Cattleman in Disguise
A Cattleman's Quest
A Cattleman's Daughter
A Cattleman's Secret Baby
To Catch a Cattleman
The Doctor and the Cattleman

To Rescue a Cattleman
A Cattleman's Heart
For the Love of a Cattleman

Bachelors and Brides Series (in order)

Matilda
Austin
Farrah
Benjamin
Verity
Denver
Ebony
Tyrone
Willow

Books by Chris Taylor
Writing as
Bella
Christian

This Is Where It Ends Series
(in order)

Jessie's Story
Ryan's Story
Holly's Story
Sarah's Story
Veronica's Story

Love audiobooks? Check out Chris Taylor Books on audio
iTunes Amazon   Audible
Join Chris Taylor's Facebook reader group/fan page and be among the
first to receive news of book releases, read and review books prior to release
and other amazing offers.

Join Now!

LCT Productions Pty Limited

18364 Kamilaroi Highway, Narrabri NSW 2390

ISBN: 9781925441130 (eBook)

ISBN: 9781925441147 (Print)

BROKEN DREAMS

Broken Dreams is a work of fiction. Names, places, characters, brands, media and incidents are either the product of the author's imagination or are used fictitiously. Any resemblance to persons living or dead, events or locales is entirely coincidental.

This book is dedicated to my son, Angus. Thank you for being a wonderful son and role model to your siblings. And thank you for your expertise and knowledge of the mining industry! I love you.
And as always, to my husband, Linden. Without your love and support, this book writing dream of mine wouldn't be possible. I love you to the moon and back.

Chapter One

Hannah Barrington's spontaneous outburst of delight was almost loud enough to rattle the glass in the windowpanes of her modest site office. She was glad she'd taken the time to close her door. It wouldn't be good for her image for anyone to overhear her jubilation.

"Oh, my goodness! Molly, you're engaged! That's wonderful news!"

"I'm glad you think so," Molly replied, sounding happier than Hannah had ever heard her.

Hannah's older sister was a paramedic attached to a busy Sydney hospital. She'd met her fiancé, Shane Lucas, on the job. He wasn't a colleague, but a former patient who'd been involved in a nasty motor vehicle accident. Thank God the other driver had finally come forward to the police.

"So, have you set a date?" Hannah asked.

"Of course not. I don't want to give Mom and Dad a heart attack. They've only just witnessed Christopher and Lexi pledging their lives to each other. Then there's Zac and Emily. Have you forgotten they're getting married next month?"

"That's right. The day before Christmas." Hannah sighed. "I guess that's kind of romantic."

"Yes, as long as it's not too hot. December can sometimes be a scorcher. At least they won't have any trouble remembering their anniversary date," Molly replied.

Hannah chuckled. She was thrilled for her sister. At twenty-six, Molly had been well and truly ready to find love. She'd never had a serious boyfriend. Not even in high school. Hannah wasn't quite sure why. Molly was gorgeous, inside and out. She'd been popular enough with the boys. But somehow, she hadn't ever hooked up with anyone. Now she sounded smitten.

Hannah wasn't surprised. She'd seen the way Molly and Shane had been at Christopher and Lexi's wedding. They couldn't take their eyes off each other. Now they were engaged. Hannah was happy for them. She might shudder at the thought of matrimony and the level of commitment that required, but she could be happy about the institution when it came to her siblings.

Seven of her eight brothers and sisters had recently found love. For all she knew, her adopted brother, Vaughan, might also have found his soul mate. Perhaps that's what had kept him all these months in Bali. Why else would he have stayed away so long?

It was enough to make her a little anxious that the love bug might be lurking in her vicinity. Molly had been the last person Hannah would have expected to fall in love. She'd be best to steer well clear of such an affliction herself. Love would only tie her down. It would mean having to take into account someone else's feelings, consult with someone else outside of her work. Share the TV remote. Heaven help her! Her life would be irrevocably changed. No, she was more than happy playing the field. She'd leave the love game to her siblings.

As she wished Molly well and ended the call, Hannah picked up the framed photo off her desk of herself, Molly, and their sister, Charlotte. They all looked alike, the three of them with dark hair and blue eyes. They took after their mother. But that's where their similarities ended. Charlotte was a hard-nosed homicide detective who didn't take nonsense from anyone. Molly had always had her heart set on helping people. She'd headed off to university to study paramedics straight out of high school. Hannah, on the other hand, had graduated with no goal in mind. She'd flitted in and out of work, going from one job to another. She'd tried waitressing, secretarial work, dog grooming, she'd been a receptionist for an insurance company, and had even done a short stint as a pastry chef. She loved to bake and had learned from one of the best. Her mother was an excellent baker. Oh, and of course, she couldn't forget the law degree. She'd gotten halfway through that before she'd lost interest and dropped out.

Hannah sighed. Although she'd enjoyed each job and at least some of the subjects she'd studied at law school, nothing had held her attention for long. This was the reason why her father, despairing his youngest child would never settle down to a career and make her mark on the world, had offered her a job at one of his mines.

Strathwaylin was a coal mine situated in the picturesque Hunter Valley, a couple of hours' drive north of Sydney. It was only one in the string of mines owned by her father. Frank Barrington made his fortune in mining. He now offered his daughter the same opportunity, coming onboard as the head of his safety department at Strathwaylin.

Hannah had been intrigued at the thought of working in a mine. Though she had no experience in mining, she'd always been good with people, and she firmly believed managing any kind of business came down to people management. Besides, how hard could it be?

A little over twelve months later and she realized there was a lot more to being group manager for workplace, health, safety, and training than she'd first thought. The mountain of regulatory compliance, the ever-present need for overseeing safety, the massaging of male egos who were put out at having a woman in charge... It had been a battle, but one she found she enjoyed. The need to prove herself in what was a traditionally male-dominated industry was a daily challenge. It was a good thing she liked to be tested.

It was the same for her relationships. Though she'd managed to steer well clear of the love bug, that didn't mean she hadn't enjoyed herself since graduating high school. There had been so many boyfriends over the past five years. It was like she was trying to make up for lost time. Like her sexuality had only just awakened and she was determined to explore it to the fullest.

Some relationships, like the one she'd enjoyed with Derek Finnigan late in the twelfth grade, lasted no more than a couple of weeks. Derek had been her first, but unsurprisingly they had gone their separate ways right after graduation. Others had been more enduring. The longest relationship she'd had was her last one.

She'd had high hopes for Chad. He was a marketing manager in a large advertising firm in Sydney. Tall, good looking, and with the sexiest laugh, he'd ticked a lot of boxes. They had a lot in common. They both enjoyed outdoor activities, country music, and dancing. He also liked to read, something Hannah enjoyed but hardly found the time for these days.

Unfortunately, after only four months, Chad had gone the way of all her other relationships. She'd realized one day that though she enjoyed his company, and he wasn't too bad in bed, she was discontented and yearned for something more. She didn't exactly know what the "something more" entailed, but she could tell she didn't have it with Chad.

Another one bites the dust...

The thought of having to seek out a new boyfriend didn't faze her. In fact, the chase was the most exciting part. Navigating the early stages of any new relationship filled her with anticipation. The nerves, the eagerness, the expectation... And the fun! She couldn't forget how much fun it was to start a new relationship.

The fact most of her siblings had found their soul mates and were headed for marital bliss didn't concern her. She loved that they were all so happy and ready to settle down and she knew just as well that she wasn't interested in being tied down. She loved having a boyfriend, someone to talk to, hang out with, but they didn't have to be her soul mate. She wasn't looking for Mr Forever. She was perfectly fine being with a sexy and fun Mr Right Now.

Someone like my open cut examiner, Nathan Garcia…

Now, he was a sight for sore eyes. The OCE had coal-black hair and laughing brown eyes that spoke to his Spanish heritage. A smile that made her pulse race. Broad shoulders, narrow hips, and a glint in his eyes that hinted at naughty things. The only problem was, he was her colleague, and she had a strict rule about dating people she worked with. When the relationship ended, as it inevitably would, things would get awkward. And in a high stakes work environment where she needed people focused, collaborative, and cooperative, that would be a disaster.

Still, she mused, if anyone could persuade her that he was worth breaking her self-imposed rule, it was Nathan. He'd been at the mine for almost as long as she had. From the beginning, she'd been aware of his interest. So far, she hadn't given him any encouragement, but now she wondered whether it might be time to change that. They'd been working closely together for months and she trusted his professionalism. Could they keep work and play separate?

As if she'd conjured him up, Nathan filled the open doorway to her office. Despite the fact he could have no way of knowing her thoughts, she blushed. Flustered, she opened the file on her desk and pretended interest in the typed pages. Nathan gave a perfunctory knock and entered. She forced herself to look up.

"Nathan. What can I do for you?" Belatedly she noticed his grim expression. Her stomach lurched. "What is it?"

He compressed his lips and strode farther into the room. He wore the standard garb for a mine worker, no matter their level of seniority, as did she. A fluorescent yellow, high-visibility work shirt and durable navy-blue work pants. He held a mine-issued, white hard hat. "There's been an accident."

Hannah's heart sank. "Oh, no. Not another one."

"Afraid so."

"How bad?"

Nathan blew out his breath. "Not too bad. A collision between an excavator and a dozer. No one injured, luckily. But a decent amount of damage. It'll have to be reported to the regulator."

Hannah grimaced. "Great. Just what we need."

Nathan's expression remained grim. He knew as well as she did what this could mean for the mine. They'd been plagued with a spate of accidents over the past twelve months, starting with the death of Evan Wilson. Despite the complete overhaul of all their safety operations since Evan's fatal accident, incidents continued to happen. Hannah was at a loss as to explain why, but she was determined to get to the bottom of it.

Nathan had a background in workplace health and safety. She'd employed him to be her eyes and ears on the ground. She also hoped his expertise would rub off on her and together, they could put a halt to whoever or whatever was causing the accidents. Safety incidents, no matter how minor, could spell the death of a mine. And she certainly didn't want another fatality.

"Grab your gear and I'll take you to the incident site," Nathan said brusquely.

Hannah nodded, appreciating his no-nonsense approach. She collected her hard hat and high-vis jacket on her way out of her office and followed Nathan to one of the mine's utility trucks. He'd parked a few yards away. Hannah opened the passenger side door of the ute and climbed inside. Nathan took a seat behind the wheel.

"Who was it?" she asked as he headed toward the pit.

"Scott Stonewall was driving the dozer. He's only been with us eight months. Still, he's had years of experience at other mines and has been driving that thing since he got here."

"Who else?"

"Paul Hammond. He was on the excavator."

"Have you spoken to either of them yet? What are they saying?"

"No. I called you as soon as I heard. I'll talk to them when we get there."

Hannah mulled over the information. The last thing they needed was another accident. The fact most of them weren't serious wasn't the issue. Safety was the number one priority at any Barrington mine, any Australian mine for that matter. Strathwaylin was no exception.

Once again, her thoughts turned to Evan Wilson. The tragic accident that had taken his life had happened during her very first day on the job. Though the ensuing litigation had now been settled and due compensation paid to the man's family, the fear of a fatal accident happening at her mine again kept her awake at night.

She might not have earned her position in the mine through sheer hard work and experience, but she was determined to make up for that. Since taking on the role of group safety manager, she'd been unwavering in her resolve to improve the operation safety record. Unfortunately, that record had just taken another hit.

Nathan pulled up beside the two machines. As she surveyed the damage, Hannah couldn't prevent a gasp of alarm. Most of the windscreen of the dozer had been crushed beneath the force of the excavator bucket. She couldn't believe the operator had escaped unharmed. Looking at the extensive damage, that seemed impossible. How it had managed to collide with the other machine was anyone's guess. From what she could see, it was an accident that should never have happened.

She climbed out of Nathan's truck and strode to the men who were gathered nearby. Most had their heads down and their hands jammed in their pockets. As soon as they spied her, they moved farther away, but remained close together, silently closing ranks.

"What happened here?" she demanded in an authoritative voice.

The men shuffled their feet and kept their faces averted. Anger licked at Hannah's belly. She asked the question again. This time, one of the men stepped forward. He had a sly look and a swagger that immediately set Hannah's teeth on edge. She'd seen that kind of attitude before on some of the men in her employ. They resented the fact she'd frog-leaped into a top job merely because she was the mine owner's daughter. They also hated that she was a woman.

To some of the men, women had no place on a mine site. Thank goodness her father wasn't one of them. Barrington mines had a number of women working for them. They were particularly sought after as drivers of the huge dump trucks because they took more patience and care with a role that involved the monotony of carrying the coal from the pit. Repair bills were always lower with a woman behind the wheel.

"Scott here was on the dozer. He called me up and requested permission to come into my swing radius. I acknowledged his request and grounded my bucket. Then I gave him permission to enter. I thought he was well out of the way before I picked up my bucket again and swung it." The man who spoke turned his head sideways and spat a globule of phlegm on the ground. He smirked at Hannah. "Appears I was wrong."

Hannah glared at him, her anger soaring into fury. With an effort, she managed to hold onto her temper and addressed the smirking man. "Appearing wrong doesn't cut it. Mine safety is about the safety of you and your colleagues. Care and precision in all actions is critical at all times. Anyone who *guesses* and *thinks* actions they take are safe has no place on a mine site!"

She turned to Nathan, gritting her teeth. "I want a full written report on my desk before the end of this shift. Understand?"

He nodded. "Of course."

With that, she turned on her heel and strode back to their vehicle, vibrating anger with every step as muttered curses followed in her wake. She pulled herself up into the passenger seat and continued to fume while she waited for Nathan to join her. Fortunately, she didn't have to wait long.

He threw her a sideways look as he switched on the ignition and put the vehicle into gear. "It could have been worse."

"It's not the accident I'm furious about!" she exploded. "It's the attitude! Did you hear what that man said? And his tone! He doesn't give a damn about the damage he's caused to that dozer, let alone the nightmare of paperwork I'm now going to be buried under. On top of that, I'm going to have to deal with the Resources Regulator. Again." She turned to look at Nathan, her breath coming fast. "This shouldn't have happened. There are too many of these incidents happening."

"You're right," he said calmly. "I'll speak to everyone involved. Don't worry, I'll get to the bottom of it."

"And what about the excavator operator? What did you say his name was?"

"Paul Hammond. He's a good operator. A first-class safety record. I don't know what went wrong."

Paul Hammond...

The name imprinted itself on Hannah's mind. The arrogant swagger, the disrespectful smirk, the challenge in his eyes... He was just the type of employee she despised.

Okay, so she hadn't been born breathing coal dust. She couldn't lay claim to generations of family members who'd made their living in the mines. But that didn't mean she couldn't do the job she'd been appointed to do. She might have been fast-tracked into an incredibly responsible position, but after more than a year at the helm, she'd earned her stripes. Too bad some of the men there still refused to accept that.

Nathan shot her another wry look. This time he followed it with a lopsided grin. "Come on, Hannah. It's not that bad. We could have been dealing with a serious injury, or a death. That would have been far worse."

"Nathan, that's not the point. The thing is, we have safety protocols for a reason. Obviously, someone failed to follow them, or the accident wouldn't have happened. You heard Hammond. He thought the dozer was clear, but he obviously didn't make sure! That attitude doesn't suggest someone with a good safety record. And sloppy approaches often result in serious accidents."

"You're right and I'll be sure to speak to both men and issue them with warnings. But as far as incidents go, it's not in the most crucial category."

"But—"

Nathan held up his hand, cutting her off. "I'll put a review of safety protocols on the top of the list for tomorrow's start-up meeting. I'll go through every manual with the men. It'll be all right, Hannah. Trust me. I've got this."

She looked at his calm and reassuring demeanor and took a deep breath. "I still need that report on my desk by the end of the shift and it had better include a reasonable explanation, otherwise jobs will be on the line. There's no room in this operation for carelessness."

`He nodded and her tension eased. She was grateful to have him as her OCE. He was prepared to get in and work as hard as she did and often stayed back to work extra hours. Better still, his casual and calm manner always managed to cut through her stress. So far, he'd been a good man to have on her side.

She glanced from his profile to his hands on the steering wheel. He drove with a lazy self-assurance that instilled her with confidence. She felt safe with him. His hands were large, capable, his fingers were long and tapered.

How would they feel stroking my body?

She caught herself as her nipples hardened in response.

This is ridiculous! I'm in the middle of a serious incident and I'm fantasizing about my OCE! Time to get a grip, Hannah. Work to be done.

They traveled the rest of the way in silence. Nathan dropped her outside her office and she thanked him and waved him off. She looked up at the sky. It was as blue and cloudless and beautiful as late November days could be in the Hunter Valley. And boy, was it heating up. Another hot Australian summer on the way. A good day for mining. She only hoped the excavator accident was the only safety breach she had to deal with that week. Now she'd spend the rest of the day filling in the paperwork and reporting the incident to the authorities.

Another black mark against the mine...and against me. Just great.

Chapter Two

Liam Hennessy flashed his government credentials at the young and attractive woman seated behind the reception desk of the Strathwaylin coal mine and introduced himself.

"Hi, I'm Liam Hennessy. I'm from the Resources Regulator. I'd like to see the group manager for WHST," he said, using the acronym for Work, Health, Safety, and Training.

He was filled with curiosity at the thought of stepping onto a Barrington Mining mine site. Had any of Frank and Evelyn's nine kids followed in Frank's footsteps and worked in the mining industry?

He'd gone to school with some of the Barrington offspring. Wade Barrington had been in his class. Zac had been in the year below him. The triplets—Trace, Charlotte, and Molly—were a year older than Wade and there were a few more who were older than him. The one that stood out in his mind for all the wrong reasons was Hannah Barrington.

Hannah was the youngest Barrington child and had been a couple of years below him in school. She'd made his every living moment there a tortuous hell. Not that she'd had any clue he existed. That had been the problem. What had become of her? Not that he cared. The less he thought about Hannah, the better. In fact, he wouldn't care if he spent the rest of his life without seeing her again.

The receptionist gave him a friendly smile. "Do you have an appointment?"

"No," he replied. "But I'm here about an incident that was reported to the Resources Regulator yesterday. I'm sure your manager will see me."

The woman picked up the phone and spoke quietly into it. Liam turned away and walked over to one wall where various framed pictures of the mine in action were displayed. They were good quality images and perfectly captured the organized mayhem and hive of activity that was most often present on a mine site.

The sound of boots coming toward him caught his attention. He turned and then froze in shock. Hannah Barrington strode toward him. She wore the same fluorescent yellow, high-visibility work shirt and navy-blue pants common to everyone who worked there. As she drew nearer, his head spun madly with a kaleidoscope of memories.

In a distant part of his mind, he acknowledged how good she looked. Tall and curvy, the promising figure she'd had as a teenager had morphed into something luscious and womanly. Even in the masculine clothing, she oozed sex appeal. His belly churned. Despite the fact this was a Barrington mine, she was the last person he'd expected to see. He couldn't believe it was her. His school days' nemesis. The woman he despised more than anyone else.

And here she was. Group safety manager of the mine site, no less. A responsible position. At the ripe old age of twenty-three. Of course she was. Her daddy owned the mine.

She looked at him without the faintest flicker of recognition which only served to infuriate him further.

No surprise she doesn't recognize me... What did I expect?

"Mr Hennessy, I'm Hannah Barrington. It's nice to meet you."

He forced himself to shake her outstretched hand. The whole time, anger burned inside him. He'd spent his final years of high school loving her from afar and she didn't even know who he was—not then and certainly not now. It might have been seven years since he'd put his high school days behind him, but the bitter memories were as fresh as if they'd walked those long and noisy corridors only yesterday.

The realization incensed him. He'd worked so hard to eradicate her from his memory and yet with the first glimpse he'd had of her in seven years, she once again saturated his mind. It was beyond infuriating. It was totally and completely unacceptable. He wouldn't let himself feel unmanned.

Damn Hannah Barrington!

He glared at her. She blinked in surprise, taken aback by his overt animosity. His predecessor had obviously had a more cordial relationship with her. Well, she'd get no common courtesies from him!

His tone was clipped. "I'm sure your receptionist informed you I'm from the Resources Regulator. I'm here about the incident you filed with my office yesterday."

"Yes. I guessed as much."

She turned on the heel of her boot and strode back in the direction from where she'd come. It incensed him all over again that she expected him to follow her without protest, like an obedient lap dog. She turned into an office at the end of the corridor and took a seat behind an enormous carved oak desk and folded her hands in front of her.

"So, Mr Hennessy. Welcome to Barrington Mining. I didn't realize Mr Warren had left."

Liam continued to stand for a moment, briefly enjoying the illusion of dominance it gave him until she indicated the chair that stood opposite the desk. He stepped forward and reluctantly sat. "My predecessor requested a transfer to be closer to his family," he replied by way of explanation, his tone still curt. "I've been appointed to take his place."

"I see." She spread her hands open, palms up. "Well, I hope you and I get along just as well as Mr Warren and I did. It certainly helps to have a respectful, professional working relationship with each other. I think it makes both of our jobs easier."

She smiled. It was the same brilliant white smile she'd had in high school. It lit up her face and shined from her deep blue eyes. He flinched as if he'd been struck and then took refuge in his briefcase to hide his reaction. Her failure to recognize him had been insulting enough. He wouldn't give her the satisfaction of knowing how much she still affected him.

Pulling out a sheaf of papers, he thrust them across the desk. Once again, she looked taken aback by his aggression.

Good. Let her wonder who the hell I am and why I'm being so rude. It will serve her right to be embarrassed when she finally works out who I am...

Then again, maybe it was wishful thinking on his part that she'd remember him at all, even later, when she'd had time to think about it. The possibility filled him with a fresh surge of anger.

"You haven't submitted all of the required paperwork," he bit out. "I'm sure you're aware of the penalties for failing to comply with our regulations."

Hannah looked at him in surprise. She frowned and sat forward. "What are you talking about? I submitted everything I was required to do."

"No," he bit out again, "you didn't. A new regulation came out last week requiring you to fill out an additional section specifically addressing the reasons why safety protocols were breached. That section was not received by me."

Hannah's eyebrows rose at his continued antagonism, but she merely drew in a breath and sat back against her chair. She was smart enough to realize she needed to do what she could to keep him on her side. If he was of mind to do it, he could make her life very difficult, to say nothing of halting production at the mine.

"Oh, I see. Well, I apologize for the oversight. It wasn't intentional. I'll get the additional paperwork to you as soon as I can."

Liam continued to glare at her. "You'd better. I need it like...yesterday."

To her credit, Hannah held his gaze, but the anger in her eyes didn't go unnoticed. "I've already said I'll get onto it. Now, is there anything else?"

Liam slowly shook his head back and forth, a humorless smile turning up his lips. When he spoke, his voice was filled with scorn. "You Barringtons are really something."

Another flash of anger flickered in Hannah's blue eyes. "Excuse me?"

His gaze narrowed, became steely-eyed. "You heard me."

Hannah stared at the man across from her. There was something perplexingly familiar about him, but for the life of her she couldn't place him. The thick blond hair, the brown eyes, the athletic physique that gave lie to the fact he spent most of his time behind a desk... He had more than his fair share of good looks and physical appeal. That alone should have made him memorable. And though his name rang a faint bell in her memory, it wasn't enough for her to know who he was or what the hell she'd done to upset him. And it was clear he was upset. Furious, even.

The Resources Regulator was a regulatory body that had been established by the New South Wales government in 2016 and tasked with the job of dealing with all mine and petroleum sites across the state. Their primary job was to act as the state's work, health, and safety regulator.

Their jurisdiction extended over open cut and underground mines, petroleum sites, quarries and extractive operations, tourist mines, opal and other small-scale mines, and mining exploration activities. They were also responsible for undertaking compliance and enforcement activities in relation to the Mining Act 1992, with a key focus on mine rehabilitation. In short, they wielded incredible power.

That was the reason she'd gone out of her way to befriend Hennessy's predecessor. Michael Warren was in his fifties and had spent most of his career enforcing work, health, and safety regulations and investigating breaches. He knew the law inside out and took his role very seriously. But he'd also been approachable, reasonable and had acknowledged the efforts made by Barrington Mining to make safety a priority. He and Hannah had enjoyed a mutually respectful relationship which had been maintained despite the recent rush of incidents.

But this new guy was over the top. It was like he had a personal vendetta against her. Or at least against her family. It was strange and more than a little disconcerting. She needed to keep the investigators who wielded the power of the Resources Regulator on their side. They could do a lot of damage to her bottom line if they chose to play hard ball, not to mention her reputation and the reputation of Barrington Mining.

With an effort, she kept her tone even. "Look, Mr Hennessy. I don't know who you are or what beef you have against my family, but if we're done here, it's time you left."

The look he gave her was so self-assured it filled her stomach with dread. "Oh, we're far from done, Hannah

Barrington. But that's it for now. Get me the rest of that paperwork ASAP." With another hard look, he pushed away from the desk and stood. "Until next time."

She didn't even bother to look up. "Good afternoon, Mr Hennessy. I'm sure you know the way out."

Hannah was still in a bad mood when she visited her parents for dinner that evening. As she drove up the tree-lined driveway that wound its way up the hill to their impressive, Hamptons-style mansion, she couldn't help but notice how fresh and green everything looked. They were nearing the end of spring and the vast manicured gardens were at their best. The lavender bed was in full bloom. The murraya hedge that followed the top curve of the driveway as it reached the house was laden with honeysuckle-scented flowers.

It was early evening, but daylight saving's time ensured there was still enough light for her to see blue wrens and other small birds flittering among the garden bed that contained a collection of Australian natives. Kangaroo paw, bottle brush, and a host of other native grevillias. All in flower. A kookaburra sat on a nearby fence.

Though her family home was a three hours' drive away from Hunter Valley, she tried to catch up with them at least once every couple of weeks for dinner, along with the rest of her family. Her mother was a superb cook, and Hannah always enjoyed the time she spent with her parents and the chance it gave her to reconnect with them and with other members of her family.

Living so far away from most of her siblings, she didn't always know what was going on in their busy lives. Coming together regularly for a family dinner was one way she managed to keep in touch. An evening with her family almost always managed to put her in a good mood, but tonight, despite the sumptuous four-course dinner and accompanying wines, Hannah remained tense.

It's all because of him. Liam Hennessy. He's the reason I'm still in such a bad mood.

As she politely listened to her brother, Zac, and his fiancée, Emily, share their wedding plans, including a lively discussion about the pros and cons of an indoor versus an outdoor celebration, her mind remained firmly fixed on the man who had the power to cause her real angst. At some point, she'd have to tell her father about the new investigator from the Resources Regulator. Any incident involving a breach of safety rules had to be reported. That meant Liam Hennessy was in their lives for the near and maybe even distant future. Hannah usually took the time to brief her father on anything interesting happening at the mine or developments of which he should be made aware. The recent accident and arrival of Liam Hennessy fell squarely into the latter.

Great.

Something in her expression must have given away her disquiet. She started in surprise when her father leaned over and covered her hand with his.

"Perhaps you should come into my office, and we can talk about what's put that dark look on your face?" he suggested in a low tone.

Hannah closed her eyes briefly and drew in a deep breath. "Is it that obvious, Daddy?"

"It is to me," he said.

Pushing back his chair, he stood and excused himself from the table. Hannah followed suit. Together, they walked to the front of the house and into the room he used as his office. The room featured a masculine décor, with plenty of dark furniture and heavy drapes that retained the scent of her father's spicy cologne. The place always reminded her of her father and it was where she felt closest to him.

He walked over to a sideboard and poured himself a glass of port. He turned to her. "Can I get you a drink?"

"Yes, please."

He handed her a glass and she took a sip. The sweet liquid slid easily down her throat and left warmth in its wake.

"So," her father said, taking a seat behind his glorious, antique Chippendale Partners Desk. "What's going on?"

Now that the moment was upon her, Hannah wasn't sure where to start. Her father had put her in charge of safety at the mine. She didn't want him to think she wasn't capable of dealing with this unexpected complication. But he also had a right to know. Liam Hennessy might just prove to be a significant thorn in their side, and they could both do without that. But for now, she'd start with the easier stuff. She nervously approached one of the burgundy chesterfield chairs across from her father and sank into its leather luxuriousness as she gathered her thoughts.

"So, production's well up on our expectations. Coupled with the high coal prices, we've already met our quotas and we're only halfway through the quarter."

Her father nodded with approval. "I'm aware of that. Good job. That's what I like to hear. But that doesn't explain the frown on your face. What else is going on?"

She bit her lip. "I'm still having a bit of difficulty with some of the men. I've been there more than year. You'd think they'd accept me by now. At the very least, the fact I'm a group manager should garner some respect."

"Did something happen?"

"Yes! I was down in the pit earlier today dealing with an issue. I addressed a group of men, asking questions to ascertain what had gone on. You should have seen them, Daddy! The way they looked at me! Like I was nothing!" she said, remembering Paul Hammond's scornful look. Even now, she burned with the need to wipe the smirk off his face.

"You have to earn their respect, Hannah," her father replied calmly. "These are tough men. They work hard. They're not used to having a woman in a position of authority. They're not going to respect you just because you want them to."

"I know that, Daddy!" she exclaimed. She pushed out of the chair and stood, trying to rein in her overriding anger and frustration. "But I work hard, too. Harder than most. I'm the first one to arrive on that mine site in the morning and I'm the last one on that shift to leave. I understand I might have been promoted well above my ability in the early days, but that was a long time ago. I've learned a lot since then."

Her father nodded. "You have and I'm proud of the effort you've put in. There isn't a piece of machinery or a section of the mine or a team you don't have some knowledge about, and I can guarantee that's made your job there a lot easier. But it's only been twelve months. And cultural change takes time."

"Of course, it does. But there are still several employees who can't get past the fact that, not only am I a woman, but that my father owns the mine. They think I'm Daddy's little girl and that's the only reason I'm in the position I'm in. It's infuriating! It's not like that anymore. I've proved my capability and leadership to get the job done."

Her father sighed. "Would you like to me to address your employees? Would that make a difference?"

"No!" she immediately protested. And then in a calmer tone, "No. Thank you for the offer, Daddy, but that would only make things worse. You riding in on your white horse to rescue me would only reinforce their mistaken belief that I'm there not because I'm the best person for the job, but because I'm your daughter."

Her father shrugged. "Fair enough. I'm glad you see it that way. It shows me how much you've matured from the flighty girl who had no idea what she wanted to do with her life a year ago. Do I have to remind you how many careers you started and then lost interest in?"

She looked away, feeling contrite. "No, Daddy."

"Hannah, look at me."

She reluctantly lifted her gaze. "I offered you the job at the mine to give you something to do, but I also knew you were capable of doing it if you set your mind to it." He paused and then smiled at her. "You didn't disappoint."

She was filled with a rush of warmth. Her father didn't often hand out praise, and when he did, he meant it.

"Thank you, Daddy. I appreciate your vote of confidence."

"Of course. I always had faith in you. Right from the start. The only thing you needed to do was to find that belief in yourself. And you've done it. You can hold your head high and take your place beside any of my group managers."

She flushed with pleasure. Hearing her father say those words did wonders for her confidence. Too bad some of the men derided her position at Strathwaylin. She'd ignore them, like she'd done in the beginning, and just get on with doing her job. Although ignoring them didn't seem to have helped. Perhaps she needed to re-think her strategy.

"How're we going as far as safety goes?" her father asked, changing the subject.

She compressed her lips and sighed. "There's a new investigator from the Resources Regulator. I met him today. Liam Hennessy. Have you heard of him?"

"No, what's he like?"

She sighed again and regained her seat. She reached for her glass and took another sip before responding. "He's rude and arrogant and overbearing. He drove all the way out to the mine just to tell me I hadn't submitted all the paperwork in relation to the latest safety breach. Something he could have easily done over the phone. What's more, he—"

"What do you mean, the latest safety breach? What happened?"

Her father's tone was harsh. Hannah swallowed another sigh. "There was a minor collision between a dozer and an excavator."

Her father exploded, as she knew he would. "What the hell? You call that a minor incident? How the hell did something like that happen?"

"I don't know, Daddy. But I'm going to find out."

Her father's gaze sharpened. "Was anyone hurt?"

"No, nothing like that. A miscommunication."

"What kind of damage are we talking?"

"The cab of the dozer was almost completely crushed. I'd estimate a hundred thousand for that. Then there's the loss of production. Fortunately, we're ahead on our production targets and we've been able to secure the hire of another dozer. We were only down for a day."

"I guess it could have been worse," her father muttered. "At least no one was hurt."

His expression darkened and she could tell he was thinking about Evan Wilson's death. The man's family had been devastated. In a strange twist of fate, her brother, Zac, had recently fallen in love with Evan's sister. They'd dated in high school but had gone their separate ways after graduation. Now they'd rekindled their romance. In fact, even though they were still debating the pros and cons of an outdoor wedding, the date was only a month away. Apparently, they were both keen to make up for lost time. Hannah could only guess Zac and Emily had worked things out between them and in particular, that they'd come to terms with the fact that Evan had been killed in a Barrington mine.

She shot her father a look of reassurance. "You're right. We can be grateful no one was injured."

"You said you reported it."

She grimaced and sat back in her seat. "Yes. I filled in all the necessary paperwork. Well, at least I thought I did."

"What do you know about this new investigator?"

"Not much. Only that he's a jerk. I've worked so hard over this past year to build a good relationship with Michael Warren and now he's been transferred." She scrubbed at her hair with irritation. "It's just that this Hennessy guy's so antagonistic. Like he's bearing a grudge. I'm sure I've never met him before, but he acts like I should know him. I can't figure it out. Are you sure you don't know who he is?"

"How old is he?"

"Mid-twenties. Maybe a year or two older than me."

"Where's he from?"

"I don't know. But he gave me the impression he knew a lot about the Barringtons."

Her father shrugged. "That's not hard. You only have to do a search on the Internet, and you can find out plenty. Not all of it's true, but that's the way it goes. And some of these people who work for the regulator—a lot of them aren't on our side. It's not just that it's their job to investigate and enforce safety, some of them take it personally, as if it's their duty to bring 'dirty' coalminers to their knees."

He paused and sipped from his glass. "There's nothing you can do about people like that, Hannah. The truth is, they're jealous of our success. They have a tiny amount of power over us and they're going to make damned sure they use it."

She reached for her drink again. "I'm not sure this Hennessy guy fits into that category. He didn't seem to care that we were rich. His aggressive attitude felt more personal than that."

"Perhaps you'd have better luck asking your brothers and sisters. They might know of him."

"Yes, I might do that. Maybe his beef isn't with me, but with one of my siblings? That might explain his antagonistic attitude."

"I'm sure you won't let him get to you, Hannah. More than that, you'll come out on top. There isn't a man on this planet who's a match for you when you put your mind to it." Her father winked. "The poor bloke doesn't stand a chance."

Hannah chuckled, her good spirits restored. For the first time that day, she looked forward to her next encounter with the very rude and insufferable Mr Hennessy.

Bring it on...

Chapter Three

Liam chopped at the tomatoes like any moment he expected them to rise off the board and attack him. All afternoon, he'd seethed with anger. It had put him in a filthy mood for the rest of the day and his bad mood had everything to do with Hannah Barrington.

"You should have seen her, Jac. It was like being sucker punched in the gut. I had no idea she worked at her father's mine. And not only does she work there, but she's the safety boss. Can you believe that? She sat behind her desk like a queen on her throne, lording it over everyone. She's as bad as she was in high school."

His older sister shot him a sympathetic look. "I can only imagine what a shock that must have been for you. It's been years since you saw her."

"Right. Not since I graduated high school. I can't believe I'm going to have to deal with her now. I've never met someone more rude and arrogant."

Jacqueline scooped up the diced tomatoes and dropped them into a hot frypan that already sizzled with onion and garlic. Liam had moved into her rented house in

Muswellbrook temporarily while he looked for suitable accommodations of his own. Her house was situated in the Hunter Valley and was central to the mines that were now under his jurisdiction. Fortunately for him, she was still single and had a spare room.

"I never thought she was rude or arrogant," Jacqueline continued in a conversational tone. "More like confident and proud. I think that's why she stood out. Most of us were desperately trying to cope with puberty, doing our best to blend in with the crowd. But not Hannah Barrington. Even though she was a few years below me, I was envious of how she didn't seem to care what people thought. And of course, she was beautiful. That helped."

Liam grimaced. "Well, she's still beautiful, don't you worry about that. Not that I took much notice. I was so instantly angry when I saw her. As well as shocked. All those memories came rushing back. Ned..." Liam shook his head in an effort to hold the anger and sadness at bay. "Surely, you remember what she did to him?"

Jacqueline regarded him curiously. "The way I remember it, Ned had a lot of problems. Not the least was an abusive father and a drunken mother who never got off the couch."

Liam's anger ignited. It took all his self-control to hold onto it. "I can't believe you just said that!"

His sister continued to regard him calmly. "Is that really what you think? That what happened was all Hannah's fault?"

"It's not just what I think! It's the truth!" he exclaimed, still aghast his sister might remember things differently.

She merely shrugged.

Liam forged on. "Come on, Jac! You were there! You know what happened!"

"It was a long time ago, Liam. Let it go. I've had a tough day at work. If you don't mind, I'd just like to cook dinner, chill out for a while, and relax."

The anger that held Liam's body taut dissipated. His sister was a nurse who worked long hours at the local hospital in the palliative care ward. It was a tough job, both physically and emotionally. Now that he looked at her more closely, he could see the dark shadows of fatigue beneath her eyes.

"Hey," he said softly. "You go and put your feet up. I'll finish this. How about I pour you a glass of wine? It looks like you need it."

She gave him a grateful smile. "Thanks, Liam. That would be great. You're right. I'm beat." With that, she took him up on his offer and after washing her hands and wiping them on the hand towel, she headed for the couch.

Tucking her legs beneath her, Jacqueline sipped on her glass of red wine. It was true. She'd had a rough day. They'd lost two of their patients. Two elderly women who'd been struggling with terminal cancer for more than a month. In some ways, it was a blessing they were now free from pain. Still, it was always hard when they lost someone, despite the knowledge of inevitability.

She'd been working on the palliative care ward for more than a year now. It was hugely demanding work, but she loved it. As Liam banged away in the kitchen, her mind went back to her years at high school. Both she and Liam had attended Broken High. The small rural town boasted a population of around five thousand, but it had a large catchment area for the high school. There were nearly four hundred kids that showed up every day. For all Liam's angst over high school, Jacqueline had only good memories of her time there.

She'd also gone to school with the Barringtons. She was a year older than Liam. She'd had the Barrington triplets in her class. Charlotte, Molly, and Trace. She remembered them as outgoing, confident, and good looking, like all the Barringtons. She'd only had eyes for Richard Mather. He'd been in her class. The most popular boy in the year. Too bad Richard had been so desperately in love with Hannah. He hadn't even noticed Jacqueline. She'd never held that against him. Most of the boys at Broken High had been in love with Hannah, including Jacqueline's brother.

Liam thought he'd been so clever at hiding the way he felt for the girl, but Jacqueline had always known. She'd thought it kind of tragic that two best friends were both in love with the same girl and even more tragic that the very same girl was unaware of either's existence.

As the memories washed over her, she sighed and took another sip of wine. Such a sad and complicated world they lived in. At the ripe old age of twenty-six, Jacqueline was only too happy to wipe her hands of love. The small taste of it she'd had in her teenage years had burned her badly. No, she was happy being single. That way she only had herself to please. Right now, that felt pretty darn good.

Liam stirred the tomato, garlic and onion and added a generous dollop of tomato paste. He flavored the spaghetti sauce with salt and pepper and tore up some fresh basil and oregano. Dropping the herbs into the pan, he gave the sauce a final stir before setting the spoon aside and turning his attention to the pasta.

He hated arguing with his sister. They usually got on well. There were only the two of them now their parents had passed. Their mother a couple of years ago from cancer. Though she hadn't said anything to him, Liam was sure that was one of the reasons Jacqueline now worked in palliative care. Their father had died only two months ago from a heart attack. He'd been all of fifty-seven.

Their father's sudden death had been the impetus for Liam to make some changes in his life. One of those changes had been leaving his hectic life in the city for a quieter country pace. It was the reason he'd requested a transfer to the Hunter Valley. Only a two-hour drive north of Sydney, the Hunter Valley was known as the birthplace of Australian wines. Famous for its exquisite varieties of Semillon and Shiraz, it was also renowned across the world as a leading gourmet getaway. For someone who liked to drink wine and cook, he was in paradise.

Though he hadn't yet had time to visit too many of the establishments on offer, he planned to do just that on his weekends off. A different place every weekend. That was his goal. And of course, being in the Hunter Valley meant he was also closer to his sister, which was important to him now that they only had each other.

He grinned ruefully. They were far closer at the moment than he'd anticipated. Right now, they were sharing a modest, two-bedroom house. Though he hoped to find a place of his own in the near future, so far, he hadn't found the time to go looking.

He sighed as he thought again of their recent argument. The thing that irked him the most was that he wasn't angry with Jacqueline. He was angry at Hannah Barrington. And angry at himself. He'd thought after all these years he was over her, but one look in her beautiful blue eyes and the feelings of love and hopelessness had come rushing back.

To make matters worse, she was oblivious to how he felt—then and now—and all he wanted was to get over her. To put her out of his mind, once and for all. To exorcise her memory and move on. Except now she was here, on his new turf.

Even more alarming, they were likely to encounter each other on a regular basis. Not only when there were incidents, but it was also his job to enforce compliance of the regulations, along with a whole raft of other things. No matter how much he wished otherwise, it looked like Hannah

Barrington was once again part of his life. That meant he had to work out some way of coming to terms with it and staying sane in the meantime. He didn't want to have to transfer again.

Hannah tucked the tail of her high-vis shirt into the waistband of her work pants and adjusted her position in her chair. No matter that she was the group manager for work, health, safety, and training and spent most of her days in an office, it was mine protocol that everyone on site dressed in protective safety gear, right down to their steel-toed boots.

Nathan sat across from her. They'd been going over the mine's safety protocols, tightening up the wording, making clearer the procedures that had to be followed every single day. It had been exactly a week since their last incident. He'd talked her out of firing anyone, but she'd been clear another incident would result in such. The mine couldn't afford carelessness. She could only hope that their run of safety breaches had come to an end.

Still, she wasn't naïve enough to believe there wouldn't be another one. With more than one hundred and thirty people working there at any given time and a large number of heavy earthmoving equipment engaged continuously on site, it was only a matter of time before something went wrong again. Minimizing the risk was key.

"We need to make sure every incident, no matter how insignificant, is brought to our attention," Nathan said.

Hannah frowned. "Surely that's already happening?"

Nathan grimaced. "In theory, yes. It's supposed to happen that way, but I've heard on the grapevine that some of the contractors get a bit slack when it comes to reporting everything."

Hannah sat up straighter, alarmed. "But that's not their call to make. *Everything* must be reported. It states that clearly in the handbook. Every single one of those contractors and their employees are taken through each step of the safety protocols at their induction. They have no excuse not to comply. Which of the contractors aren't reporting properly? I'll need to speak with them and put them on notice. If they're not reporting, they need to be replaced."

Nathan held up a hand in a placating gesture. "Whoa, Tiger. I have no definite proof of anything. Only rumors. If you go charging in half-cocked and accusing them of breaching safety standards, we'll have a mass walk-out. We can't afford for the contractors to put down tools for even a day, let alone anything longer than that. And where are you going to find fifteen dump trucks overnight? We need those contractors to supplement our operators."

Hannah refused to be mollified. "Then what do you suggest? That we turn a blind eye to what might very well be safety breaches?"

Nathan's tone remained calm. "No, of course not. Leave it with me. I'll make a few discrete inquires. See if I can find some evidence of wrongdoing. As you say, any contractor deliberately ignoring the safety protocols doesn't deserve to be here, no matter how many machines they're supplying."

"In fact, the more machines they have, the greater the risk of something going wrong if they're ignoring safety protocols," Hannah muttered.

Nathan flashed her a smile that reminded her how attractive he was. "You're right." He winked. "That's why they pay you the big bucks."

Feeling slightly irritated by his comment, Hannah turned her attention back to the most recent incident.

"I submitted the additional paperwork to the Resources Regulator. I'm still waiting to hear whether they intend to launch an investigation. Let's hope they don't. How are we going with repairs to the dozer?"

"The mechanics and fitters have been working around the clock. There was a bit of a hold up on the glass, but I'm led to believe the dozer will be back in action in another week."

Hannah pursed her lips. "Then it's just as well I was able to source another one so quickly. Two weeks down is a lot of lost production time."

"Yeah." Nathan started scrolling through his phone.

Irritation surged through her again. He was meant to be her second in charge and he couldn't have appeared less interested.

"Nathan!"

"Yeah?"

He didn't even bother to look at her. She clenched her jaw and tried to hold on to her temper.

"Are you listening to me?" she asked through gritted teeth.

This time he looked up and flashed her another smile. "Of course, I am."

"It doesn't look that way."

"Hey, you're concerned about contractors picking and choosing which incidents they report. I get it. I'm concerned too. All the incidents over the past year have involved contractors. For some reason, they don't seem to be getting the safety message. But I'm on it. You don't have to worry. I'll poke around and find out what's going on. Then we'll know how best to address it."

She sighed on a weary breath. "Thank you. In the meantime, I'd appreciate it if you attend the general communications meeting at the start of each shift for the next couple of weeks and reinforce the need for every single person on this site to be familiar with our safety protocols. We need to get on top of this. In fact, I think I should be there too."

Nathan reached across the desk and covered her hand with his. "There's no need for both of us to attend. I promise, I'll see to it."

Hannah blinked at the unexpected contact. She looked at him in surprise. Nathan merely grinned and removed his hand.

"You've got this, boss. And you've got me here to help you. I'm there for you every step of the way. Don't forget that."

Another cheeky wink and he was gone, leaving her to ponder the wisdom of hiring such a good-looking offsider. The attraction was downright distracting and right now, distracted was the last thing she could afford to be.

I need to keep my mind on the job. Now isn't the time to be preoccupied by a pair of teasing eyes and a cheeky grin, no matter how tempting... Best remember that the next time the handsome devil's in my office...

A reluctant smile tugged at Hannah's lips. For all of Nathan's irritating inattentiveness, she couldn't deny she enjoyed working with such a sexy man. His HR record had indicated that he was single. In the time he'd been there, she'd heard no talk of a girlfriend. He was just the kind of guy she found attractive: good looking, charming, sexy... She swallowed a groan.

Focus!

The sound of her mobile phone ringing interrupted her musings. She pulled it out of her pocket and checked the screen and then blinked in surprise.

"Nathan. What did you forget?"

"I'm afraid I have bad news."

His words and the grimness of his tone made her heart skip a beat. Tension of a different kind tightened her stomach.

"What is it?"

Chapter Four

Hannah drove into the pit and made her way over to the site of the accident Nathan had just called in. Her belly felt weighted down with dread. Nathan had been sparing in his details, but one thing he'd made clear was that this time someone had been injured. Straight away, that put this in a more serious category. She could only imagine the field day Liam Hennessy would have with this, especially coming so soon on the heels of the last incident.

Great. Just what I need. Thank goodness no one was killed...

She was grateful for that. As she climbed out of the truck, Nathan came toward her.

"What happened?" she asked without preamble.

"It's not as bad as it could have been," he replied.

"Is that supposed to make me feel better?" she snapped, pulling on her hard hat as she strode toward the workshop.

Nathan didn't respond. Instead, he began to tell her what had happened.

"One of the maintenance fitters received a laceration to his cheek while he was removing a cross-member from the engine bay of a haul truck."

"How did that happen?"

"Two of the fitters were removing the cross-member by jacking from below and lifting it with a crane. The man who was injured was reportedly moving electrical cables from the path of the cross-member when it came loose. It appears that the tension applied by the slings, combined with the pressure from the jack, allowed the cross-member to rise quickly and strike the fitter across the face."

Hannah gave him a hard look. "Again, I ask: How did that happen?"

Nathan averted his gaze and shrugged. "It appears the incorrect procedure was being used for the task."

Anger rushed through her. She looked around at the mine workers who'd gathered in small groups around her. The logos on their work shirts indicated they were employed by a contractor.

"Who are these men employed by?" she demanded.

"Hume Earthmoving," Nathan replied. "They were given the contract by your father after Joseph Rodriguez was fired."

At the mention of Joseph Rodriguez, Hannah's stomach clenched. Rodriguez had employed Evan Wilson. The contractor had been fired only hours before the accident that had claimed Evan's life. It had happened on Hannah's first day on the mine site. Technically, Evan's death had occurred on her father's watch, but that didn't bring her comfort.

Now another contractor's employee had been injured and this time all eyes would be on her. The buck would stop with her and that's how it should be. She wouldn't hide behind her father. She'd never been that kind of girl.

"Where's the contractor now?"

"His name's Colin Hume. I understand he's not on site this morning. Had a prior engagement in town."

"So, who's in charge here?"

"That would be Paul Hammond."

Hannah frowned sharply. "Hammond? Wasn't he one of the men involved in last week's collision?"

Nathan nodded briefly. "Yep."

"Well, that's one incident too many. You talked me out of firing him."

"He was stood down for a week."

She glared. "Only a *week?*"

Nathan shrugged. "As I told you at the time, the current labor market's tight. Everyone's finding it difficult to find staff. Especially staff with as many years of experience as Hammond. We can't afford to fire people over minor incidents."

Hannah turned on him, incensed. "*Minor* incidents?"

Nathan eyed her steadily. "Yes. Minor incidents. No one was hurt the last time."

Hannah's fury boiled over. He just didn't seem to get it. "And I still don't know how. It was a miracle nobody got hurt. We haven't been so lucky this time. Look at that man!" She pointed in the direction of the worker who stood to one side surrounded by his colleagues. A thick padded dressing stained with blood had been taped across his cheek. "He could have been killed!"

"But he wasn't," Nathan replied in an infuriatingly calm tone. "It's okay, Hannah. Don't make this out to be more than it is."

"How can you say that, Nathan?" she exclaimed. "It's not just *this* accident. Have you forgotten how frequently these incidents have been occurring? Have you forgotten about the fitter who was struck a few months back by a steel pin? I was on site when that happened. I attended the scene of the accident. I saw the bone sticking out of his leg. The unimaginable pain that man must have been in. It's something I'll never forget."

Nathan's face remained impassive. His lack of reaction irritated Hannah no end. Her anger continued to rise.

"In the past twelve months, there have been two dozers and an excavator tip over on this mine site," she said, her voice clipped. "That's an extraordinarily high number and I don't mean that in a good way. Okay, so there was no loss of life, but that was pure luck, not good management. We both know any of those incidents could have resulted in a fatality. Worse still, they all could have been avoided if the correct safety procedures had been followed."

Seemingly unperturbed by her outrage, Nathan merely shrugged. "Accidents happen all the time, Hannah. You only have to read the daily reports issued from around the world to know that."

Hannah stared at him, unable to believe his dismissive attitude toward something that could result in having the mine closed. She clenched her jaw tight against a wave of frustration. For the first time, she wondered if she'd chosen the best person to be her eyes and ears on the ground.

Drawing in a deep breath, and noting the men listening in, she drew away and beckoned Nathan to follow as she made a conscious effort to control her anger. "You don't seem to understand the seriousness of these events, Nathan. Okay, so mine sites are dangerous. Everyone knows that. But we've had more than our fair share of accidents of late and they haven't gone unnoticed. We have a new investigator from the Resources Regulator. He's been breathing down my neck. It's obvious he's just itching for an excuse to shut us down." She gave him a hard stare. "Is that what you want? For everyone on this mine site to be out of a job? Including you?"

Nathan chuckled and shook his head. "Hannah, come on. You're getting hysterical. Okay, so there have been a few incidents—"

"Don't you dare patronize me, Mr Garcia. A few? What about that collision the other day? Or the service truck that overturned a couple of months ago? The operator lost control of the vehicle while descending a ramp. Okay, so the road was wet. But the question is, *why* was it wet? Who authorized the water trucks to have that haul road so wet it caused a truck to slide and overturn?"

Nathan shrugged again. He couldn't have looked more disinterested. Hannah threw up her arms in frustration.

"That's my point exactly. Nobody knows. And from where I'm sitting, it seems like nobody cares. It's your job to know. Your job to find out. Your job to minimize the risk of further incidents."

She made a conscious effort to quell her frustration and underscore the depth of her concern. He needed to take her seriously. "These safety breaches have gone on for far too long," she said in a calmer tone. "It's time to make some changes. From now on, whenever there's a safety breach that results in a reportable incident, I'm going to be the one to interview the people involved. That's the only way I can be assured the right questions are being asked and that we'll get to the truth of what happened. And if contractors need to be fired, then so be it. Understand?"

Nathan's expression turned sulky. "You put me in charge of investigating safety breaches. Don't you trust me to do the job properly?"

Hannah's initial reaction was to respond in the negative. That's how angry and frustrated she was. But then she softened. Nathan had been instrumental in helping her navigate the complexities of managing mine safety. She couldn't have done it without him, or at least not as quickly as she had.

"I trust you," she replied in a mollified tone. "But I need to see for myself the response of the contractors to the safety procedures you're underscoring with them. There appears to be no measurable improvement. There have been too many accidents. Something's not right."

"I tell you, I'm on top of it. You don't have to worry about it. Besides," he added, lowering his voice. "I mean no offense, but the men will probably be more forthcoming with me about what happened. Most of them don't take too kindly having to answer to a female group manager."

And just like that, Hannah's fury returned. Anger burned her cheeks. "Well, if they don't like it, they can find work elsewhere. This is the twenty-first century. Many mining contractors are now employing women as operators, including at other Barrington mines. Women on mine sites are no longer the exception. I'm sure you know that."

Her tone was scathing. Nathan held up his arms in a sign of surrender. "Hey, don't shoot the messenger. I'm just telling you how it is. Between you and me, I love having a female boss." He winked and sent her a grin so sexy it had the power to curl her toes. Too bad for him she wasn't in the mood for seduction.

Ignoring his overture, she looked directly at him. "You're also my messenger and safety controller. Your job works both ways and you need to do it."

On her way back to her office, she couldn't help but wonder about Nathan. He'd been employed by Barrington Mining for nearly a year and he hadn't yet managed to put a halt to the safety breaches. He kept telling her he was on top of it, but all indications were to the contrary. After all, one of his main roles was to investigate those very same incidences. But they kept happening. She couldn't imagine how humiliating it would be to have to tell her father she was responsible for the mine being closed.

Maybe it's time to get more involved...Nathan's ego be damned... Especially with that jerk of an investigator hanging around...

Dropping into the chair behind her desk, she scrubbed at her hair and tried to come up with the best plan of attack. She didn't want Nathan to think she was undermining him and no doubt he had a point about the men being more reluctant to open up to a woman, but she had to do something to stem the flow of incidents before they turned into something she could no longer control. That possibility had become more of a reality with the arrival of Liam Hennessy.

She had to come up with a game plan for getting him on her side, and fast. But what? He was already treating her like the enemy. Getting him on her side wouldn't be easy when the very sight of him got her defenses up. She'd have to work on that. Be as friendly as possible and above all, professional.

Feeling grim at the prospect, she drew her keyboard toward her and checked her email. The name Liam Hennessy snagged her attention. She clicked on the email and opened it, scanning the contents. Her stomach sank.

"I'll be out there tomorrow to launch an official investigation into the excavator incident."

Great. And he doesn't even know about the latest one... This one's even more serious. He's going to have a field day. Great. Just great.

Liam pulled into the Strathwaylin mine carpark and came to a halt. The early morning sun already felt warm on his face. It was going to be another hot day. As he climbed out of his truck, his gut churned, both at the thought of seeing Hannah again and from the purpose of his visit. Not every incident reported to the Resources Regulator gave rise to a formal investigation, but Liam couldn't pass up the opportunity to get one over the woman who still twisted him up in knots. It was petty and immature and smacked of revenge, but he'd never imagined he'd have the opportunity to lord it over Hannah Barrington. It was time she realized how that felt.

He announced himself to the receptionist and waited while she informed Hannah via the telephone of his arrival. Fortunately for Hannah, he didn't have to wait long. She surprised him by greeting him with a friendly smile and handshake and then invited him back to her office.

"Simone, will you bring us some refreshments, please? Mr Hennessey, would you like tea or coffee?"

Liam blinked, slightly startled, and then responded. "Coffee, thanks."

Hannah turned to nod at her receptionist and requested a pot before bestowing upon him another smile.

"You must have gotten an early start from Sydney this morning. It's barely eight o'clock."

Liam inclined his head. "Actually, I'm living in Muswellbrook with my sister. So not too far to come."

She merely nodded and showed him into her office. She pointed to the familiar seat opposite her desk. "Please, take a seat. Simone won't be long."

Her courtesy knocked him off-balance. He hadn't been expecting that. He was there to investigate a safety breach. She had to be aware of the seriousness of that and the even more serious ramifications if he chose to make life difficult for her. He expected her to be just as rude and unfriendly as she'd been before. Then another thought occurred to him.

Maybe this was all an act? Her way of buttering him up? Treat him well so he went easy on them. He wouldn't put it past her. No matter what his sister said, Hannah had always had a conniving side. Ned knew that better than most. Still, he wasn't going to pass up a fresh cup of coffee. Any efforts she might make toward softening his opinion of her or his approach toward the investigation would fall on deaf ears. It had taken him a long time, but he was no longer a heartsick youth. He was now completely immune to the charms of Hannah Barrington.

The receptionist arrived with a tray containing a stainless-steel coffee pot, two mugs, a jug of milk, a bowl of sugar, and a plate of petit fours that looked both delicate and delicious. Liam's stomach growled. In his haste to get out to the mine first thing, he'd skipped breakfast.

"Thank you, Simone. That will be all."

After the receptionist had left, Hannah poured them both a cup.

"Milk? Sugar?"

"No, just black." He noticed she took hers the same.

She handed him a mug. Their fingers brushed. A spark of electricity fired between them. Liam suppressed a gasp. He glared at her, annoyed by his involuntary reaction. Her expression remained passive. It was obvious he was the only one who'd felt the spark.

Typical. Hannah Barrington has always only been aware of herself. Everyone else could go whistle Dixie... It's obvious she's still like that. I'm well rid of my stupid attraction to her...

He took a sip of coffee. It was hot and strong, just how he liked it.

"Would you like a cake?"

Her sugar-sweet tone was in direct contrast to the challenge in her eyes. She was almost daring him to say no. He held her gaze, equally defiant. There was no way she hadn't heard his stomach growling. A part of him wanted to refuse her offering. He didn't want to feel indebted to her for anything. But he wasn't stupid. He wouldn't say no to cake. Not when he was hungry and they looked so good and besides, that's exactly what she wanted him to do.

"Thank you, I don't mind if I do." He ate four in quick succession. One bite of each and they were gone. Then he licked his fingers clean. All the while, she watched him.

"Good?" she asked derisively.

"Yes. Very good. My compliments to the baker."

She inclined her head. "Thank you."

He frowned in sudden comprehension. "You?"

"Yes." A light blush colored her cheeks. "Are you surprised?"

"Yes," he answered honestly. "I didn't think someone like you would know their way around a kitchen."

Her expression darkened. "What do you mean, someone like me? Do you think because I work in a mine that I don't know how to bake?"

Liam shot her a deliberately bored look and merely shrugged, knowing that would incense her further. Still, she'd surprised him. Maybe there was more to the spoiled princess than he'd realized. He quickly put a stop to that line of thought.

"We're getting off track here. This isn't about whether you have baking skills. I'm here to continue with my investigation of the incident you reported last week."

Hannah surprised him again by looking guilty. He tensed.

What's she done that she feels guilty about?

Before he could put the question to her, she spoke.

"Um, actually, before you arrived, I was in the process of submitting a report about another incident that occurred yesterday afternoon."

She said the words in a rush and kept her gaze fixed somewhere over his shoulder. He frowned, incredulous.

"*Another* incident?"

"Yes. I'm afraid so. I'll provide you with all the details in my report. I haven't quite finished with it yet, but I promise I'll get it to you later today."

"Was anyone hurt?" he asked.

She nodded. "Yes. Not seriously," she added quickly. "A cut to the cheek. The worker was given first aid at the scene."

Liam stared at her in disbelief and slowly shook his head. "This is...unbelievable. What sort of a business are you operating here?"

He crossed his arms over his chest and leaned back in his chair. "I've reviewed your safety history. There have been a number of concerning breaches over the past year, including a fatality a little over twelve months ago." He narrowed his eyes at her. "It seems to me you're willing to overlook almost any safety requirement if it means increased production. Do you have *any* consideration at all for worker safety?"

Anger flared in Hannah's eyes. She opened her mouth as if to protest and then closed it again. When she remained silent, he goaded her again.

"What? Nothing to say?" He leaned forward and gave her a menacing look. "*You're* the one in charge here. *You're* the one responsible for the safety of every man and woman on this site. When an accident happens, it comes back to *you*, no matter who was there at the time. Like it or not, the buck stops with *you*."

She looked at him coldly. "I don't need *you* to tell me about my responsibilities and I'm well aware of our recent poor safety track record. I can assure you I take safety *very* seriously and I'm doing all that I can to reduce our incidents. In fact, it's my goal to reduce our incidents to zero. Whether I'm successful, only time will tell, but I'm going to do everything in my power to make that happen."

By the time she was finished, her cheeks were flushed, and her breath came fast. Liam tried to remain unaffected by her passion, but it was difficult. Cool, calm, and collected she was beautiful. In the middle of an impassioned response, she was spectacular. Her blazing blue eyes were even more stunning, like the deepest cobalt sea, shot through with fire. The color on her cheeks only served to emphasize her strong bone structure and the line of determination in her jaw. It took all his self-control to remain unaffected. That only served to irritate him further.

"I require immediate access to the pit and to any worker who was involved in or a witness to either of the incidents," he said in a clipped voice.

"Of course, you have my permission to go anywhere you see fit. I'll call in our open cut examiner," she replied brusquely. "You'll have our full cooperation."

He shot her a hard look. "I wasn't asking for your permission, Hannah."

She glared at him but remained silent. They both knew she had no authority to refuse him access.

"I also expect a copy of your report on this latest incident emailed to me within the hour. Do you understand?"

He eyeballed her. She eyeballed him right back. Whatever had happened to her in the years since he'd left high school, she hadn't lost any of her grit. He could only admire her for that.

Admire her? What the hell am I thinking? Of course, I don't admire her. I can't stand the sight of her. Every time I look at her, I think of Ned...

That was all the reminder he needed to get his thoughts about Hannah Barrington back firmly where they were meant to be. She was the enemy. Always was and always would be. Best he remember that the next time he started to feel anything near admiration for her. He stood abruptly, indicating to her he'd wait for her OCE outside.

Chapter Five

As soon as Liam Hennessy was out of hearing, Hannah cursed long and loudly. It had taken all her self-control not to lose her temper in front of him. The man was infuriating! He'd been in the job five minutes and already he pretended to know everything about her and the way she ran her business. Her initial impression of him had been right. He was an asshole. It was too bad he wielded so much power over her life—at least her working life. Even more infuriating was that he knew it.

"I wasn't asking for your permission, Hannah," she said in a sing-song voice, pulling a face as she waited for her OCE to answer her call. When he did, she got down to business.

"Nathan, Mr Hennessey, the investigator, has just left my office and is heading to the pit. I need you to assist him around the site and keep me posted. He knows about yesterday's accident and will want to interview witnesses to both incidents and likely take photos."

She heard Nathan draw in a sharp breath before he reassured her that he was on it. He hung up before she could say more. She chewed her lip in worry. Hennessey would draw his own conclusions and if his attitude was anything to go by, they wouldn't be good for Barrington Mining. He had a job to do, but some investigators took that job a little too seriously and for some reason this investigator had taken a disliking to her. Not like Michael Warren.

Hennessy's predecessor had been one of the good guys. He investigated what he had to, but he'd respected the efforts Hannah and her staff went to in order to keep the mine a safe workplace. Some days they got it more right than others. Michael Warren accepted that on such a big mine site, some accidents were inevitable. He viewed everything through a lens of reasonableness. It seemed this new investigator looked at everything through the lens of accusation and would likely go out of his way to hold her personally responsible.

Great.

She stared at the plate of cakes. So much for winning him over with her baking, although there was no denying he'd enjoyed them. At least it had appeared that way. Perhaps it was only for show? More gamesmanship from the man who was fast becoming a thorn in her side.

With a disgruntled sigh, she picked up her half-finished coffee and took a sip. It was nearly cold. Too bad it wasn't something stronger. She could do with a stiff scotch. That only made her more irritable. She hoped her OCE was up to the task of reassuring Hennessy about the mine's stringent safety procedures and practices.

Is Nathan Garcia up to the task or am I on my own? God help me...

She could do nothing at this stage but wait for Nathan to report back. Determined to put the annoying investigator out of her mind, she reached for the pile of incident reports Simone had left on her desk. One of Hannah's jobs was to review every safety breach that had occurred in the previous twelve hours at mine sites all around the world. It served as a sobering reminder to those in charge just how easily safety issues could arise and how important it was to have airtight practices in place in order to avoid them. And not only to have stringent safety protocols in place, but to ensure those protocols were being followed. It was all about mitigating risk. Learning from others was part of that process.

It annoyed Hannah no end to discover a number of people over the past twelve months had breached the carefully thought out, strenuously implemented culture of safety she was so proud of at Strathwaylin. Safety had always been their number one priority, despite the fact there had been an increasing number of incidents. There was something going on that she was unaware of, and neither was her OCE if he was to be believed, but she was determined to get to the bottom of it. As the Resources Regulator's unpleasant investigator had relished reminding her, the buck stopped with her.

That reminded her of the report she needed to write. She'd already wasted too much time thinking about him. With a sigh, she set aside the world-wide mine safety reports and pulled her keyboard toward her.

Liam tossed the folder containing his investigation notes onto the back seat of his truck and then climbed behind the wheel. He'd interviewed most of the people who'd either been involved in or had witnessed the two most recent accidents and had taken a bunch of photographs. Though he didn't have all the details of the most recent incident, after speaking to several witnesses, including the injured man, he was pretty certain he had a good idea about what had happened, and it didn't look good for Hannah Barrington.

While he'd been in the pit, he'd come across a man who introduced himself as the open cut examiner. Nathan Garcia was a pretty boy whose soft hands told Liam the man spent most of his time behind a desk. Garcia advised he was the safety controller.

"Then you're just the man I need to talk to," Liam said.

"The boss told me you're here to talk about those safety incidents."

"Did she? You took your time finding me. I've already spoken to the men involved, but I'm interested in hearing what you think happened, given your role as the safety controller," Liam said. "What assessments have you made? Did you witness anything?"

"No, I wasn't there on either occasion. I only heard about them afterward. I spoke to everyone concerned and ascertained it was just one of those things. Sometimes accidents happen."

Liam was taken aback by the man's casual attitude. Along with Hannah, he was meant to be in charge of mine safety. Surely, he should be more determined than that to get to the bottom of any accident. If for no other reason than to make sure nothing like that happened again. Wasn't his job at stake? What sort of show were they running?

Just something else to take up with Hannah Barrington...

Liam had also taken the time to review the mine communications recordings and had listened to those recordings that related to the first incident. It was quite clear that neither the excavator operator nor the dozer operator had made positive communications with each other prior to the collision. Though no one had been hurt in that incident, it was still a serious breach of safety protocols. Had her OCE bothered to listen to the recordings? Had he told his boss?

Positive communications on the mine radio between heavy machinery operators was standard procedure and a basic safety requirement. In that situation, the dozer operator had a responsibility to communicate with the digger driver prior to coming within the digger's swing radius. The digger operator should have then responded, acknowledged the dozer operator's request, and grounded his bucket. Not until that interaction had taken place should the dozer operator have proceeded forward. It was obvious none of those things had happened. The fact that Hannah had two workers on her site who either didn't know or had blithely ignored the safety protocol reflected very poorly on her as the group manager for work, health, safety, and training and on the mine's overall safety record and it was up to Liam to remind her of that and of the precarious position she'd put the mine's operations. He also had some serious questions about the capability of her OCE.

He pulled into the carpark outside the portable building that housed her office, spoiling for a fight. Simone's desk was empty. With hardly a pause, he strode down the hallway and into Hannah's office. She was on the phone with her back to him when he entered. He dropped his folder of notes on her desk with a loud thump. She jumped in her chair and turned around, her eyes widening with surprise and irritation as she caught sight of him.

With a pointed stare and narrowed eyes, she ended her phone conversation with a hurried promise she'd call straight back and then glared at him from the other side of her desk.

"What the hell are you doing in here? You can't just walk into my office."

With casual indifference that masked his anger, he dropped into a seat and regarded her coolly. "I thought you might like to hear my preliminary findings now that I've had the opportunity to make some inquires."

She swallowed and made a visible effort to restrain her anger. Her chest rose and fell on a deep breath. She folded her hands in front of her and rested them on her desk. She looked the epitome of calm professionalism. He had the power to close her mine, costing her millions of dollars in lost production, and yet she regarded him with a haughty arrogance, as if she were his equal. Though her attitude annoyed the hell of out him, a reluctant stab of admiration went through him.

There it is again... That annoying admiration for a woman I despise...

"What can you tell me?" she asked in a level voice.

He leaned back in his chair and folded his arms across his chest. "Let's start with the first incident. I understand the excavator operator was a man by the name of Paul Hammond and the dozer operator's Scott Stonewall, correct?"

"Correct."

"And they're employed by the mine?"

"No. They're employed by a contractor. Both the excavator and the dozer are owned by the same contractor, Colin Hume."

He narrowed his eyes at her. "You are, of course, ultimately responsible for everyone on this mine site, including your contractors."

"Of course. It might not look like this to you, Mr Hennessy, but everyone at Strathwaylin, including me, take safety very seriously. I'm appalled at what's happened here and I intend to get to the bottom of what's going on. Our people, and that includes our contractors, are fully briefed on every aspect of safety every single shift. We don't cut corners. We don't allow others to cut corners. These accidents should never have happened. Both me and my open cut examiner are working to find out why they did."

She held his gaze, her eyes bright with determination. Once again, admiration for her poked at him. He deliberately pushed the feeling aside.

"The mine communication recordings make it clear the dozer driver failed to positively communicate his position to the excavator operator," he continued. "Neither did the excavator operator respond. You talk about safety being your utmost priority and yet that's a breach of one of the most basic safety requirements. How do you explain that?"

She lowered her gaze to hide a sudden surge of anger toward her OCE. How could Nathan not have told her? Surely, he'd listened to the recordings?

With an effort, she pushed the questions aside and responded. "I don't know. Like I said, we're very strict on reviewing and enforcing our safety protocols at every start-up meeting. They're constantly reinforced. I don't know how both men failed to abide by the rules. There's no way they weren't aware of the correct procedure. Have you spoken with my OCE, Nathan Garcia? He's looking into the incident."

"I have and he seemed to think it was just one of those things. A rather casual view compared with your earlier impassioned statement. It's a miracle no one was injured that time but you didn't get so lucky in the second incident."

She grimaced, ignoring the dig about her OCE. She had her own increasing concerns on that score. "You're right about the second incident. And before you ask, I emailed you my report a few minutes before you walked in. I assumed you'd leave after you'd conducted your investigations."

Though her tone remained perfectly polite, the flash of scorn in her eyes reminded him of how she felt about him being there. He felt a sudden rush of satisfaction that he'd gotten under her skin.

Good. I'm glad she's annoyed. After what she did to Ned, that's the least she deserves.

His gut clenched with pain. It had been seven years since Ned had taken his life, but the memory of it still had the power to upset him and it was the woman who sat across from him who was responsible. The reminder sent another surge of anger rushing through him and he glared at her again.

"I haven't checked my emails, but I've interviewed a number of witnesses. I'm confident I know what happened. Again, you were very lucky no one was killed."

She inclined her head, her expression somber. "I'm very aware of that, Mr Hennessy."

Her calm demeanor only served to increase his anger. "And yet, like your OCE, you don't seem too concerned."

She opened her mouth as if to protest, but he cut her off. "I reviewed your safety protocols with regard to that specific piece of the plant. They're grossly inadequate," he bit out.

Once again, she opened her mouth to respond, and once again, he cut her off. "The mechanical engineering safety protocols must set out the control measures for risks associated with the unintended release of mechanical energy by considering safe work systems for people dealing with plant or structures. You failed to do that at every instance."

His lip curled up with disgust. "This is basic stuff, Hannah. You have a responsibility to regularly review how workers and supervisors are trained to recognize the potential hazards associated with all energy sources, including the load introduced by lifting equipment on the plant and your safety protocols must reflect that. This is especially important when there's the potential for stored energy to be released without warning and this failure on your part is the reason why that man was hurt."

Twin spots of anger suffused her cheeks. She glared at him, her breath coming fast. "Are you done? I'd like to be given the chance to respond."

He held out his hand. "Be my guest."

She pushed away from her desk and planted her hands on her hips. She turned slightly away from him and drew in a deep breath. Satisfaction surged through him, knowing he'd rattled her carefully constructed calm.

When she turned back to face him, her eyes were icy. Her voice shook with the force of her anger.

"Let me start by saying, Mr Hennessey, that it's Ms Barrington to you. I have *never* put anyone's life at risk. I went over every single one of those protocols when I first took over the safety management of this mine. A few were decidedly lacking in detail, and I made sure they were all comprehensively brought up to date. That practice has continued under my leadership. If the manual you reviewed was deficient, all I can offer by way of explanation is that you were given an outdated edition. Why that happened, I can't say. I wasn't there when you were provided it. Who gave it to you?"

He held her gaze and tried not to notice how beautiful she was when she was angry. "I have no way of knowing if that's the truth," he bit out, ignoring her question. "Hand over the most current manual and that might go some way to supporting your argument."

She reached for her phone and stabbed at the screen. Turning her back on him, she spoke to someone on the other end. He caught the words "manual" and "right away" before she ended the call and turned back to face him.

"I've just asked Mr Garcia to bring it to me ASAP. If you'd care to wait around a little longer, I'm sure you'll have it in the next ten minutes."

He nodded in response and settled back to wait. Hannah's lips tightened and he was sure she wanted to ask him to wait outside, but she remained silent. He suppressed a callous grin. He guessed she wasn't used to not having the upper hand, especially here. This was her domain, where she ruled over anyone and everyone who entered her kingdom. Too bad for her he didn't follow her orders and had the authority to do and go anywhere he liked on that mine site. The best thing was, they both knew it. He could only imagine how galling it was for her to have to surrender her power to him, at least temporarily.

She remained standing with her back to him, staring out the window from behind her desk. Her face was set in a frown and she had her arms crossed over her chest. She could have simply excused herself and left him there to wait on his own, but she'd see that as a sign of weakness and if there was one thing Hannah Barrington wasn't it was weak.

A few minutes later, there was a brief knock on the door and then it was opened. The same broad-shouldered, buffed, pretty guy Liam had met in the pit filled the opening. The newcomer's gaze went straight to Hannah and his face broke into a smile.

"You wanted the safety protocols, boss?"

Liam tensed at the possessive way the man's gaze roved over her. She was dressed in the standard-issue, high-visibility shirt and pants, but somehow even the gender-neutral clothing looked good on her. The pants cupped her shapely ass. The shirt stretched across her generous breasts. The two top buttons were undone and revealed a glimpse of smooth, tanned skin. His fingers itched to touch it. His fists clenched instinctively, and he forced himself to relax.

Hannah turned and offered the man a tight smile. "Thank you for coming, Nathan. Mr Hennessy, I believe you've met the mine's open cut examiner?"

Liam watched as the man named Nathan turned toward him and held out his hand. The action was accompanied by another wide smile, but it felt as fake as the man's straight, white teeth.

"Nice to see you again," Nathan said, his tone as insincere as the look in his eyes.

Liam shook the man's hand briefly.

She looked at Nathan. "Did you bring the manual?"

"Yes. Here you go."

He walked around Hannah's side of the desk and handed her a binder. He stood close enough that their arms brushed. Hannah looked at the man and frowned slightly but didn't move away. Nathan looked at Liam and smirked.

Liam tensed again. It was obvious the man was sending him a message: *She's mine.* He glared at Nathan, not because he was interested in Hannah, but he refused to let the man think he was intimidated. Seemingly oblivious to the undercurrents, Hannah shifted away and took a seat back behind her desk.

She opened the binder and scanned the first page before offering the manual to Liam.

"This is the most recently updated protocol. I'm not sure why you were given the wrong one. Do you know who gave it to you?"

"I think he said his name was Rodney Valentine."

"Hm," was all Hannah said. Once again, she turned her attention to Garcia. "How long has Valentine been working at this mine?"

"Ah, I'm not sure off the top of my head."

"Give me a ballpark," Hannah said dryly.

"Maybe eighteen months."

"Hm," she said again, looking decidedly unimpressed. "Anyone who's worked here that long should know which manual is the current version. In fact, older protocols are destroyed so there's no confusion. I'm not sure why that didn't happen this time." She frowned at Garcia again. "Do you know anything about that?"

The man shook his head and offered a fake attempt at a disarming smile. "Sorry, no. But I'll find out."

"Please do that. It's your job as safety controller to ensure only current versions of our protocols are available," Hannah replied.

Liam watched Garcia. The smiles never reached the man's eyes. There was no doubt about his interest in his beautiful boss, but whenever she wasn't looking, his gaze became as cold and watchful as a snake, as if just waiting for the right moment to strike.

Liam wondered about Garcia's background, how long he'd worked for Barrington Mining and in particular for Hannah, and just where his true loyalties lay. He also wondered if Hannah had any idea about the kind of guy her OCE was and that he might not be as loyal to her or to her family as she thought.

Then Liam cursed silently and pushed the thoughts aside. He shouldn't care less who she employed and whether they were loyal or not. That was her problem. His job was to get to the bottom of the safety breaches and decide what disciplinary action, if any, would be taken. That was his only concern. Hannah could deal with the rest of whatever nonsense was going on there on her own.

As if aware of his thoughts, she looked at him. Aware that it would infuriate her, he deliberately let his gaze drift to Garcia before shooting her a knowing look. Color suffused her cheeks. He couldn't tell if it was from embarrassment or anger. Not that he cared. She could sleep with whoever she liked.

Although it was interesting that she'd shifted away from Garcia. Perhaps she wasn't as interested in the guy as he was in her? Whatever. It didn't matter. As soon as Liam had done what he'd come there for, he'd leave and hopefully never have anything to do with Hannah Barrington again.

Chapter Six

Hannah stared at Liam and suppressed a groan. It hadn't escaped her notice how the tension had suddenly ramped up in her office with Nathan's arrival. The two men had immediately looked each other up and down, taking each other's measure. Typical men. Like two alpha males sizing up the opposition, ready to draw blood if necessary. It was ridiculous. Just as ridiculous as Nathan's none-too-subtle attempt to warn Liam off by deliberately brushing up against her.

For heaven's sake…she needed to remind him of who was in charge.

It had been a ludicrous show of testosterone. She might have given some consideration to taking on Nathan as a lover, but he hadn't been privy to those thoughts. As far as he was concerned, they were work colleagues, nothing else. Besides, she refused to be any man's possession. She didn't belong to Nathan. She didn't belong to anyone. And she certainly didn't appreciate Nathan's subtle attempt to suggest otherwise, no matter that it was Liam he'd been trying to warn off.

She didn't like Liam, but she refused to let Nathan think he had a claim on her. Just to make sure he got the message, she glared at her OCE again and deliberately stepped away from him before addressing Liam directly. To her annoyance, he sent her a knowing look.

Hannah gritted her teeth. She could tell Liam thought she and Nathan had something going on. She didn't care what he thought, but it irked her he'd obviously drawn that conclusion and was judging her for it.

How dare he judge me! He doesn't know anything about me!

With an effort, she tamped down her anger and handed him the manual. He barely looked at it. Instead, his attention remained focused on Nathan. No doubt the investigator was still musing about her relationship with the man. And then Liam pushed his chair back from the desk and stood. He tucked the binder under his arm and looked at Hannah.

"Thanks for this. I'll go through it and make sure it complies with the current regulations."

"I'm confident you'll find it does," she replied. "Nathan and I went through every one of those protocols ourselves. They're all up to date." She paused and then dared to ask, "Does that mean you're satisfied there's nothing more to be done here?"

To her annoyance, the man threw back his head and laughed, his eyes wide with disbelief.

"You're joking, right? Two serious safety breaches in the space of a week and you think nothing's going to come of it? What kind of fantasy land do you live in?"

His brown eyes blazed with anger. It was all Hannah could do to hold his gaze. Dread filled her stomach.

"You don't seem to understand what you're dealing with here," he said, his tone harsh. "Workers who have consistently failed to follow safety protocols and injuries that could have easily resulted in a death. And these aren't isolated incidents. These breaches have been happening time and time again and all of them on your watch. That tells me there's a serious problem here and it seems to be coming right from the top."

His eyes narrowed. His breath came fast. Alarm ran through her like a charge of electricity, leaving her nerve endings tingling.

Oh, God... He's going to close us down... Please, God. No. I can't let that happen...

As he continued to glare at her, her chest went tight. Her breath halted. She was suffocating. And then the words she dreaded came from his mouth.

"The way I see it, you'll be lucky if I don't make a recommendation that we close this mine down."

It was all Hannah could do not to explode. As much as she wanted to rail at him about the unfairness of his statement, that wouldn't aid their cause. In fact, it might just make things worse. He and his department held the mine's future in their hands and boy, did he know it.

She hated feeling so powerless and she hated him for making her feel that way. On top of that, she hated that she was attracted to him with about the same amount of passion that she wanted to kill him. She thought about his predecessor and couldn't help wishing the man had never left. Michael Warren hadn't always made decisions in their favor, but he'd been so much more reasonable, so much more malleable than this! He'd also been in his fifties and had never once sparked her interest.

She needed to pull on her big girl panties and suck it up and be professional. She had to take a constructive approach starting with getting to the bottom of what was happening in her mine and why her OCE was without answers. She'd learned more from the annoying investigator than from the colleague who was meant to have her back.

There was more going on here, including with the investigator who seemed to have a personal grudge against her. She had to start digging into Liam Hennessy's background for answers. And she had to get to the bottom of why safety protocols were not being followed. The existence of the outdated manual was a worry.

Liam watched the emotions chase themselves across Hannah's face and was filled with a surge of satisfaction. Yes! Let her feel angry, confused, and bewildered. It was no more than she deserved. Let her fret over the fact he might very well recommend the closure of her mine. He had no doubt her father had taken a leap of faith when he'd entrusted such responsibility to his youngest daughter, and he was just as certain Hannah wanted very badly to prove to her father that his faith in her had been justified. Liam hadn't yet decided whether he'd recommend closure or not, but it was somewhat satisfying watching his adversary struggle with the possibility. As far as he was concerned, she only had herself to blame.

I'm doing this for you, Ned. RIP, my friend...

He thought about what his sister had said and was annoyed by a twinge of guilt. Jacqueline believed that Ned's decision to end his life had been Ned's choice and his alone. And that was true. Ned had struggled with addictions and to be frank, he'd had a terrible home life. Even before he'd become infatuated with Hannah, his life had been far from great.

But that was beside the point. It was Hannah's callous disregard for Liam's friend that had tipped Ned over the edge. Ned had told Liam that. No, there was no escaping her culpability regarding Ned's tragic death. And it was up to Liam to make her pay. And boy, make her pay he would.

Every time Hannah thought of Liam Hennessy, she fumed all over again. It had been three days since their last conversation, and she still hadn't heard whether he intended to recommend closure of her mine. The not knowing was doing her head in. So was the fact that her OCE hadn't been able to provide her with any satisfactory answers. She was now on her way to another family dinner, which meant another briefing with her father. She dreaded telling him about the latest developments and how the new investigator seemed determined to ruin them.

Dinner with her family was the usual mix of loud conversation, laughter and the tinkling of crystal glasses and silverware. Zac and Emily's wedding preparations were progressing nicely. They'd opted for an outdoor wedding. Now they only had to decide whether it would be held in the impressive gardens at the Barrington Estate or somewhere closer to the city, where they could accommodate a larger number of guests.

Hannah barely listened to the conversations that were going on around her. Her mind was fixated on the upcoming briefing with her father. She'd swallowed every morsel on the plate in front of her, but for the life of her, she couldn't recall what she'd eaten. In fact, the hard knot of dread in her stomach had made it almost impossible to eat anything, but if she didn't, it would only cause her mother to ask questions and Hannah wasn't up for having to reveal to almost every member of her family the current turmoil in her life, particularly when it was of her own making.

Liam was right. As the group manager for work, health, safety, and training, she was ultimately responsible for everything that went on there from a safety perspective. She might have open cut examiners and supervisors she delegated to, but that didn't remove her liability. The fact someone in her team, or maybe there was more than one, had let her down wasn't the point.

Swallowing a sigh, she reached for her glass and finished the last of her wine. She prided herself on being a bit of a wine connoisseur and living in the heart of wine country in the Hunter Valley, she'd taken it upon herself to supply her family with wine at their family dinners. She liked to bring home something different every time. This one was a fine, dry Semillon that tasted of honey, lemon, apple, and pear. Normally a blending grape, this one was perfect on its own.

"Can I give you a refill?" her sister Molly asked.

Hannah smiled gratefully and held out her glass. Molly filled it up before shooting Hannah a sideways glance.

"Everything all right, little sis?"

Molly's question was pitched low enough that it wouldn't be heard over the general hum of dinner table conversation. Even still, Hannah blushed. It was one thing to reveal her struggles to her father. He owned the mine. He deserved to know. But confessing her shortcomings to her siblings...

They'd all been skeptical when she'd announced she was going to work at the Strathwaylin mine, and rightly so. She was all of twenty-three and had no experience in the mining industry, other than the very occasional times she'd visited her father in his on-site office when she'd been younger. She'd understood their skepticism. She'd been a little overawed herself. But she'd always been up for a challenge, and this was no different. She'd spent every waking moment from the time she accepted the position to when she'd taken over the reins studying everything there was to know about coal mining, including the hundreds of pages of regulations, mostly dealing with safety.

Safety was paramount. That much had been clear. And just in case she hadn't picked that up from her research, her father reiterated the same thing so often there was no way she couldn't have gotten it into her head. She'd taken her responsibility to her employees and contractors seriously, along with her need to prove herself capable to her father. He'd entrusted her with something no one else ever had and she didn't take that trust lightly.

The last thing she wanted was to repay him with a mine closure. The very thought made her sick.

"What is it, Hannah? You look ill."

Once again, Molly's concerned gaze filled her vision. She reached for her glass and managed a tight smile.

"Nothing I can't handle," she deflected. "Don't worry about me."

"But—"

"Hey, so tell me about what's happening with you and Shane. Did I tell you how I think he's a dream boat? You sure got lucky there. I can't believe you're engaged! I'm so happy for you both."

To Hannah's relief, Molly took the bait. Her answering smile was luminous. "You're right. He *is* a dream boat. The best man a woman could hope for. And did you hear? The Law Society has reinstated his license to practice. He's going to be able to work as a lawyer again."

Hannah smiled, genuinely happy for her sister. "That's great news! Congratulations to Shane! You must be both so thrilled."

"Yes. I'm so happy for him. He loves being a lawyer."

"What kind of law did he used to practice?"

"Family law. That's how he knows Flynn Craigdon so well. They worked together at Sydney Legal."

"Isn't that where Charlotte's fiancé works?"

"Yes. Grayson. But he's an estate and probate lawyer. I think they know each other in passing. They work on different floors."

"So is Shane hoping to get back into family law?" Hannah asked, pleased to keep the conversation off herself.

Molly shook her head. "No. He wants to go into criminal law. He's going to be a defense lawyer."

Hannah nodded. Given that Shane had spent two years in jail after accidentally running over and killing a cyclist, she could understand how he might be drawn to helping people who also found themselves on the wrong side of the law.

"That's great," she murmured.

Molly merely smiled, her eyes shining with happiness. "Yes, isn't it? He's just the most amazing man."

Once again, Hannah nodded. She was genuinely pleased for her sister. She knew her family had secretly wondered if Molly ever would find a boyfriend, let alone a husband. Of course, no one felt like that about *her*. Hannah had brought so many boyfriends home over the past five years, everyone had lost count. But it had never been that way for Molly and now that she'd found her special someone and was head-over-heels in love, it left a warm feeling in Hannah's heart.

What's it like to feel so completely and totally connected to one person to the point that no one else matters? That you're happy to commit for life to them? Will the time ever come when I'll want to find out?

Before she contemplated that any further, her father wiped his face with his napkin, set it aside, and cleared his throat. Then he looked at her. "Are you ready for our briefing?"

She swallowed against a sudden rush of nerves and nodded. "Of course, Daddy."

Pushing away from the table, she reached for her mostly full glass of wine and then collected the opened bottle in her other hand.

Molly grinned. "Thirsty, Hannah?"

"You've no idea," Hannah mumbled.

Thankfully, she'd packed an overnight bag and planned to spend the night in her old bedroom upstairs. Swallowing a sigh and bracing herself for what was to come, she followed her father into his office.

"So, what's been happening?" Frank Barrington asked as he poured himself a whiskey and then settled in behind his desk.

For a minute, Hannah thought about putting off the bad news and instead spending some time regaling him with the usual uneventful updates, but that would be cowardly, and she'd never been one of those. Besides, she was only delaying the inevitable. Sooner or later, she'd have to tell him about the latest disaster to befall the mine on her watch.

Just do it.

Drawing in a fortifying breath, she swallowed a gulp of wine and then set both her glass and the wine bottle down on the desk. She took her familiar place in the chesterfield chair opposite and compressed her lips.

"Well, it's been a bit of a tough week, to tell you the truth."

Her father's gaze remained steady on hers. "How so?"

"There was another accident."

Her father's gaze sharpened. "*Another* one? In one *week*? What happened?"

In a calm and detached manner, she recited the facts as she knew them. By the time she got to the arrival of Liam Hennessy, her temper got the better of her. Just the thought of him drove her wild!

"This guy is out of control, Daddy! He threatened to close us down! Okay, so we've had a higher number of safety breaches than usual, but they've all been properly dealt with and apart from Evan Wilson, none have resulted in fatalities. I mean, talk about an overreaction! It's clear he's the new kid on the block who feels the need to prove himself and throw his weight around. Well, I'm not putting up with that! I'm going to lodge a formal complaint!"

By the time she'd finished speaking, her face burned, and her breath came fast. As much as she'd tried to remain cool and calm, the very thought of Liam Hennessy got her blood boiling.

"Calm down, Hannah. The last thing we need is to get the regulator offside. I don't need to remind you how much power these government bureaucrats yield. Okay, from what you've told me, this guy sounds like a prick who's trying to make a name for himself as a tough investigator. No doubt he gets a bonus every time he makes life difficult for one of the big bad coal mine owners."

Her father sighed and scrubbed at his thick white hair. "The thing is though, we have to keep our nose clean and play by the rules. No matter how big an asshole this guy is, he can make life very difficult. Not only that, any closure, no matter how short, will cost us big time. You know all this, Hannah. And quite frankly, I don't care what it takes. You have to find some way to get this guy back on our side. What does Garcia say about it? What's his take on the incidents?"

"Nathan thinks these incidents are nothing to worry about. I'm not so sure, but I need to trust that he knows what he's doing. As for the regulator, I agree, Daddy. But it isn't as easy as you make out. Whatever's going on with this guy, it's personal. The most recent safety breaches aren't in the most serious category. The investigator has other options. He could issue a warning or a fine. He doesn't have to shut the mine, not even temporarily, and yet that's what he's threatened."

She sucked in a breath. "I need to find out what's behind this. Who he is. What his beef is with our family. There's more to it than just him being an asshole."

Her father reached for his glass and took a sip of whiskey, contemplating her from across the top of his glass. "Do you want me to talk to him?"

For the tiniest millisecond, she was tempted to take him up on his offer, but then she set that temptation aside. She was the group manager for WHST. This was *her* fight.

Determination surged through her. She narrowed her eyes. "Thank you, Daddy, but no. I'm the boss." She picked up her glass and drained it, then set it back down on the desk. "He's all mine."

Chapter Seven

The next morning, as Hannah worked methodically through the never-ending paperwork that was piled high on her desk, her mind remained firmly fixed on the problem of Liam Hennessy. She'd spent a restless night at her parents' house canvassing various options in her mind and dismissing them almost as quickly. The thing was, she had no power to have him removed from his position. Neither was he on the verge of retirement. Short of him coming down with some terrible illness—and she truly didn't wish that on him—he wasn't going away. No, she had to find another way to get him to work with her in coming up with other solutions rather than mine closure.

It annoyed her that she hadn't managed to find out anything about him. He wasn't known to her father. Neither was his name familiar to any of her siblings. She hadn't been able to speak to all of them, but she'd asked Molly and Charlotte and two of her brothers, Lincoln and Trace, and no one had been able to shed any light on the matter.

Who is Liam Hennessy? What's his beef against my family? Why is he so antagonistic toward me?

The answers to those questions remained infuriatingly out of reach. She sighed, at a loss as to how to move forward. When she'd been in this situation in the past, she'd always resorted to pouring on the professional charm. She prided herself on being quite good at that. But she'd already tried the charm offensive on this man, and it hadn't worked. She needed more information.

Drawing her keyboard toward her, she opened a search engine and typed in Liam's name. She scrolled down the page until she found a hit. It was an industry news report written on or around the time he was first appointed to the Resources Regulator. The accompanying photo showed a smiling Liam that commanded her attention. He looked a few years younger, fresh faced, bright-eyed and eager. He smiled at the camera. It was a good photo. The type of photo someone would use on a job application.

She scrolled down farther and clicked on another link. This one was from his social media page. A picture of Liam with his arm around the waist of a woman with model-looks filled the page. Tall and slim and perfectly proportioned, her dark auburn hair and alabaster skin was in perfect contrast to her smiling green eyes. There was no doubt she was beautiful. Hannah ignored a twinge of jealousy and scanned the post. Liam Hennessy and his date, Georgina Wakehurst, had been photographed outside the State Theater, enjoying the Bjorn Again ABBA tribute concert.

So, he likes ABBA. And maybe he has a girlfriend...

Hannah made a sound of disgust in the back of her throat. What did she care if he was spoken for? She had no interest in him. All she was trying to do was find a way to appeal to him so that he eased back on his aggression. So, what if her skin had tingled when their fingers had brushed. That didn't count for anything.

She scrolled down the page and found another photo. She groaned. Another picture of her nemesis looking gorgeous and relaxed in a designer suit and with yet another glamorous woman on his arm. This one was blond and blue-eyed, but just as tall, just as leggy.

No doubt another model... What is it with this guy and models?

Once again, she was annoyed with the direction of her thoughts, but her gaze returned to the picture again. She couldn't deny he was good looking. All blond hair, brown eyes, and tanned skin. Shoulders of an impressive width that looked like he was familiar with the inside of a gym. And that look in his gaze—confident, direct, challenging. She couldn't help but react to it.

If she hadn't already met him and knew he was an asshole, she'd be both interested and intrigued. He had an air of mystery about him that drew her in. At least, in the picture. She'd be tempted to stalk him on social media and arrange for an "accidental" meeting. She'd done that kind of thing before.

She'd always believed in going after what she wanted. Be that a house, a car, or a man. She wasn't one to wait for the planets to align to make things possible. Hell, no. She went out and made things happen. She created the opportunities herself. And she was proud of that.

Life didn't reward losers and those caught napping never achieved their dreams. But sex appeal and exceptional good looks couldn't make up for Liam's personality flaws. As far as she was concerned, nothing could be done about them. Still, she needed to come up with something. The current situation was untenable. She couldn't have him threatening closure every time there was an incident. Though she was determined to get their incident rate down, it wouldn't happen overnight. In the meantime, she needed an investigator with some genuine understanding of her position, and some respect for her wouldn't go astray either.

She looked at the picture again and scowled. She couldn't imagine dating a man like that. What did those women see in him beyond the sex appeal? Maybe that was enough for them. Who knew what beautiful women like that were after? Then again, maybe they saw a different side to him. She'd been lucky enough to get the rude and overbearing Liam. Perhaps he had a charming side?

She grimaced. Who said anything about dating? All she wanted to do was to get him to lay off his heavy-handed treatment of the mine. The irony was, safety was just as important to her as it was to him, but he hadn't seemed to accept her word on that. Okay, so he had a job to do, and the outdated safety protocols provided by one of the contractors was a concern, but there were more constructive ways and means of going about addressing the issues. Muscling in and dishing out orders and ignoring her pleas for understanding didn't sit well with anyone, least of all, her.

So, what do I do to win him over?

A nice dinner at the best restaurant in Muswellbrook might be a start. He'd told her he lived in the town. So did she, and she knew the perfect place to take him. It was classy without being over the top. Best of all, it served to-die-for food. A neutral place in which to discuss the issues and plead her case couldn't do any harm, surely. Mind made up, she reached for her phone and drawing in a fortifying breath, she dialed his number.

Liam ended the call from Hannah and stared down at his desk, bemused by her unexpected dinner invitation. Once again, she'd taken him by surprise. The last time they'd spoken, they'd been distinctly at odds, and as far as he knew, nothing had changed since then. In fact, the more he looked into Strathwaylin's safety record, the more concerned he became.

For a long time, the mine had experienced no more safety incidents than any other mine of that scale. But the past year was different. The incidents were frequent and though they were often only minor in nature, each time they were caused by a series of events that should never have happened.

What's going on out there?

The sheer number of incidents was way out proportion, especially compared to their earlier safety record. The only thing that had changed was the management. The incidents had ramped up in volume and frequency ever since Hannah had taken over at the helm. Now she'd invited him to dinner.

What's she up to?

She'd already tried to charm him with coffee and homemade cakes. Was this another attempt to get him to soften his approach? It wouldn't work, but no matter how much he disliked her, that didn't mean he'd turn down dinner at the fanciest restaurant in town... Or the chance to spend time in Hannah's company.

He scowled. He hated that he was still attracted to her, as drawn to her as he'd always been. Seven years had passed, but it might as well have been yesterday. Looking at her, being around her... It was like taking a punch to the gut. His attraction on seeing her again had been instant and uncontrollable. No matter how much he told himself to remain aloof, to think of all the pain she'd caused, it didn't seem to make any difference. He wanted her every bit as much as he had in high school.

The realization churned his gut. He didn't want to feel that way. Somehow it felt like a betrayal of Ned. Every leap of his pulse, every acceleration of his heartbeat... He had to find a way to overcome them. What he needed to do was remember the tragic loss of his best friend the next time he felt even the slightest shaft of desire for Hannah Barrington. That ought to do the trick.

Hannah's stomach swirled with nerves and anticipation. In less than half an hour, she was due to have dinner with Liam.

It wasn't that she was scared of him. Hannah wasn't scared of anything or anyone and she'd always thrived on a challenge. It was more that she was concerned about the impact he could have on her father's business. This meeting needed to go well. Liam had more power over the mine than anyone alive. Then there was the annoying fact she found him attractive. She'd disliked him from their very first meeting, but her libido didn't care that he was a jerk. Or that he only seemed to date models.

She didn't have the kind of looks that would grace the covers of glossy fashion magazines, but neither was she ugly. She liked her long dark hair and she was often complimented on her blue eyes. She had good skin, a tidy figure, and at five foot nine, she wasn't exactly short.

She'd also always had a healthy sex drive and was prepared to seek out physical pleasure whenever she got the urge. She loved hanging out in bars and nightclubs, dancing, drinking, and having a good time. It had been a bit harder to let her hair down in a town of less than twenty thousand people, but she still managed to get out most Friday nights, and a lot of the time, she managed to run into someone new. She didn't go home with someone every Friday night, but she was always open to the idea, except of course when she was in a relationship. She wasn't a cheater. Neither did she do married men.

She'd lost count of the number of boyfriends she'd had, along with the relationships that had barely lasted a few weeks. When she met an available man she was attracted to, she had no qualms about making a move. Sometimes things lasted a few months, like her relationship with Chad, sometimes a whole lot less. Hell, she was only twenty-three. She wasn't looking for long term.

She didn't kid herself; the challenge of overcoming Liam's antagonism and bringing him over to her side wasn't going to be easy, but she remained confident in her people skills. Of course, she wasn't going to try to seduce him. No matter that she found him attractive, she couldn't imagine sleeping with him. He wasn't just a desirable male to be picked up on a Friday night. He held the survival of her mine in his hands. She needed to stay sharp and focused. There was no way she'd complicate matters by getting romantically involved and given that every time they were together he made her blood boil, she didn't think there was much chance of that happening anyway.

Hopefully, by the end of the night, they'd at least part as courteous professionals, each recognizing and respecting the job they had to do but agreeing to work together to find solutions to returning the mine to being a safe workplace. That's all she wanted. She was just as concerned as he was about the current spate of incidents. They both wanted the same outcome.

She'd taken extra care with her appearance, while still maintaining a professional look. Her hair was pulled back in a knot with casual tendrils around her face. She'd applied her makeup to emphasize the almond shape and blue of her eyes and had glossed her lips an icy pink that highlighted the cool tones of her olive skin.

She tried to pretend that she hadn't spent so much time getting ready because she wanted him to desire her. She knew deep down that she wanted to set him back on his ass. But she also knew she was at her most confident when she felt good about herself.

That was one of the reasons she'd chosen to wear a form-fitting, black Chanel dress. The soft, expensive fabric felt good against her skin. Though the neckline was low enough to provide a glimpse of her generous breasts, the hemline kissed the tops of her knees. It was modest and not over the top, but sexy and elegant just the same. A perfect combination.

Now for the next challenge...

She'd made the dinner booking for seven and was pleased when he arrived at the restaurant right on time. It was a weeknight and there were only a few other tables occupied. Soft music played from a hidden speaker. The waiter showed him over to their table. Determined to be her shining best, Hannah smiled as he took the seat opposite her.

"Thank you for coming," she said. "It's nice to see you again."

He shot her a quizzical look, one eyebrow raised. "Is it? I got the distinct impression you didn't particularly care for my presence."

She refused to feel annoyed. Instead, she held his gaze steadily and kept her smile in place.

The waiter hovered beside him. "Can I get you something to drink?"

Liam glanced at the glass of white wine near her hand. "I'll have what she's having."

The waiter nodded and moved away. Hannah smirked. "You don't even know what I'm drinking."

"Doesn't matter. I drink just about anything. Besides, we're in the heart of wine country. I've already had the opportunity of sampling a little of the local offerings. I can't imagine anything I'm served here won't be good."

She half-shrugged, impressed despite herself. "Fair enough."

Liam looked around him. "This is a nice place."

She nodded. "Yes. Have you been here before?"

"No. I haven't been in town that long. I haven't yet eaten out anywhere."

"Well, it's definitely not Sydney, but there are a few decent bars and restaurants and the people out here in the country are so warm and welcoming. I'm sure you'll enjoy yourself." She paused and then asked, "How long are you intending to stay?"

"I'm not sure. I moved here to be closer to my sister. She's all I have as far as family's concerned."

Hannah frowned. "Your parents are dead?"

"Yes."

He didn't expound any further and she didn't respond except to offer condolences which he accepted with a slight inclination of his head. She wasn't there to get to know him better, though it was sad he'd lost his mom and dad. She couldn't imagine losing her parents when she was still so young.

The waiter arrived with Liam's wine and then handed them dinner menus. Hannah busied herself scanning the options. It was safer than feeling sympathy for him. That was way too dangerous.

The menu offered contemporary Australian fare which reflected a cultural fusion of flavors. Liam ordered a coriander prawn and honey bok choy starter and squid ink pasta with salmon and roe for his main. Hannah opted for roasted tomato soup with crusty bread and the restaurant's signature dish, an in-house aged Tasmanian eye-fillet steak with truffle oil mash. For dessert, she ordered a Belgian chocolate tart with fresh cream and a raspberry coulis. Her dinner guest declined dessert. The waiter took their orders and left.

Liam's gaze raked over her. "You don't look like a woman who indulges in dessert too often."

She tensed at the personal comment but then shot him an arch look. The whole point of this meal was to get him on her side.

"That's where you're wrong," she murmured huskily and then looked at him from beneath her lashes. "I indulge as often as I like." She shot him a challenging look, daring him to question her further over what kind of indulgences she was talking about, but he merely changed the subject. She was annoyed at herself for feeling disappointed and disappointed in herself for stooping to flirtation. This was, after all, a business dinner.

"So, how does a woman like you end up a group manager? Apart from the fact your father owns the mine, that is."

Anger surged through her. She reached for her glass and took a sip of her wine, deliberately using the time to keep her temper under control. He sure had a way of keeping her libido in check. She supposed that was a good thing. She really wasn't trying to seduce him, but getting into another argument with him before they'd even had the appetizers wasn't a good start.

She forced a smile. "You're right. My father owns the mine, but that's not the reason I got the job. He knew I could do it and I've proved to him many times his confidence in me wasn't misplaced."

He cocked an eyebrow at her, silently challenging her statement. "But you had no prior experience in the mining industry, right?"

Beneath the table, her hands clenched into fists. *He's deliberately goading me...* It was all she could do not to tell him to take a hike. *Deep breaths, Hannah. Deep breaths...*

Once again, she held on to her temper and offered him a strained smile. "That's right. But what you don't know is that I do my best work under pressure, and I've always been up for a challenge. Apart from that, I'm a fast learner and I have a talent for being able to get the best out of people. That combination of skills has seen production in the mine increase by twenty percent these past two quarters. I'm sure you'll appreciate, that's no mean feat."

She eyed him steadily, daring him to disagree. She was sure someone who took their job as seriously as Liam Hennessy would have done his homework. He'd know exactly how much coal was being dug out of the ground at Strathwaylin, just like she was sure he knew every single safety breach that had occurred on her watch. She swallowed a sigh.

His lip curled up in a sneer. "Oh, yes. Production. It's no surprise your safety breaches have increased along with your bank account. There's nothing like record coal prices to motivate a coal manager to cut corners. It's all about the money for you people. You don't care who gets trampled along the way."

The fury that washed over her was hot and quick and immediate and it was all she could do to contain it. Here it was again, his damned attitude. *To hell with this.* Tired of dancing around the issue, and with her temper barely restrained, she cut to the chase.

"What the hell is your problem? I'm trying my best to foster a civil relationship and yet you're determined to scorn me at every turn. You know nothing about me or my family. You've marched into my life with preconceived notions of who I am and what I stand for, and I've had enough. Either get over yourself or—"

She broke off, unsure of what to say. She could threaten him all she liked. That wouldn't remove him from her life. He'd been appointed by the Resources Regulator over her patch of turf. No matter what she said or who she complained to, that wasn't likely to change. And he knew it.

He merely raised an eyebrow in silent, arrogant query. "Or?"

She glared at him across the table, her chest tight with anger. "I don't know why you're being such an asshole," she said in a slightly modified tone. "I understand you have a job to do, but so do I. Despite what you think, I care about my staff, and I do my best to avoid accidents. I don't know why they've suddenly increased in number, but like I've told you before, I'm doing everything I can to get to the bottom of that and bring it to an end. I appreciate your role in the safety chain, and I agree it's a very important one, but the best thing for all concerned is for us to work together constructively to make the mine a safe place for everyone. Fighting with me, getting me offside—how does that achieve anything?"

By the time she'd finished, her breath came fast. Her fists were still clenched, and her face burned. Liam's expression had frozen. It was like staring at stone. Anger glittered in his frosty brown eyes.

"Are you done?"

Chapter Eight

Liam had never been so angry. Even when he'd lost his father so soon after his mother and had raged at God over the injustice of it, that still didn't compare to this. Of course, it was typical of Hannah Barrington. When did she ever think of anyone other than herself? She hadn't changed a bit over the past seven years. No, that wasn't right. She'd changed on the outside at least.

Gone was the slim and girlish teenager. She'd been replaced by a tall and elegant woman who'd filled out in all the right places. The expensive black dress she wore was cut low enough to enhance her generous cleavage. The fabric followed the curves of her body so closely it looked like she'd been glued into it. Her long legs were encased in black stockings that only emphasized their shapely form. She'd teamed the outfit with a pair of impossibly high stilettos, the sight of which sent blood straight to his cock.

He hated that his body was hard and yearning; that he wanted nothing more than to crush her against him and kiss her full lips until they were both breathless. It was a betrayal of the worst kind. They were enemies and always would be. He needed to tell his cock that.

It annoyed him even more that she still hadn't recognized him. Well, he was going to change that. Right now. She wanted to know what his problem was. She was about to find out. He narrowed his eyes in a glare.

"I can't believe you don't know who I am."

Her brow furrowed in confusion. "Excuse me?"

He continued to glare at her. "You heard me."

She glared right back. "From the moment I met you, you've been throwing out these cryptic remarks, acting like I should know you. I'm sorry to dent your ego, Mr Hennessy, but no, I don't know who you are. I'm sure I'd remember meeting someone as rude and insufferable as you."

He sneered. "Typical."

Anger flashed in her eyes. Her mouth tightened. "For heaven's sake, just spit it out. It's obvious you think we've met before. Forgive me for not remembering." She gave him a scathing once-over. "Whenever it was we're supposed to have met, I'm afraid you didn't leave a lasting impact on me."

He tensed. The remark was deliberately insulting. It only fueled his anger. He shot her a scornful look.

"You were always so full of yourself, Hannah Barrington. I've never met a more rude or arrogant woman. I shouldn't be surprised. You were like that all the way back in high school. Some people never change."

Her frown deepened. He could almost see her thought processes as she tried to place him. "You knew me in high school?"

He continued to regard her with scorn. "Yep. Although I wasn't in the popular crowd. Nor was I rich. No doubt that's why I never made a lasting impact on you," he said, deliberately throwing her words back at her.

Hannah's eyes widened with disbelief and confusion. It was obvious she truly didn't remember him. He ignored the stab of hurt and disappointment.

Of course, she never noticed you... She was everything you weren't... Rich, popular, and surrounded by friends. You were a nobody.

She reached for her glass and emptied it in two large gulps, then signaled to the waiter for another. As she waited for her drink to arrive, she drew in a deep breath and then looked at him. Her expression appeared genuinely apologetic.

"I'm sorry. I wish I could say I remember you. Were you in my year?"

"No. I was two years above. With your brother, Wade."

She nodded. "Okay. So, how did we know each other? Did you play football?"

"Yes, but I only made the reserve team. I can't remember ever seeing you at one of our games."

She offered a self-deprecating smile. "You're right. My brothers played first grade. They dragged me along to their games, but I only went because they wanted me to. I didn't really care for football. To tell you the truth, I wouldn't know a halfback from a hooker." She smiled again.

Despite everything, he couldn't help but be reminded of how beautiful she was. Blood pumped spontaneously to his groin. He scowled. His body's reflexive reaction only made him more irritable. All at once, he wanted to strike out at her.

"Do you remember a boy by the name of Ned Harris?"

She screwed up her face in thought. "Ned Harris. I don't think so. Was he in my year?"

"No. He was in mine. We were best friends." As memories overwhelmed him, Liam's anger rose, along with his voice.

"He thought you'd hung the moon and stars and when he told you how he felt, you cut him to the quick. He never got over your rejection. It's your fault he's dead. Oh, you didn't pull the trigger, but you might as well have."

Hannah stared at him. Her eyes went wide. Her mouth gaped. Her hand came up to press against her chest. "What... What are you talking about?"

Anger tore through Liam's chest. He shook his head in disgust. "See! Even now you don't remember him! My best mate. Ned Harris." His lips twisted in a grimace. "He was in love with you all through high school, like most of the boys. He told me you'd encouraged him to tell you how he felt, gave him hope you might reciprocate his feelings. He finally screwed up the courage to approach you one day and gave you a love letter declaring his feelings. You dismissed him with hardly a glance in his direction and crumpled up the letter and threw it away. Right in front of him. Right in front of your friends. And then you ran off, laughing. Ned topped himself shortly after. It was all your fault."

Liam's breath sounded harsh in his ears. His heart pounded. His face was hot. The pain of that awful time came crashing around him, filling his head with images he'd rather forget. Though he hadn't been the one to find Ned, as soon as he'd been told, he'd charged over to his friend's house and had raced into Ned's bedroom. He'd arrived there before the police. It was a scene he'd never be able to erase.

When he dragged his gaze back to Hannah, her face was chalky. The shock in her eyes couldn't have been manufactured. She looked...shattered. Exactly how he'd felt all those years ago when he'd been confronted with the harsh and graphic reality of Ned's death.

"I... I'm so sorry," she gasped. "That's devastating. I had no idea."

Liam stared at her. She sounded so genuine. He delved behind her shocked gaze for the truth. She reached for her glass and then stopped when she realized it was empty. She ran a hand through her hair and then clenched her hands into fists. She drew in a shaky breath. Her shoulders slumped on a heavy sigh. And then she looked at him again.

"I'm sorry, Liam. I really am. I can't imagine how hard that must have been for you. For anyone. For that to happen to your best friend..." She shuddered and her eyes filled with shadows. "How old was he?"

"A week shy of turning eighteen," Liam rasped.

Hannah shook her head. "I can't imagine having to go through that, or what it must have done to you. Now I understand your antagonism. I understand your anger. You think I'm responsible for your friend's death."

Her voice was ragged with emotion. He tried not to let the shock and disbelief that lined her tone affect him. She was the enemy. The one who'd driven Ned to suicide. Okay, so he'd had other problems, but Hannah's rejection had tipped him over the edge.

"I'm sorry you feel that way," she continued in a low voice that still shook with emotion. "I don't know what to tell you. The only thing I can say in my defense is that it wasn't like you remember."

Liam tensed. There was nothing wrong with his memory. Every single awful minute of that time was singed into his brain. It wasn't something he'd ever forget.

"I remember him now," Hannah continued softly. "Yes. Ned. I don't think I ever knew his last name. Tall, thin, glasses. A nice smile." Her lips turned upward as she appeared to recall his friend.

"I only knew him to look at," she added. "As you said, he was a couple of years above me in school. I don't know why you think I gave him encouragement. That's not true. We didn't hang out in the same circles. We had no mutual friends. I'm sorry to say, but I barely knew him."

She raised her gaze to Liam's. Her eyes were clear and direct. "I certainly didn't know he was in love with me."

"But he gave you a love letter," Liam persisted. "You encouraged him to pour out his heart to you. He told me."

She held his gaze. "No, I never did that. But you're right about the letter. I remember that now."

"See! You balled it up and threw it back in his face!"

She shook her head. "No! I stood there and read it in front of him. I was so surprised and embarrassed. I mean, he'd declared his undying love. I didn't even know him. I remember pushing the note into my backpack and trying to get out of there. I certainly didn't laugh in his face. My friends might have teased him. I can't remember. All I remember is wanting to get away from there and hide. I didn't want a boyfriend. I certainly didn't want someone declaring their undying love. I was more interested in baking than dating. I didn't date anyone back then."

Liam compressed his lips, anger still swirling inside him. He'd always thought the reason she'd remained single throughout high school was so that she could keep stringing all the boys along, including him. It fit with her self-absorbed personality. And yet she appeared genuinely shocked at the thought he held her responsible for Ned's death.

What if she's telling the truth about that?

No! He refused to believe that. He'd been there when Ned had told him about the humiliation he'd experienced at Hannah's hands. The way she and her friends had laughed and made fun of him. How dare Ned Harris think for even an instant he had a chance with the beautiful and popular Hannah Barrington!

The memory cut short any concerns that Liam might have gotten things wrong. He eyed her coldly.

"Forgive me for not believing you. I was there when my best mate cried his heart out over your callous rejection. He was a mess. Those feelings of worthlessness didn't come from nowhere." He pushed away from the table and stood. "Please excuse me. I've lost my appetite."

Hannah gaped after Liam's departing back, shocked for the second time that night. She couldn't believe he thought she was lying about his friend. Worse still, there was nothing she could do about it. The name "Ned Harris" hadn't meant anything to her. It wasn't until Liam had mentioned the love letter that she'd recalled him. But the way things had transpired was so different from what Ned had told his friend, she didn't know what she could do to make Liam believe her.

She'd long ago lost touch with her girlfriends who'd been with her that day and even if she could track one or two of them down, there was no guarantee they'd remember. They had no reason to. No, there was no way she could produce a witness and Ned wasn't going to be offering up any other explanations.

She was surprised to discover it upset her to witness Liam's distress. All they'd done since they'd met was butt heads and yet, she cared that after all these years, he continued to carry around so much grief. It was obvious the tragic loss of his friend still hurt. He was still so angry about it; angry at *her*.

The thought weighed her down. She'd never felt so helpless. Taking the blame for something she hadn't done went against everything she believed in, but what else could she do? She'd told him the truth and he didn't believe her. There was no point insisting. That would only be wasted breath. Until he accepted his friend had been less than honest about what he'd told Liam about her, there was nothing she could do. Unfortunately, there was no guarantee that would ever happen. The knowledge was depressing.

Liam spun the tires of his Mercedes coupé as he exited the car park of the restaurant. His head was still full of thoughts of Hannah. She was unbelievable. Even after all these years, she couldn't admit to the part she'd played in Ned's death. It was infuriating. Liam hadn't expected her to beg forgiveness, but he'd at least thought she might shoulder some responsibility.

He tore down the quiet suburban streets, barely noticing the iconic blue heeler cattle dog statue that sat upon a high sandstone brick platform in the center of town. His anger hadn't diminished by the time he pulled up in his sister's driveway. Jacqueline's Honda was in the carport. She'd told him she was having a night in. She'd been curled up on the couch in front of the TV when he'd left. As he came through the front doorway, he noticed she was still there. The TV was tuned to an episode of "Suits". She turned her head and looked at him in surprise.

"What are you doing home so early? I thought you were going to dinner."

Liam grimaced and walked farther into the room. With a weary sigh, he threw himself down on the couch beside her.

Jacqueline gave him a half-smile. "That doesn't sound good. I take it your date didn't go exactly as you'd planned?"

He pulled a face. "Firstly, it wasn't a date. I told you it was a business meeting."

With one eyebrow cocked, she eyed his designer shirt with the two top buttons undone and his jeans. "Really? You didn't dress for a business meeting."

Liam flushed, but doggedly held her gaze. "I only accepted because I was intrigued by her invitation. We've been at loggerheads since my arrival. Being invited to dinner by Hannah Barrington was the last thing I expected. I was curious about how far she'd go to butter me up."

Jacqueline winked. "Given that you've only been gone about an hour, I take it she didn't go as far as you would have liked?"

Liam choked. The fact that he'd had to fight to keep his libido in check from the moment he'd spied Hannah seated in the restaurant only made things worse. He didn't want to be attracted to her. Not when he was a teenager and certainly not now. Too bad his cock had other ideas.

"You have it all wrong," he said, eager to set his sister straight. "After what she did to Ned, I can barely stand to be in the same room with her."

Jacqueline sent him a knowing look. "Whatever you say, little brother."

Liam's anger ignited. "How could I want a woman like that? A woman who played with Ned's feelings and then cut him to the quick! She's the reason he's dead!"

Jacqueline sent him a somber look. "We've been over this, Liam. You know that's not true."

His frustration boiled over. "I don't know anything of the sort!" he exclaimed, jumping to his feet. "You know, she didn't even recognize me. I had to tell her we'd gone to high school together."

"Well as far as I can recall, you didn't exactly run in the same circles. You weren't even in the same year. And you have filled out since high school," Jacqueline murmured.

Liam barely listened. Anger coursed through him. With clenched hands and jaw, he began to pace the living room.

"I mentioned Ned to her. She didn't even remember him! Can you believe that? It was only after I told her about the love letter that she recalled who he was and then she had the gall to tell me she barely knew him." Liam shook his head with disgust. "She's even more narcissistic than I thought."

Jacqueline sat up straighter on the couch. A frown marred the smooth lines of her forehead.

"Hang on a minute, Liam. You seem to forget it was Ned who was in love with her. I don't remember ever hearing the feeling was reciprocated. How do you expect her to remember the guy? It's not like they were an item."

Liam stared at his sister. "I can't believe you're defending her! What is it about this woman that has everyone jumping to do her bidding?"

"I'm not jumping to do her bidding. I'm trying to make you see reason. You're hellbent on holding Hannah responsible for Ned's death. I'm just reminding you that there were other factors involved."

"But Ned told me she'd encouraged his attentions! That's why he found the courage to write that letter. When I put that to Hannah, she denied it. Said she never gave Ned any encouragement."

Jacqueline regarded him somberly. She opened her mouth to speak and then closed it again, as if she'd changed her mind. Liam tensed.

"What is it? What were you going to say?"

His sister sighed quietly and then took her time in replying. "I had a conversation with Ned a few months before he died."

Liam shrugged. It wasn't unusual for his sister to talk to Ned. His mate had spent plenty of time over at their house. "Yeah, so?"

Jacqueline drew in a deep breath and eased it out. "So," she said, drawing out the word. "Ned told me he was in love with Hannah. He also told me he knew he could never have her. She was way out of his league. She barely knew he existed. He told me she was always sweet to him if they happened to pass in the hallway and he said something to her, but that was because she had a kind heart. He could tell she wasn't interested in him, and she'd never given him the slightest encouragement."

Liam stared at his sister in shock. "I don't understand."

"Let me finish." She dragged in another breath. "Ned was hopelessly in love with Hannah. She was all he could think about. I was worried he bordered on the obsessive, but I didn't see the harm in it. He wasn't the first teenager to pine after a pretty girl and live with unrequited love. I thought he'd eventually leave high school and get over it.

"A couple of weeks before he died, he told me he couldn't finish high school without letting her know how he felt. He said he was going to write her a letter, lay out his feelings and take his chances. He didn't hold out much hope that she'd be open to his declaration of love, but he was determined to risk humiliation to tell her how he felt before it was too late."

Liam braced himself for what was about to come. He knew where this was headed. "Let me guess. He gave her the letter, bared his heart, she laughed in his face and humiliated him in front of her friends. He was so torn up, he went home and shortly afterward, took his life. Am I right?"

He glared at his sister, even though his anger was firmly directed toward Hannah. Then Jacqueline surprised him.

"No, Liam. You're wrong. That's not what happened. I don't know what Hannah told you, but I spoke to Ned that day. I found him behind the toilet block at that park across from our house. He was beside himself. I asked him what was wrong, and he told me he'd given Hannah the letter. He stood by while she read it. Then she shoved it in her bag and left.

"He was in an agony of not knowing how she felt, but he could tell from her reaction that his declaration of love hadn't been received very well. She'd been embarrassed that he'd written her a letter. Her friends gave her a hard time over it, but Hannah ignored them and got the hell out of there. I don't know that she ever spoke to Ned again."

Liam felt like he'd been poleaxed. All these years, he'd believed Ned's story and now he had to accept his friend hadn't told him the truth.

"Why would he lie to me?" he asked, dazed. "We were best friends."

"Maybe he wanted to save face," Jacqueline suggested quietly. "You were his best friend. What was he going to do? Admit the girl of his dreams didn't love him?" Jacqueline shot him a sideways look before adding, "Ned was a smart guy. Maybe he knew you were also in love with her. Maybe he thought you might have a better chance with her? What better way to ensure you didn't even think about making a play for her, than by painting her in such an awful light?"

Liam reeled back in shock. "What the hell? Firstly, I wasn't in love with—"

"Please, Liam. It's me you're talking about. Quit the bullshit."

Liam blinked. His sister rarely resorted to curse words. When she did, she meant business. He drew in a deep breath and blew it out on a weary sigh and then dropped back onto the couch beside her. With his elbows on his knees, he dropped his head into his hands.

"Okay. You're right. I was in love with Hannah. Probably as long as Ned. I always knew how he felt about her. That's why I never said a word to him about my own feelings."

Jacqueline gave him a gentle look. "You didn't have to. We both knew."

Liam shook his head. "Ned told you?"

"He didn't have to, but yes, he told me."

Liam's shoulders slumped on another sigh. All these years he'd thought he'd kept his love for Hannah a secret from his best friend, from everyone. He should have known better.

"Do you really think Ned blackened Hannah's name so I wouldn't go after her myself?"

Jacqueline compressed her lips and gave him a sad look. "Yes, Liam. I do. And it worked."

Jacqueline was right. It *had* worked. He'd hated Hannah with a vengeance from that moment on. Even more so after Ned took his life.

She's innocent in all of this...

Right on the tail of that realization was another one: *I owe her an apology...*

Leaning back against the couch, he scrubbed at his hair and grimaced. So many years wasted feeling angry at Hannah Barrington, when all the time his anger should have been directed toward his friend.

Ha! Some friend! What kind of friend does that to a mate?

Liam was overcome with sadness and regret. He'd never get to have that conversation with his friend; never get to rant and rail; never get to demand an explanation or an apology. All he could do was to try and mend bridges with Hannah. It wouldn't change the way he approached his job, but it would go some way to alleviating the antagonism he'd felt toward her up until now. He just hoped she understood and accepted his apology. There was nothing else he could do.

Chapter Nine

Hannah finished reading through the last report on her desk and filed it in the folder that contained all the other reports that had come in overnight from mines around the world. After being abandoned the night before by Liam, she'd fixed up their bill, apologized to the staff, and taken her leave, all the time fuming that she'd been put in that predicament. She'd invited him to dinner in an attempt to smooth things over and call a kind of truce, but her efforts had failed miserably. He was angrier at her than ever. At least she now knew why.

Ned Harris.

Though Hannah was sad that Ned had so tragically taken his life, she refused to feel guilty or accept that she'd played a part in that. She was disappointed Liam seemed determined to believe Ned's version of events. Not that she could blame him. After all, the two boys had been best friends. No one expected to be lied to by a best friend. But that also meant she was fighting with two hands tied behind her back when it came to persuading Liam to recognize the truth.

None of that would matter if he wasn't so integral to her success as a group manager and the ultimate success of her father's business. To say nothing of the more than one hundred employees she had relying on her to keep the mine profitable and ensure their wages kept being paid. All of that was under threat every time Liam considered the possibility of closing the mine.

The sound of her phone ringing interrupted her thoughts. She scrambled around in her handbag and finally located it. Checking the screen, her heart somersaulted with a combination of nerves and anticipation.

"Mr Hennessy. What can I do for you?"

"Hannah. I wanted to call and apologize."

"It's fine. I'm a big girl. I can cope with being left high and dry in a restaurant."

Her quip didn't make an impact on his somber tone. "That's not what I meant."

"Oh, so you're not sorry for leaving me alone, looking like a shag on a rock?"

"Of course, I am. But that's not what I feel sick to my gut about. I want to apologize for what I said to you about Ned. I was wrong."

It was obvious from his tone how difficult it was for him to make that admission. For an instant, she was tempted to make him suffer further, but she'd never been the kind of person who got off on being vindictive or enjoyed seeing other people hurting.

Instead, she said simply, "Thank you. Does this mean you believe me?"

"Yes. I'm sorry. I... I've always thought Ned told me the truth about that day. It's difficult for me to accept that he lied. Or at least slanted the whole sorry episode his way." He sighed. "Poor Ned."

She heard the sadness and pain in his voice and her heart filled with compassion. Forget about the fact they were on different sides of a battle. She couldn't sit back knowing he was hurting and not say anything.

"I can't imagine the pain Ned must have been in to get to the point of taking his own life. I wish I'd known him better, known how he felt."

"Would it have made a difference?" Liam replied hoarsely.

Hannah paused. "To the way I felt about him?"

"Yes."

"No. I'm sorry. I wish I could tell you differently. But like I said, I wasn't into boys back then. They were hardly on my radar. I was busy with school and sport and friends. My weekends were mostly filled with baking. I used to spend hours poring over recipes, adding my own slant on them, experimenting. Cupcakes, cookies, pasties, and pies. I was interested in learning to bake everything."

Once again, she heard him sigh wearily. "I wish Ned had told me the truth. I wish I hadn't spent so many years blaming you. It wasn't fair. You weren't responsible for Ned's death any more than I was. Ned was in a terrible place. He had a lot of underlying issues."

"Like what?" she asked softly.

"He had a terrible home life," Liam said quietly. "His parents were dysfunctional, to say the least. He'd turned to alcohol and drugs to escape. I knew it was happening, but I also knew why. I understood why he felt the need to numb the pain in whatever way he could. I remember feeling so helpless, wishing there was something I could to do help him, but I was just a kid too."

His voice cracked with emotion. Her heart clenched. "I'm sure he valued your friendship," she murmured.

"Yeah, I guess."

He sounded far from convinced. She felt another urge to comfort him. "Of course, he did," she insisted. "You were best friends. You told me that he told you everything."

"Except now I know he didn't always tell me the truth."

She had no argument for that. "What happened that you changed your mind?"

There was a pause and then he answered. "I talked to my sister, Jacqueline. You probably don't remember her, either. She's a year older than me. I think she went to school with the Barrington triplets."

"Okay. I'm sorry, but I don't remember her, but I'm sure Charlotte, Trace, and Molly will," she said. "Next time I talk to them, I'll ask them."

"That doesn't matter. All I meant is that Jacqueline was the one who made me see the truth of things."

"How so?"

Liam told her how Jacqueline had confessed to having a conversation with Ned about the letter he'd given to Hannah and how Hannah had reacted. She was quietly relieved Ned had at least told someone the truth.

"I see," she said when Liam finished.

"I'm sorry again that I didn't believe you."

She sighed softly. "That's okay. Honestly. I understand why you'd believe your best friend over me. After all, you know nothing about me. Or at least, only what you think you know, and that's been forever tarnished by what Ned told you."

"That's true." He sighed. "There's something more. After I talked to Jac last night, I had a lot of time to think about this. The reason I blamed you so hard was because it made it easier than blaming myself."

"No, Liam. That's not fair. It wasn't your fault."

"I was Ned's best friend," Liam continued as if he hadn't heard her. "I should have seen something, known how close he was to the edge. You wouldn't believe how guilty I felt all these years for letting my friend down, for not recognizing the dark place he was in, for not getting him help! But even if I'd known, even if I'd spoken to Ned, there was no guarantee I would have been able to stop it. I see that now. Ned made the decision to end his life and he did that on his own."

Once again, his voice cracked with emotion. Hannah's heart went out to him. "You're right. As tragic as that is, there's no one else to blame."

Hannah heard Liam drag in a shaky breath and blow it out. "Thank you. I have no right to expect you to be so gracious about this. I treated you abominably and said some terrible things."

"It's fine, Liam. You were acting under a misapprehension," Hannah murmured.

"I ruined your dinner," he said wryly. "Please let me make it up to you. Are you free tonight?"

Hannah blinked in surprise. She was suddenly beset by a weird combination of nerves and excitement. She couldn't deny she was attracted to him. Now that they'd gotten to the bottom of his antagonism and had established a fragile peace, she wanted to get to know him better. Not because that might give her the opportunity to work on him to soften his approach toward the mine, but because she was intrigued by him.

For so long, she'd steered clear of serious relationships. The four months she'd given to Chad was longer than she'd given anyone and when things came to an end, she'd been relieved. It had been well and truly time to move on.

But with Liam, she'd already ridden the emotional highs and lows and while much of it had been in relation to the mine, their interactions had also felt personal. He was different. He wasn't a man she'd picked up in a bar looking for a good time and who knew the score. She had more respect for him than that. More importantly, he was integrally connected with her professional life. If things didn't work out and their relationship soured, that could potentially impact the mine. *Is that a risk I'm prepared to take? The stakes are high.*

"Please let me take you to dinner," he urged. "I really want to make it up to you."

The quiet sincerity in his tone touched her. Despite her better judgment, she found herself agreeing.

"Great!" Liam breathed. "I'll meet you there at seven. Let's do things right this time."

Liam spent the rest of the day poring over the notes and photographs he'd taken during his investigation into the two separate incidents at the Strathwaylin mine. Despite the way he felt about Hannah, he had a job to do, and he took that responsibility seriously. A mine was a dangerous workplace. There were any number of things that could go wrong and when they did, there was a high chance they'd result in serious injury, or even death.

It was his job to ensure those running the mine did so with safety at the forefront of their minds. If that meant issuing fines or shutting the place down, then so be it. He hoped that wouldn't be necessary with Strathwaylin, but if the evidence supported such a decision, then he wouldn't hesitate to do it and he'd face the fallout with Hannah.

Hannah.

He was still coming to terms with the realization that she wasn't the malicious, spoiled, little bitch he'd always thought she was. No, that wasn't right. He hadn't always thought of her that way. It was only after what Ned had told him about her that his love for her had morphed into hate. He'd spent seven years cursing her for what she'd done. It would take time to recalibrate.

Inviting her to dinner seemed like a natural first step toward mending bridges. He'd already made it clear that nothing she said or did would alter his attitude toward doing his job, but he was willing to temper his antagonism and call a truce. They might even become friends. She'd had a good relationship with his predecessor. There was no reason the same couldn't happen between them. But for now, he had to complete his investigation.

He didn't know if it was mere coincidence that the first fatality at Strathwaylin had occurred on the first day the mine was under Hannah's control. Liam had read through the contents of the report on the death of Evan Wilson. It was a sad fact that the accident should never have happened. A young man had lost his life. A family grieved the loss of their son and brother. While nothing would bring him back, Liam was pleased to discover the family had been adequately compensated.

Ever since that day, the number of safety breaches resulting from a range of incidents had been steadily increasing. Not all of them had been serious, but it was the sheer volume of accidents that concerned him. It also made him suspicious. The mine had once been a relatively safe workplace. Something in the past twelve months had changed. The first explanation he'd thought of was the change in management, but he now wondered if there was more to it than that.

He picked up a report from an incident the previous month and scanned its contents. The name "Paul Hammond" leaped out at him. Hammond had been involved in the two most recent incidents, as well as a few other less serious ones. Given his penchant for breaching safety regulations, Liam wondered why the man was still employed. On impulse, he put the man's name into a search engine and then sat back to wait for the results.

He reached for his coffee and sipped at it while he waited for the pages to load. Scrolling through the entries, he clicked on the one that appeared highest in the list. It was a media report put out by one of the newspapers on an incident at the mine. The accident had resulted in a fully-loaded dump truck tipping over and had been serious enough to raise the interest of the mainstream media.

Most mining incidents remained in-house. Employees were under strict instructions not to speak of anything that happened there. Neither were they allowed on their phones. And yet somehow the media had gotten wind of the story. It was interesting that Paul Hammond's name was mentioned.

Was he the source for the story? If so, what did he have to gain? If his employer had discovered the leak had come from him, he should have been immediately fired.

And yet, Hammond remained employed at the mine. Not directly by Barrington Mining, but he was employed there just the same. It almost seemed like he was untouchable.

What does he have over those in charge?

Determined to dig further, Liam clicked on other links that mentioned Paul Hammond. He discovered the man was twenty-eight, single, and lived in Singleton, another mining town in the Hunter Valley about an hour up the road from Muswellbrook. Hammond's social media pages provided even more information.

There were a large number of photographs with him and other people Liam presumed were his friends and work colleagues. Many of them wore high-visibility clothing and had the typical look of coal miners. In a lot of the photos, they were drinking and obviously having a good time. Nathan Garcia showed up often enough in the collection that Liam could only presume the men socialized outside of the workplace.

At the sight of Hannah's open cut examiner, Liam frowned. He'd taken an instant dislike to the man, but he was honest enough to admit that probably had more to do with Garcia's possessive attitude toward Hannah than anything else. No doubt the man was good at his job, or else he wouldn't be employed there. Still, as the OCE, Garcia was just as responsible for safety breaches as Hannah was. As such, he also warranted some looking into.

Clearing his browsing history, Liam entered Nathan Garcia's name into the search engine. Almost immediately, the page started loading with a number of hits. It seemed Garcia had a significant online presence. Most of the hits related to personal aspects of Garcia's life. There were numerous links to social pages, with Garcia photographed at various high-end society events.

There were glamorous charity events, football finals, nights at the Opera House, and horse meets at Randwick Racecourse. Garcia was often photographed with celebrities, politicians, and other high-profile members of Sydney society. Each and every time, he wore a different designer suit. His silk ties cost a week's wages alone. His expensive clothes were in sharp contrast to the high-vis shirt and pants he wore on the mine site. Liam couldn't help but wonder just who Garcia was.

Well-heeled, perhaps independently wealthy, or else he was being financially supported by someone else. His parents? Who knew? The sheer number and type of social events he'd attended in the past couple of years indicated he was someone who didn't necessarily have to work for a living. He was definitely somebody who was well connected.

So, what's he doing working at Strathwaylin?

Intrigued, Liam clicked on yet another article on Nathan Garcia. This one showed him at a business dinner hosted by the largest, privately owned mining company in Australia. There was a picture of Garcia standing shoulder to shoulder with an older gentleman and an attractive younger woman with shiny blond hair. Liam didn't recognize either of them. He scanned the article and discovered Garcia's dinner companions were a man by the name of Joseph Rodriguez, and his daughter, Ruby.

Joseph Rodriguez... He filed the information away and continued reading. There was also a picture of Frank Barrington and his wife, Evelyn. And then he saw a smaller picture of Hannah. She stood with her arm around the waist of a good-looking man about her age, smiling at the photographer and looking every inch the beautiful and sophisticated woman she was.

Liam was annoyed by the stab of jealousy that flashed through him. He had no call on Hannah and no say about who she did or didn't date. He ought to be happy she had a significant other in her life. The way the man was looking at her, it was obvious he was enthralled. Liam knew the feeling.

With a muttered curse, he clicked out of the article and returned to his notes. Paul Hammond and a couple of other names—Rodney Valentine and Scott Stonewall—cropped up, over and over again. That had to be more than mere coincidence.

What if this isn't Hannah's fault? What if someone's deliberately creating situations that lead to mishaps and purposefully sabotaging the mine?

The more he thought about it, the more he felt he was onto something. At the very least, it warranted further investigation. Hannah was adamant the safety protocols were not only kept rigorously up to date, but that every single person who worked on that mine site was made aware of them on a regular basis. If that were the case, the accidents wouldn't be occurring. At least, not in the numbers they were.

Something was awry and he intended to get to the bottom of it. In the meantime, he had dinner with Hannah Barrington to look forward to.

Chapter Ten

Hannah took particular care with her appearance as she dressed for her date that night. No, not a date. Dinner with Liam Hennessy. She merely wanted to get him on her side so that their working relationship was more amiable. That would not only help her, but it would also help the mine.

Still, there was no denying she was attracted to him and though her more sensible self told her it would be foolhardy to have a fling with an investigator from the Resources Regulator, her wilder side wanted to throw caution to the wind. It had been nearly a month since she and Chad had parted ways. Almost that long since she'd had sex. Investigator or not, being around someone as sexy as Liam would put her self-control to the test.

What harm would there be in it, anyway? We're both adults. He can always say no. It's not like I'm going to force myself on him. Heaven forbid!

She finished off her makeup with a slash of red lipstick that emphasized the lush curve of her lips and then took a moment to step back from the mirror and survey the results. Her low-cut, stretch-knit dress hugged her body and drew attention to her generous cleavage. The deep blue fabric brought out the color of her eyes. She wore a simple gold chain around her neck that matched the gold hoops in her ears and the three bangles on her wrist.

Returning to her bedroom, she slipped on stilettos that elevated her height to six feet. She wouldn't be as tall as Liam, but close enough. She knew from the pictures she'd seen of him in the social pages that he preferred tall women. Then she pulled a face, immediately annoyed with herself. So much so, that she was tempted to take off the heels and wear flats. She wasn't trying to vie for his attention. It wasn't like she was interested in him that way.

Liar.

She compressed her lips and briefly closed her eyes. She couldn't deny the truth. She was interested in him all right. So interested she'd pretty much already made her mind up that she'd have a fling with him and to hell with the complications that might follow. He was an attractive, appealing man who filled her stomach with butterflies. What harm was there in slaking her physical needs with him? She'd always been the type of woman to go after what she wanted, and that included men. Why should that change now?

However, she did need to keep focused on the primary goal—talking him into cooperating with her in getting to the bottom of why accidents were occurring so frequently at the mine.

With a final look in the mirror, she collected her handbag, keys, and phone and let herself out of her house. Climbing into her BMW, she headed to the restaurant to restart the night before. She only hoped things turned out better the second time around.

Liam was waiting for her at the bar when she walked inside. Her eyes zeroed in on him and her heart did a little dance of excitement. He looked good in another designer shirt and Levis that clung to his long legs. His RM Williams boots were polished to a high shine. He looked the epitome of a clean and wholesome, wealthy, country gentleman. Not the usual sort of guy she dated. But heck, who said anything about dating?

She smiled and strolled over to where he sat. He stood as she drew closer. For a moment, he looked as though he didn't know whether to offer his hand in greeting or kiss her. She saved him the trouble by holding out her hand.

His skin was warm with a few calluses attesting to outdoor work. Her fingers tingled at the contact. He smelled good too. Fresh and woodsy. Her libido jumped another notch. Nerves bounced around in her stomach. She caught a glimpse of tanned skin through the open buttons at his neck before she forced herself to let go and settled herself on a bar stool.

"Hi, how are you?" she asked.

His answering smile reached his eyes. "I'm doing okay. Thanks for coming. You look great."

His gaze raked over her. Heat trailed across her skin in its wake. Her nipples pebbled reflexively and need pooled low in her belly. She was a little put out that her body reacted so instantly to him, but she'd never been one to question physical desire when it struck. Then it was only a matter of deciding whether she liked the guy enough to spend the night with him.

Before Hannah could order a drink, the waiter arrived to show them to their table. Liam led the way. Hannah couldn't help but notice how the other women in the room turned their heads as he walked by. She was conscious of a surge of pride and even more surprisingly, a foreign feeling of possession.

The place was more crowded than it had been the night before. The background music could hardly be heard over the sound of conversation. The tinkle of glassware, the occasional bark of laughter. Candles had been lit on each table, lending the room an intimate glow. A waitress passed by carrying two plates laden with food. It smelled delicious. Hannah's stomach growled.

"Can I get you a drink, madam?" their waiter asked once they were seated.

Hannah scanned the wine list. "Yes, please. The Brokenwood Semillon. Do you sell it by the bottle?"

"Yes, madam. Of course."

She looked at Liam. "Is that all right with you?"

He smiled. "I think I already told you, I'm happy to try anything."

She nodded and returned her attention to the waiter. "Could you bring us a bottle, please?"

The waiter nodded and disappeared. A few moments later, he returned with the bottle of wine and poured some into a glass. He offered it to Hannah to sample. She sniffed, swirled, and tasted and then nodded.

"Thank you. That's perfect."

The waiter filled her glass and then served Liam before placing the bottle in an ice bucket nearby. He handed them dinner menus. "I'll be back in a few minutes to take your order," he said, before disappearing once again.

"I think I'll order the same as last night," Liam said, closing his menu. "With a bit of luck, I might get to taste it this time."

The wink that accompanied his comment helped to ease the flash of embarrassment that heated Hannah's cheeks. She looked across at him. "I'm sorry. Last night was…"

"There's no need to apologize. It's all on me. If you're okay with it, I'd like to clear the slate and start again."

She smiled. "I'm okay with that."

He nodded and appeared relieved. "Good. Shall I propose a toast?"

He picked up his glass. Hannah did the same.

"To old friendships…and new."

They clinked their glasses together. Liam's eyes held hers. They twinkled with good humor and something else. Something deeper, more intense. Something she couldn't quite define. Whatever it was, his expression did weird things to her insides; made her nervous. Which was strange. She was always supremely confident around men, especially ones she found attractive.

What is it about this man that makes me so jittery? I'm almost breathless with anticipation… I'm also uncertain how he feels. That's even more ridiculous! I'm never uncertain about whether a man finds me attractive. I can usually tell right away.

But with Liam things were different. She'd caught more than one admiring glance from him, but he hadn't ogled her like other men did, nor had he made it clear that he desired her, through words or action. If she wasn't as confident in her own appeal as she was, she'd be having doubts.

The play of emotions across Hannah's face intrigued Liam. *What's she thinking?*

The way she looked at him, like he was a tasty morsel, heated his blood, but building a friendship was way too important to him to mess it up by letting his libido get in the way. She gave every sign that she was aware of him as a man, but he didn't want to read too much into that. At least not before he'd had more time to get to know her, to feel her out.

Life at the mine would be much easier for her if he were on her side. He didn't yet know if her attempts to charm him had more to do with that, or if they were genuine. As much as he wanted to satisfy the white-hot desire that raged through his veins, he didn't want to be used. That was the way of heartbreak. And he'd already felt that unrequited pain in high school.

Heartbreak? Really? Does she still have that much power over me?

The short answer was yes, but not for the same reasons. For years, he'd loved her from afar. The kind of all-encompassing, overwhelming love of a teenager. But now he could see it for what it was. A crush. Of course, she'd consumed his every waking moment and many of his dreams, but time and maturity now allowed him to see things through a different lens.

He thought he'd been head-over-heels in love with Hannah and yet he'd never known her. Not the real her. He'd never spoken more than a dozen words to her in all that time and that had only been in passing. His attraction had been based on nothing more than the physical—a typical teenage boy response. He could see now that all the love and passion he'd felt for her in high school had been nothing more than teenage lust and what he'd thought was a broken heart had been nothing more than a bruised and battered ego.

That didn't mean he wasn't still enthralled with her. For so long, he'd focused on hatred for what she'd done to Ned. Now that the hate was gone, he felt exposed, completely without protection; more vulnerable than he'd ever felt in his life. Though his teenage self might have only crushed on her, at twenty-five, he was well aware that it wouldn't take much for those feelings to become a good deal more. Especially if he took the time to really get to know her. He'd already been in lust with the teenage Hannah. The woman was so much more a threat to his heart. So, no matter how much he yearned to make love with her, the best thing he could do was to retreat while his heart remained intact. He needed to keep things professional and ... friendly.

Picking up his glass, he sipped at his wine. All the while, he regarded Hannah coolly over the rim.

"Tell me again how you came to be a group manager at the ripe old age of twenty-three."

He saw a flash of annoyance in her eyes and her lips turned down briefly with disappointment, but to her credit, she smiled briefly, then answered.

"I didn't know what I wanted to do when I left school. I loved baking, but not to the point where I wanted to open a shop. I tried a few different things, including getting halfway through a law degree, but nothing kept my interest for long. My father needed a manager. He offered me the job."

"And just like that, you rose to the highest echelons," Liam said dryly, deliberately baiting her.

Once again, her eyes flashed with irritation, but just like before, she remained courteous.

"It wasn't quite like that. I worked for a year doing various jobs at other mines my father owns. I drove machinery, did paperwork, oversaw safety operations. During that time, I became really interested in all facets of mining. My father decided I was ready for the top job and here I am, twelve months in and doing a darn fine job, at least as far as production goes."

She shot him a look filled with challenge, as if daring him to disagree. He merely sipped again from his wine before setting the glass back down.

"So, what got you interested in mining?" she asked. "How did you end up at the Resources Regulator?"

He debated for a moment how much to tell her. He was still wary of letting her get too close. She had the potential to break his heart and he refused to let that happen again, no matter that with the benefit of hindsight and maturity, he now saw his previous infatuation for her for what it was. But the whole point was to get to know her better. He wanted her to know more about him. To see him as more than a man she'd gone to high school with. To see him as a man, period. And how contrary was that!

"I actually started work as a plant operator at a mine in Mudgee working for a contractor."

Surprise flooded her face. "Really? I had no idea you had real-life experience on the ground."

"There's a lot about me you don't know," he murmured.

She tilted her head. "Tell me more."

"I drove dump trucks, excavators, and scrapers. For a time, I worked at the coal handling plant. I worked long hours. It wasn't easy, but I enjoyed it and no one could argue about the money."

She grinned wryly. "Hey, I've seen the weekly wages bill. You won't get any argument there from me." She reached for her glass and took a sip. "So, how did you go from being a plant operator, to an investigator? It seems to me like you switched sides."

He shrugged. "Maybe I did. The thing is, while I was working as a plant operator, I saw so many safety breaches. Every day. Every week. Every month. One resulted in a fatality. It was just good luck there weren't more."

He scrubbed at his hair as familiar frustration poured through him. "It was like there were all these rules and regulations, but nobody much cared if they were followed or if people were injured as a result. It made me so angry." He drew in a breath and stared at her. "So, I decided to do something about it. I was determined to make those people responsible accountable."

Her expression had grown somber. He could tell she agreed with what he'd said. She had a safety problem herself. She knew all about people who refused to pay heed to safety regulations, including one incident that had ended in a fatality.

"You probably know about Evan Wilson."

He nodded. "The man who was killed at Strathwaylin."

"Yes. It happened on the first day I'd taken over as safety manager."

"Yes. I've read the report."

"Then you must know nothing was proven. Even the Resources Regulator couldn't come up with someone to blame. But my father suspected a contractor who'd been fired that very day for continuous safety breaches. Joseph Rodriguez. Of course, nothing could be proven against him, but to this day, my father's certain he had something to do with it."

Liam frowned. *Joseph Rodriguez.* That was the man he'd seen pictured with Nathan Garcia.

I need to revisit that. Especially now that I know that Frank Barrington had his suspicions about the man and it's not just my instinctive dislike of Garcia...

Hannah cleared her throat, drawing his attention back to her. "No matter what you think, I care about the lives of the people who work at my mine. I care about their safety. I want them to go home each and every day to the people who love them. I don't know who or what's behind these safety breaches, but I'm going to get to the bottom of them."

Her cheeks were flushed. Her breath came fast. He reached out and touched her hand. A tingle of awareness arced through him, but he steadfastly ignored it.

"I believe you," he said, holding her gaze.

She looked startled and then swallowed and then drew in a deep breath. Before she could respond, the waiter appeared and took their orders. Like him, Hannah ordered the same food as she had the night before, except for the Belgian chocolate tart.

He lifted an eyebrow in silent query. "No dessert this time?"

She blinked and her expression cleared. Then she smiled and gazed at him with a bold look in her eyes and ran her tongue slowly across her lips. "Maybe later. I haven't decided yet."

The throatiness of her tone, coupled with the look in her eyes, heightened the desire that rushed through him. Their discussion about mine safety was instantly forgotten. Blood raced to his cock, hardening it instantly. All the while, he urged himself to play it cool. A woman like Hannah could have any man she wanted. She knew that as well as he did. But he wanted more from her than a one-night stand.

So, instead of taking her up on the blatant invitation in her eyes, he took a quick swig of wine and changed the subject.

"So, you were too busy to date anyone in high school. Wasn't that kind of boring? Especially when you could have had your pick."

Once again, she appeared disappointed he hadn't acknowledged the undertone of sexual chemistry that simmered between them, but then she shrugged and offered a response.

"No, it wasn't boring at all. Like I said, I wasn't interested in boys. I loved school. I loved learning. I'm a bit of a nerd, to tell you the truth. I might not have known which career path I wanted to take, but I always tried hard in school. That took up a lot of time."

Then she gave him a wry smile. "There's also the fact I have six brothers. Most of whom were at high school with me. I also wasn't brave enough back then to express interest in a boy. Could you imagine? They'd have made it their business to scare him off long before it could go anywhere. That would have been beyond embarrassing."

She laughed and the husky sound of it reverberated all the way through him. Once again, heat centered in his groin. He cursed under his breath. No matter that he was determined not to be just another notch on her belt, it was almost impossible to avoid the pull of desire between them. He felt it, and from the knowing look she sent in his direction, so did she.

He hated that she still had so much power over his emotions that with a few looks, a few offhand comments, she could turn him into a blithering mountain of need. Then their eyes locked. Her expression turned somber. His heart stopped. His breath caught in his throat.

"They wouldn't have scared me off."

The words fell out of his mouth. He couldn't believe he'd said them. Hannah's eyes widened in comprehension and surprise. She stilled. Then she flushed. She continued to stare at him. Slowly, her eyes filled with questions. Liam's heart thumped.

Do I tell her? Do I finally tell her the way I used to feel? The way I still feel? Do I take the risk that she'll laugh at me, or worse, sleep with me out of pity?

His palms went sweaty. His chest grew tight. His mouth dried like a sand dune. He'd been in lust with Hannah

Barrington for as long as he could remember. Definitely since the ninth grade. Up until recently, he thought he'd been in love. A whole decade later and he still felt the same.

As the silence stretched out between them, he decided to throw caution to the wind. They'd established a fragile rapport. They were two adults now, no longer teenagers. While they were sharing true confessions, he might as well take hold of his courage and come clean.

His gut clenched with nerves at the thought of what he was about to do. He drew in a deep breath. She must have seen something in his sober expression. Lines of confusion furrowed her forehead. She looked away momentarily and sought out her wine glass before gazing at him again. An uncertain smile hovered over her lips.

"Liam? What is it?"

"Ned wasn't the only one who was in love with you in high school."

Her eyes flared with an indefinable emotion that sent another surge of blood rushing to his groin. Her mouth parted on a silent sigh. She continued to regard him with surprise and something else. Holding on to his courage, he spoke again.

"I fell for you the very first day I saw you walking into school. You were in the seventh grade. You'd just climbed off the bus with your brothers and sisters. Your hair was shorter and darker than it is now. It was loose and flowing around your shoulders. You were the most beautiful girl I'd ever seen. You're still the most beautiful girl I've ever seen."

Hannah reached for her wine again and this time she drained it and then filled the glass again. She was silent for so long; Liam began to regret being so candid.

What an idiot! Why did I go and do that? Hell, now I have to live with the embarrassment every time we meet. Why couldn't I just keep my mouth shut? Keep this as nothing more than a dinner between friends?

As the thoughts chased themselves around his head, his cheeks flamed. He could no longer bring himself to look at her, too embarrassed to see if there was shock and revulsion on her face. It was one thing for her to find him physically attractive. It was quite another for him to bare his heart.

Oh, hell.

Then the waiter appeared with their appetizers, and Liam had never been so glad to see anyone. At least with his mouth full of food, he'd have an excuse not to speak. He picked up his fork and speared a fat prawn and shoved it in his mouth as the silence lengthened between them.

Hannah stared at Liam in shock. She couldn't believe what he'd just said. This was the man who'd been rude and obnoxious and impossible toward her from the first day he'd walked onto the mine site. Now he was telling her he'd been in love with her in high school! Not only that, but he'd said she was beautiful. It was hard not to feel flattered by that. It was also hard not to reciprocate. For whatever reason she'd failed to notice him in high school, the same couldn't be said now.

She'd been aware of him right from the beginning. Those broad shoulders, slim hips, long legs. The antagonism between them hadn't changed that. Knowing he thought she was beautiful sent a fresh surge of desire through her veins. He might have been avoiding her signals all night, but if he'd been in love with her in high school, there was a fair chance he at least still found her attractive. His admission was the assurance she'd been seeking. It was like he'd given her the go-ahead to take things to another level. Need centered in her core.

A little voice in her head urged caution. This wasn't just some guy she'd picked up in a bar on a Friday night. This was Liam Hennessy. A man who'd just professed to once being in love with her. More importantly, he was the investigator in charge of every incident that occurred at her mine. It would be unwise to mix business with pleasure. If things didn't work out between them, he could make life even more difficult for her.

Am I prepared to take that risk?

She reached for her wine and took another healthy gulp. She'd lost count of the number of glasses she'd had, but whatever the number, it had been enough to give her a decent buzz. Enough that she didn't stop herself from reaching out and covering his hand with hers and giving him a flirty smile. All the time, she kept her gaze fixed on his, making it clear with her eyes how very much she desired him. The surprise on his face was quickly followed by a scorching look. His gaze swept over her, pausing deliberately on her breasts. Heat trailed in its wake.

Is this the reason I've been so worked up about his antagonism? Because all this time I've wanted to tear his clothes off?

The thought made her smile. She was a hot-blooded woman with sometimes ravenous needs. Right now, she was so turned on she thought she might combust, and he hadn't even touched her. The thought of how hot and passionate it might be between them left her tingling with desire.

I want him. I want him now. Dinner and the mine, be damned.

She'd deal with both later. Earlier, she'd thought she was hungry. Now she was ravenous for something else entirely. She needed to get hot and heavy and naked with the man who sat across from her and was doing his best to set her nerve endings on fire with nothing more than a look.

Heaven help us both! This is going to be an experience neither of us will forget... Time to get out of here and find a room. It looks like another good dinner's gone to waste... Oh, well...

She looked him in the eye. "You should know, I have a healthy sexual appetite. I enjoy sleeping with sexy men. I also go after what I want. And right now, I want you. Are you okay with that?"

Chapter Eleven

Despite Liam's determination not to be just another notch on Hannah Barrington's belt, his body had other ideas. Her bold declaration sent desire ricocheting through his veins. His cock was so hard, it was painful. Her words… That look she'd given him… It was all he could do not to sweep away everything on the table and take her there and then, candles and the crowd be damned.

With dinner now the last thing on his mind, Liam pushed away from the table and stood. Hannah did the same. As she briefly leaned forward, he was gifted with a glimpse of her cleavage—generous breasts that almost spilled out of the front of her dress. His cock twitched.

She strode toward the exit in front of him and then deviated toward the reception desk. He enjoyed watching the sexy sway of her hips. She wore heels that were impossibly high, but she walked with a confidence that was just as alluring as her fine figure. He took a moment to toss a few bills down on the bar to cover the bottle of wine and their dinner and then joined Hannah at the door.

He was slightly dazed from the speed of what was happening. A moment ago, they'd been discussing high school and he'd confessed to having had feelings for her. Thank God he'd stopped short of admitting he still felt that way. But she didn't seem to mind his use of the past tense. In fact, from the sultry looks she kept sending his way, she couldn't wait to get him naked. Hannah Barrington, all grown up and now flushed with desire, was someone he had no power to resist.

While she waited for him to open the door for her, she moved closer and casually slid her hand across his crotch. It was so unexpected, so erotic, it snatched his breath and left him silently gasping. His stomach clenched. His cock jerked. He had a sudden embarrassing image of himself coming way too soon. Heat spread across his face.

Though he was far from celibate, it had been a while since he'd last had sex. Moving in with his sister hadn't been conducive to bringing girls home. Now he was going home with Hannah Barrington.

Well, maybe not home. He certainly couldn't take her to his place. This early in the evening, his sister would still be up. The last thing he needed was for her to see Hannah and ask awkward questions. Maybe they could go to Hannah's place? He didn't know how far away she lived or what her living arrangements were, but it was obvious she wanted to have sex. He could only assume she had a plan.

Maybe she wants to do it in the carpark?

The thought sent a ripple of desire down his spine. He wasn't normally an exhibitionist, but having sex in a public place, even under the cover of darkness, held a certain appeal. He opened the door and held it for her while she stepped through and then followed closely behind. She turned slightly and reached for his hand. Her skin was soft and warm against his.

She shot him another one of those sultry looks. "You ready?"

He stared at her, his gaze intense. "I'm ready if you are."

She winked and his gut took another nosedive. Nerves swarmed in his stomach. He cleared his throat and fought to maintain a casual tone. "Your place or mine?"

She smiled. "Neither. I just paid for a room right here at the hotel."

She lifted her free hand, and for the first time, he noticed a key dangling from her fingertips. She tightened her hold on his hand and pulled him in the direction of the accommodation. It adjoined the building that housed the restaurant. She found the room without trouble. *Has she been here before?* Then she pulled him inside the room and pressed him up hard against the closed door. The moment her lips touched his, he forgot about everything but the feel of her in his arms.

She kissed him with passion. Sliding her arms up around his neck, she slid her tongue into his mouth. She tasted of sweetness and wine. He cupped her ass and dragged her even tighter against him, pressing his cock into the softness of her stomach. He burned with the need to bury himself deep inside her but kissing her with such abandon felt pretty darn good too.

Then she began working on the buttons of his shirt and tugging it out of his waistband. When the last of the buttons were loose, she spread the fabric wide and flattened her palms against his pectorals. Her fingers flicked at his taut nipples. He trembled beneath her touch. Her hands slid lower, over his stomach and paused at the top of his jeans.

With their lips still locked together, she worked the clasp and his belt and finally, she tugged his zipper down. When her hand slid under the waistband of his boxers and closed around his cock, he couldn't help but sigh with relief.

"Hannah…" he groaned.

She pulled slightly away and grinned at him. "You like that?"

"Hell, yeah."

His voice was rough with desire. He couldn't remember the last time he'd been so turned on. And she appeared to feel the same. There was a desperate urgency in her kisses, in the stroking of her hand. In the beating of her heart against his chest. In the catch of her breath. He dragged her back to him and kissed her again, hot, passionate, unrestrained.

His hands went around her back and he felt for the zipper of her dress. He eased it down and her dress parted. She quickly shimmied out of it. At the same time, he pulled off his boots and socks and kicked his way out of his jeans. He took her in his arms and walked her backward until her legs came up against the bed.

With a laugh, she tumbled onto the mattress, and he quickly followed her down. She wore nothing but matching lacy, black underwear. The sheer sexiness of it drove him wild. He buried his face between her breasts, filling his hands with her soft flesh. As desire overtook him, the only thought he had was to get them naked, to lie there pressed against her, skin to skin.

As if she could read his mind, she reached behind her and unclasped her bra and tossed it over the side. Freed from their constraints, her breasts bounced against her chest. Before he had time to focus on their beauty, she lifted her hips and pulled the scrap of lacy black underwear down her hips. That also went the way of her bra.

His eyes raked over her nakedness. She was perfect from head to toe. She lay back against the pillows, a look of challenge in her eyes.

"You like?" she asked.

"I like," he rasped.

On a surge of impatience, he pulled off his boxers and stepped out of them. Then it hit him. No condom! Seeing his hesitance, Hannah pointed to her purse she'd dropped on the floor. He grabbed it up, quickly opening it at her nod, and found a string of them. He quirked a brow and she gave him her flirty smile. His girl liked to be prepared. Quickly sheathing himself, he returned to the bed and gathered her against his side. Their lips met in another scorching kiss.

She moved restlessly against him, her silky legs entwined with his. The center of her femininity was pressed against his thigh. He felt the heat of her, the moistness and it drove him insane with desire. He flipped her onto her back and used his body weight to hold her there. Then he licked and suckled her nipples until she arched off the bed.

She clung to his shoulders, digging her nails into his skin. Breathless whimpers of need told him she wanted this as much as he did. Her legs fell open in silent invitation and it was all the encouragement he needed to position himself between her thighs. With one hard thrust, he plunged all the way inside her. They both gasped.

"Oh, Hannah…"

With his gaze fixed on hers, hot and intense, he moved inside her. Long, slow strokes designed to drive her wild. Her arms tightened around his shoulders and her legs came up around his hips. Their gazes locked. Something indefinable passed between them. He trembled from the force of it. She met his thrusts with wild abandon, urging him on all the way with mindless murmurs. A few moments later, she closed her eyes and cried out and her body tensed. She arched up against him and then shuddered and sighed with relief.

The sight of her reaching her climax tipped Liam over the edge. He increased the thrust of his hips, pounding into her. And then he was there, at the precipice, shouting out his own release as he collapsed against her. Breathing hard, it was long moments before he had the strength to shift his weight off her and roll to his side. He turned to face her. She looked flushed and satisfied. She reached out and took his hand and threaded his fingers through hers.

"That was just what I needed," she said and winked.

He managed a tight grin. All the while, inside he was flooded with disappointment.

What did I expect? A declaration of love? Reassurance I was the best she'd ever had? Regret that we'd wasted so many years…

Fool.

This was nothing more than sex for Hannah and from the confident way she'd engaged in their lovemaking, it was clear this was far from her first time. She'd been upfront about going after who she wanted. Not that he cared how many men she'd slept with, but a ridiculous part of him, the part that had wanted her for so long, was hurt. He wanted her to tell him how wonderful that had been. How she'd never felt closer to anyone. How she couldn't wait to do it again. All the things he felt…

Fool.

Before he could respond any further, she rolled away from him and stood. Gathering her clothes, she turned away and headed for the shower.

Apparently, they were finished.

Hannah stared at the page in her hand and cursed under her breath. She'd read the same paragraph three times and still didn't know what it said. The problem was Liam. She couldn't stop thinking about last night.

Though a tiny part of her regretted complicating things by sleeping with him, she was mostly pleased that they'd come together so well. Given the fireworks between them whenever they were in her office, she wasn't surprised the sex had been so good. Not only that, but there had also been a moment when she'd felt truly connected to him, like this was as much an emotional coupling as a physical one. And that was the main reason her thoughts kept returning to him again and again. She'd never felt like that before. She wanted to sleep with him again. Not that she wanted commitment. Her life was great just the way it was. Free. Easy. Uncomplicated.

As much as they were on different sides in their professional life, there was no denying the sexual chemistry between them. She'd been with a lot of guys. None of them had been as good in bed as Liam. And they were only just beginning. Imagine how good it would be once they'd gotten to know each other better, took time to love each other slowly, thoroughly, without the urgency that nearly always accompanied a one-night stand.

Perhaps it's time to re-think the whole Friday night pick-up routine? It might be nice to spend time with just one man for a while. Let him get to know me. Maybe even date...

Heaven forbid!

She could hardly believe where her mind had wandered. She wasn't into dating. The four months she'd spent with Chad had been plenty. More than she usually did. Anything long term got boring. That was the reason she'd broken things off. Four months in and the sex was no longer exciting. No, casual relationships were her thing. She might have been slow to start, but now she knew what a thrill it was to seek out a worthy companion for the night and set off fireworks, she was loathe to give that excitement up.

Except with Liam, things felt different, and she couldn't explain why. Perhaps it was because he'd known her since she was in high school? Perhaps it was because he'd confessed he'd once been in love with her. That was pretty heady stuff; a real boon to her ego and though she had a healthy self-esteem, it was always nice to be around someone who'd once thought that highly of her.

But am I willing to give up my casual Friday nights for a possible relationship? Am I ready for that?

The thought of Liam having sex with other women made her frown. Almost immediately, she shook her head. She had no call on him. He could sleep with whoever he liked. They'd had sex. Big deal. But somehow, she couldn't seem to dismiss what had happened between them as nothing more than that.

She was still pondering that remarkable realization when her phone rang. She picked it up and checked the screen but there was no Caller ID. After a slight hesitation, she answered it.

"Hannah Barrington."

"Hannah. It's Liam. Liam Hennessy," he added.

Her heart immediately picked up its pace. She smiled wryly. "Did you think I wouldn't remember your name?"

"Yes. No. I don't know. Force of habit, I guess."

"And do you make it a habit of sleeping with a girl you only just met?" she teased.

"We met in high school. And no, I don't make it a habit of sleeping with women I barely know. You were...an exception."

His somber tone took her aback. She'd been expecting to trade sexual innuendos and then make plans for when they could get together again. But this cool and distant tone... It confused her.

Maybe the sex wasn't as good for him as it had been for me?

The thought momentarily immobilized her, but then she shook it off. No. There was no way he hadn't enjoyed himself. Maybe it was her running off straight after her shower that had upset him. She'd never been into idle chit chat, especially after sex. She hadn't given much thought to how he might have felt about her quick getaway.

A stab of guilt went through her, taking her aback. She didn't normally feel guilty about leaving her lovers so abruptly. But Liam was different. She still couldn't work out why, but she wanted to offer him an explanation.

She drew in a deep breath. "About last night—"

"It was a mistake," he interrupted before she could finish.

Hannah tensed. That was the last thing she'd expected him to say and something no man had ever said to her before. She was equal parts hurt, disappointed, and furious.

How dare he say our night together was a mistake!

"A mistake?" she repeated, her tone decidedly cooler.

"Yes," he continued, as if oblivious to her growing anger. "I'm investigating two workplace incidents that occurred at your mine. Given your track record, there will likely be more in the future. I'm not only under an obligation to remain impartial, but I also can't allow the possibility of a personal relationship with you to cloud my judgment, or at least have the appearance of that. It's quite simple," he said in a matter-of-fact tone. "It's a conflict of interest. I can't be involved with you. I'm sure you'll agree. What happened last night can't ever happen again."

Hannah felt like she'd sustained several body blows all at once. Of course, she understood his reasoning, but it still hurt just the same. Last night was nothing more than sex for him. And for her, too. So, there was no need to feel upset or disappointed or any of the tumult of emotions that now coursed through her. She wouldn't dare be so foolish as to suggest that there might be more to this, that they had something special. No, that would be stupid. Far better to approach the whole situation like he had. Like it meant nothing, and it would be best for all concerned if they didn't repeat it. Ever.

If she concurred with him, she'd salvage her pride. That was one thing at least. No point in trying to pretend their night together meant something to him when he'd made it obvious it didn't. Even though he couldn't see her, she forced a smile that felt both tight and plastic.

"You're right," she said at last, her tone brusque. "Last night was nothing more than a pleasant interlude between two people who wanted to get laid. No need to turn simple sex into something it isn't. And given your position with the Resources Regulator and your obligation to investigate safety incidents at my mine, I agree. The best thing for both of us is to pretend last night never happened. In fact," she added, "I've already forgotten all about it."

She heard his sharp intake of breath but refused to feel guilty about it. The comment was unnecessarily nasty, and would no doubt be a blow to his pride, but he certainly hadn't done a thing to protect hers. A snarky comment that might damage his ego was the least he deserved.

Ending the call abruptly, she clenched her jaw as anger won the battle over hurt. Okay, so she'd been the one to initiate sex, but he'd been a willing participant. They'd both known the score. Surely, he could have gotten an attack of conscience *before* they'd gotten naked and saved them both the trouble.

Groaning aloud, she thumped her desk and then cried out as pain reverberated up her forearm. The truth was, she was madder at herself. She'd known who he was and how tricky things could get if she took their relationship to such a level and yet she'd done it anyway. And all for a few minutes of mindless pleasure. Now she had to live with the consequences. She just wished the sex hadn't been so good. It would be so much easier to dismiss him if that were the case. Instead, she'd be reliving those magical moments of unadulterated desire for a long time to come.

Damn you, Liam Hennessy! Go stick your conscience where the sun doesn't shine! I don't want to have anything to do with you. In fact, you can go to hell!

If only things were that simple…

Chapter Twelve

L iam set his phone down on his desk and cursed long and loudly.

Damn, Hannah Barrington!

She'd proven herself to be just as selfish as he'd always thought. They'd spent a magical night together and she had the audacity to tell him she couldn't even remember it. She was lying. She had to be. Her callous words had to be a reaction to him not wanting to take things any further, like the hurt he'd felt at her abrupt departure. That, coupled with their work situation was what had driven him to make that call. But even if she were oblivious to his hurt feelings, surely, she understood his reasoning from a professional point of view?

He was the investigator in charge of her mine site. There were current incidents in which he had yet to make a determination. Given the propensity for accidents at Strathwaylin, it was only a matter of time before there would be another, and once again, it would be his duty to investigate it. No matter his decision, it wouldn't look good if it became public knowledge that he and Hannah were involved. He cursed again.

It's my own fault. I should have kept my cock in my pants and stuck to my original game plan. I have no one to blame but myself.

Knowing that didn't make him feel better. He sighed. There was no point in feeling regret. What was done was done. The only thing to do was to put the whole sorry episode aside and focus on what he could do: getting to the bottom of the investigations.

With that thought in mind, he dragged his keyboard closer and entered the name "Joseph Rodriguez" into a search engine. Liam was intrigued by a picture of Rodriguez and Garcia together at the gathering of mine executives. How well did the men know each other?

The more Liam dug, the more he was convinced someone was going out of their way to cause the accidents. There could be no other explanation. The safety protocols were all up to date. The daily meetings with staff included safety briefings every single time. Every person who stepped on that mine site was given a comprehensive safety induction. And yet the accidents kept happening.

A few moments later, the screen filled with results. He clicked on the first link and scanned the news article. It seemed Joseph Rodriguez was a medium-sized earthmoving contractor who'd mainly made his money as a subcontractor to mining companies. His most recent contract had been with Barrington Mining, until the contract had been terminated a little over a year earlier.

The article was vague on the specifics of the termination, but it hinted at safety concerns the mine owner had with the operations of Rodriguez Contracting. Whatever the reason,

Rodriguez Contracting was given the boot and had since struggled to secure another mining contract.

Liam understood why. The mining industry was tight. The executives and mine owners were under an obligation to keep themselves informed of what was happening on other mine sites, both in Australia and around the world. Safety was paramount. If there was even a hint that a contractor had been terminated over safety concerns, that would be enough for most mine owners to give that contractor a wide berth.

It seemed that's exactly what had happened to Rodriguez. That kind of shunning had to bite. Mining contracts were lucrative. There was a lot of money to be made. More than what could be made in other industries. And with coal prices at record highs and demand for the stuff seemingly endless, despite the increasing focus on renewable energy as an alternative, the loss of that contract would have had disastrous results on the contractor's profits.

Liam thought back to what Hannah had said about her father. Though Frank Barrington hadn't been able to prove a connection between Rodriguez and the accident that had taken Evan Wilson's life, to this day he remained suspicious. Rodriguez had suffered serious financial penalties after having his contract terminated by Frank Barrington. No doubt he'd also suffered embarrassment and though nothing had been proven against him, neither were any of the other mine owners prepared to take him on.

Those weren't minor matters. Rodriguez must have been furious at Frank Barrington. Not only had the man destroyed his current prospects, but he'd also damaged future prospects as well.

Just how angry is Joseph Rodriguez? Angry enough to try and sabotage the Barrington mine? But how would he accomplish that? The man and his crew are no longer allowed on site.

Liam returned to his initial search and scrolled farther down the page. He clicked on another link, this one a piece from an online social site. The reporter had covered the sixtieth birthday celebrations of Joseph Rodriguez. The article was dated two years earlier, before Rodriguez's fallout with Barrington Mining.

Liam scanned the text. There were several photos of Rodriguez and his wife and children. Two boys and a girl. The same attractive blond who'd been pictured with him and Garcia. All three children looked to be in their thirties. All looked confident, rich, and beautiful as they stared into the camera lens. There were other photographs of Rodriguez with some of the one hundred guests that had attended the exclusive birthday bash. As Liam looked at them, his gut clenched.

One of the pictures showed Rodriguez standing beside Nathan Garcia. The men had their arms around each other's shoulders and were laughing. Liam read the text below the picture.

Joseph Rodriguez and his nephew, Nathan Garcia.

"Holy shit," Liam muttered. *His nephew?*

Liam knew from staffing records that Garcia had been employed as Hannah's OCE shortly after she took over management of the mine. Her first day there had coincided with the sacking of Rodriguez. One of Garcia's responsibilities was to oversee mine safety and yet for all the time he'd been there, accidents had been occurring with increasing frequency.

Liam had placed the blame on Hannah's shoulders, but what if Garcia were to blame? What if he were part of a scheme cooked up with his uncle to see the mine closed? What better way to get revenge on Frank Barrington?

Liam's mind reeled with the possibilities. No matter which way he looked at it, his theory made an awful kind of sense. Garcia had ingratiated himself with Hannah to the point where she was blinded to his faults. On top of that, Garcia was a handsome devil. Just the kind of man Hannah went for. She'd told Liam she had a healthy sexual appetite. That she enjoyed sleeping with sexy men. He didn't know if she and Garcia were an item, but there was a fair chance they were, or had been in the past, and that explained a lot.

Liam had to give it to Garcia. What better way to fly under the radar than to be sleeping with the boss? If she were enamored with the guy, she'd be less likely to question anything he said and her judgment would be clouded. Could that be the reason she hadn't connected the dots? That she hadn't stopped to think why the spate of incidents kept occurring on Garcia's watch?

He hated the thought that she might have taken Garcia as a lover, but that seemed more and more likely. Liam hadn't forgotten the way the man had brushed up against her in her office or the possessive way he'd looked at her and the way he'd silently warned Liam off. It all pointed to one thing. He tried not to let the knowledge affect him. He was falling in love with Hannah Barrington, this time for real, but she'd never had time for him. They might have had sex, but for her, that had been nothing more than a physical release. Hadn't she as good as dismissed it as such?

The best for all concerned was for him to get to the bottom of his investigations, draw evidence-based conclusions and then submit it all in a formal report to his supervisor, along with the action (if any) he suggested they take. In the meantime, he'd do his best to steer clear of Hannah and minimize her effect on his overall emotional wellbeing. That way, he could do his best to hold her at a distance, and more importantly, keep his heart intact.

Liam's determination to stay out of Hannah's path was put to the test the very next time he arrived at Strathwaylin. It had been nearly a week since he'd seen her and he didn't want to see her then, but safety protocol demanded that he check in with the office and advise them of his presence. He'd hoped to merely speak with Hannah's receptionist, Simone, but as luck would have it, he found Hannah standing beside the front desk when he entered.

His initial reaction was to turn tail and head back to his truck, but a stubbornness took over and he continued forward. He was there to do a job and he refused to let her interfere with that. The sooner he brought the investigations to an end, the sooner he could return to his office and his day-to-day responsibilities, which with a bit of luck didn't involve investigating incidents at the Barrington mine or coming into close contact with Hannah. Unfortunately, that day wasn't today.

She had her back to him as she continued to speak to the receptionist. Then Liam saw the young girl's gaze shift in his direction. She smiled in recognition. Hannah turned around. Her eyes flared wide with surprise but were just as quickly shuttered. Her face went blank.

"Mr Hennessy," she said coolly. "To what do we owe this pleasure?"

Her lips twisted, making it clear to everyone that this impromptu meeting was far from pleasant. Her icy tone reinforced the fact.

Refusing to be intimidated, Liam smiled back, although it felt more like a grimace. "Ms Barrington. It's nice to see you again. I'm conducting further inquiries into those incidents. I need access to the pit."

Her lips tightened. The disapproval in her gaze only served to make him more determined to see this through to the end. He thought for a moment about telling her about his suspicions that someone was deliberately causing accidents and then decided against it. If Nathan Garcia was indeed behind it, Liam needed more proof before he presented her with his findings. If she *was* intimately involved with her OCE, there was every possibility she wouldn't believe him. No, better to wait until he had irrefutable proof. He just hoped finding such proof was possible.

His gaze raked over her. Though she was dressed in the usual high-vis work garb, in his mind's eye, all he could see were her luscious breasts, her erect nipples, her long, silky, naked limbs wrapped around him as he plunged his cock into her wetness...

The erotic images had an immediate impact on his body. Blood flowed to his groin. He silently cursed his instant erection. He might be falling in love with her, but he wasn't a masochist. She'd made it clear their sexual encounter had been nothing special. She'd agreed it was a mistake. He'd thought her quip that she'd already forgotten about it was just her way of covering up her hurt, but from the way she now treated him like he was just another person she had to deal with, it was clear he'd read that wrong.

It was time he accepted that for her, their night together had truly been nothing more than sex. The thought was depressing, but he refused to allow her to see how much it upset him. No doubt he was just another notch on her bedpost. A wave of resolve went through him. He should have stuck to his guns and never slept with her. He wouldn't make the same mistake again.

He'd learned from his lesson. Hannah Barrington did whatever took her fancy and to hell with the consequences, or who she hurt. If he'd learned anything from their encounter, it was that she didn't feel anything for him past the physical and no doubt never would. There was no point pining for someone who didn't pine for him. That was sheer lunacy.

He had to do whatever it took to bring the investigations to an end. Then he'd write up his findings and hopefully never see Hannah again. At least not until he'd had a chance to regroup, set his armor firmly back in place. In the meantime, he'd do his best to keep his distance. His heart couldn't take too many more confrontations with the woman. Neither could he afford to have his judgment clouded or risk an allegation of bias. That would damage his career and now that the possibility of Hannah feeling the same way he did had been blown apart, his career was all he had left.

Chapter Thirteen

Hannah retreated to her office the moment Liam disappeared. She left Simone to deal with the key pass he needed to access the pit. Her hands still trembled from their confrontation. She wished he didn't have that kind of power over her. That his mere presence could affect her like that. But it was true. Ever since they'd slept together, something had changed. At least, it had for her. He was evidently oblivious. To him, it had obviously been nothing more than sex. A mistake, he'd said.

I should never have slept with him...

But how was she to know it would be so much more than sex? That she'd feel connected to him in a way she'd never felt with anyone else? Only for him to dismiss the whole interaction as nothing special, a mistake, in fact. She hated that he felt like that. She hated even more that his attitude upset her.

She was the one who set the rules, who flitted in and out of relationships, who eagerly participated in one-night stands. So why was she so put out that Liam felt that way too? She ought to be pleased he was the kind of guy who enjoyed no-strings-attached sex. Wasn't that what she lived for? What she preferred?

Yes!

Only, where Liam was concerned, the one-night-stand gig didn't hold the same appeal. It irritated her to discover she wanted more from him than that. It had been nearly a week since they'd slept together and she still couldn't get him off her mind. In fact, he'd consumed her thoughts to the point where she could barely think of anything else. It was infuriating. Especially when it was clear he didn't feel the same.

With a groan of frustration, she dropped into her chair and rested her elbows on her desk. It was Friday afternoon. The end of her working week. On any other Friday, she'd be making plans to go out for a drink, take in some of the local nightlife, maybe even find a bed partner for an hour or two. But that was before Liam.

No, she refused to let that man ruin things. She wouldn't give him so much power over her life. If she wanted to go out, have a few drinks, flirt with other men, then by God, she would. Liam Hennessy could go to hell.

With that thought in mind, she pulled out her phone. Deliberately setting aside her earlier reservations, she called Nathan. He was charming, sexy, and interested. Right now, that was all she cared about.

He sounded surprised to receive her invitation but was quick to accept. She agreed to meet him at the most popular bar in town. As she ended the call, she smiled. Nathan was just the man to have some fun with. With a bit of luck, he might help her forget all about Liam Hennessy.

Liam was in a bad mood. He was bored and irritable and out of sorts. It was Friday night and instead of being out with mates, enjoying a drink or two and letting his hair down, he was at home alone, with nothing but the TV for company. Jacqueline was on an evening shift. She'd left him a note wishing him a good night, along with a bowl of chicken and mushroom pasta. Though the dish looked enticing, and he appreciated the effort his sister had gone to cook extra for him, he didn't feel like eating.

The reason was Hannah. He couldn't stop thinking about her. From the time he'd left her office to the moment he'd left the site, his mind had been consumed with her. It was driving him insane. He had to stop thinking about her. It wasn't healthy. It was bad enough that he'd slept with her, all the time knowing she didn't feel the same way about him.

The best thing he could do was to forget about her and everything that had gone on between them. Making love with her had been an amazing experience, but it wouldn't happen again. It was time to accept that and move on from Hannah Barrington once and for all.

On a sudden surge of determination, he jumped off the couch and strode down the hall toward his room. What better way to exorcise her from his memory than by sleeping with someone else? It wouldn't mend his broken heart, but it would go some way to erasing the memory of her body, her sweet kisses, her soft sighs...

Throwing open the door to his wardrobe, he pulled out jeans, clean underwear, and a plain white T-shirt. Then he jumped under the shower. He washed his hair and shaved his face and soaped all over. After rinsing and drying off, he got dressed. A few minutes later, he surveyed himself in the mirror.

The jeans fit snugly around his hips and the denim emphasized the length of his legs. The tight T-shirt clung to his broad chest and clearly delineated his pectorals. The short sleeves showed off his biceps. He liked being fit and he worked out regularly at the gym. Since he'd relocated to Muswellbrook, he hadn't been as often as he usually did, but he was determined to change that. He needed to get back into his old routine. That would also help to eradicate Hannah from his thoughts and put her firmly where she belonged. In his past.

His hair was still damp from the shower. He finger-combed it roughly into place. He patted some aftershave on his cheeks. He looked good. Young, confident, and with a glint in his eye that he hoped would telegraph that he was available. Exactly the look he was going for. Hannah Barrington and the hold she had over him could go to hell.

He spied his car keys on the dresser. His hand hovered over them. If he drove, he wouldn't be able to drink. At least, not as much as it would take for him to stop thinking about

Hannah. Then again, in a small town like Muswellbrook, taxis were in short supply. It wasn't like the city. They weren't on every street corner. Did he really want to be stuck at a bar with no way of getting home in the event that no one interesting caught his eye?

Jacqueline lived in one of the newer subdivisions that was quite a way from the center of town. At least a five mile walk from any of the bars. That was a fair distance to walk late at night. Best to play it safe. He could always leave his car outside the bar and come back for it later if he found someone he wanted to go home with. Decision made and feeling better than he had all week, he picked up his keys and left.

Hannah was already regretting inviting Nathan out. As they stood together at the bar talking over drinks, his hand kept finding its way to her ass. She'd discreetly shifted it twice already and she was almost certain that wouldn't be the last time she'd be forced to do that. She understood how Nathan might have gotten the wrong impression. Hell, she'd wanted him to think that way. But now she was there with him, she realized she'd invited him under false pretenses. As suave and good looking as Nathan was, he didn't hold a torch to Liam.

Where Nathan was all gloss and superficiality, Liam was the real deal. Where Nathan had picture-perfect, impossibly white, straight teeth, Liam's were slightly crooked. Where

Nathan was evenly tanned from hours spent in a solarium, Liam was tanned only where his skin was exposed to the sun. She knew firsthand that his stomach was pale, along with his ass. Although she'd never seen Nathan in the buff, she'd bet every dollar she had that he was the same golden color all over. Once upon a time, that kind of self-absorption wouldn't have mattered to her, but now she realized she preferred the real deal over the fake.

In short, it was Liam she wanted, not Nathan, and she wished it was Liam who was here with her now. Only Liam didn't want her. He'd told her that spending the night with her had been a mistake. Talk about how to put a dent in a woman's ego. Oh, he'd hidden behind the excuse that he'd put his career on the line if he got involved with her, but she didn't believe that for an instant. Liam Hennessy struck her as a man who did what he wanted. If he truly wanted her, his career would have been the last thing on his mind. It annoyed her to waste even a second thinking otherwise. Which brought her back to Nathan.

She swallowed a sigh and gulped at her wine. She'd already decided to bring her night to an end just as soon as she'd finished this glass. No matter how hard Nathan flirted, Liam had spoiled her for other men. The knowledge only made her feel more irritable.

"So, do you have any plans for the weekend?" Nathan asked, frank interest in his eyes.

She thought about her reply. If she said she didn't have plans, that might initiate an invitation. Spending more time with Nathan was now the last thing she wanted to do. If she made up some imaginary plans on the spot, he might question her further about them and she'd end up getting caught up in her lies.

As she cast around for something to say, she spied Liam out of the corner of her eye. She froze momentarily and then blinked in surprise. He was the last person she expected to see there. Of all the bars in Muswellbrook, he happened to come to the one where she was. He stood near the door, letting his eyes adjust to the dimness. Then he started scanning the room.

Their eyes locked. Something indefinable flashed in his. Her heart leaped in her chest and then her pulse took off at a gallop. She watched as he looked from her to Nathan and his expression immediately changed. A look of comprehension flooded his face. His upper lip curled in disgust.

It was obvious he thought they were together and though he'd drawn the wrong conclusion, all at once, she was filled with the need to strike back. Setting her glass down on the bar, she grabbed the lapels of Nathan's jacket and drew him close. Tilting her head, she pressed her lips against his.

Kissing him through his initial surprise, she clung to his jacket and kept her lips locked on his for as long as she could stand. When Nathan's surprise morphed into desire and he started kissing her back, she broke away. Flustered and overwhelmed with guilt, she took refuge in her drink.

The moment Liam spied Hannah with Nathan, jealousy tore through his gut. *Fuck.* His initial instincts had been right. They were a couple. He turned away, unable to bear watching their public, passionate display. All the erotic moments he and Hannah had shared that he'd replayed over and over in his mind had been reduced to ashes. This was proof their night together had meant nothing to her.

Though he already knew how she felt, it was like the scab being torn off all over again. The hurt was just as fresh as it had been the first time. Though his first instinct was to turn and run, he refused to let her have that much power over him. Instead, he strode to the far side of the bar, out of sight of Hannah and her boyfriend, and ordered a beer. It arrived a few moments later and he downed it in four quick gulps and then asked for another. It was only after his third drink that the jealousy and hurt that raged inside him began to ease.

Hannah was a free agent. He had no call on her. If she wanted Nathan Garcia, then so be it. Her actions only served to reinforce his belief that she hadn't changed from the teenager she'd once been. The spoiled brat who'd enjoyed watching boys turn themselves inside out over her.

No. That wasn't fair. She'd told him she hadn't been interested in boys back then and he'd believed her. No doubt she'd been oblivious to the attention she garnered. Still, that didn't change anything. It was clear she felt nothing more for him past the physical. So be it. He didn't need her in his life. Taut with anger and hurt, he downed the last of his beer, tossed some bills on the bar and turned on his heel and left.

Hannah watched Liam's departing back and swore under her breath. She was gripped with guilt. What she'd done was stupid and immature, only designed to hurt. And from the fierce look of anger and betrayal she'd glimpsed on Liam's face, her actions had had the desired effect.

Just as bad, Nathan now looked at her like he was already picturing them in bed. He stared at her with a mixture of confusion and delight. His eyes were bright with desire and anticipation. She couldn't blame him. She'd just kissed him for all she was worth. How was he supposed to know it had all been an act?

He reached out and put his hand on her hip and drew her forward, obviously intending to go in for another kiss. She tensed and pulled away. He frowned.

"Hannah?"

She saw the questions in his eyes and compressed her lips, once again flooding with guilt. This was all her fault. She'd hurt Liam terribly and she'd also done the wrong thing by Nathan, but there was nothing she could do about that now. All she wanted to do was to tear out of there and find Liam and tell him the truth and beg for his forgiveness. But first, she owed Nathan an apology. She just hoped he'd accept it and that it wouldn't affect their relationship going forward.

"I'm sorry, Nathan. I shouldn't have done that."

He shot her a half-smile, his eyes still clouded with uncertainty. "Hey. No need to apologize. You can kiss me like that anytime. Hell, you can kiss me, period."

She eyed him somberly. "I'm sorry. I've given you the wrong idea. It's all my fault. I... I like you, Nathan. I like you a lot. But not in that way. We work so well together, but that's all I want."

His frown deepened. "I don't understand."

Conscious that every moment she spent there delayed her ability to go after Liam, Hannah swallowed a groan and tried again.

"I should never have kissed you. It was wrong and it wasn't fair to you. I understand your confusion and that's on me, but please, can we just forget it ever happened and go back to being friends?"

His expression darkened to something ugly. Anger glinted in his eyes. "Friends? You kiss me like that and then expect me to believe you only want to be friends?"

She shrugged, feeling helpless. There was no way she could tell him she'd done it to make another man jealous. "I'm sorry."

"Sorry?" Nathan shook his head, eyeing her scornfully. "There are names for women like you, Hannah."

She winced but didn't argue. Nothing she could say would make this better. The best thing to do was to leave. Picking up her handbag, she slid the strap over her shoulder.

"I need to get going."

Nathan's lip curled in disgust. "Yeah. You do that."

With her stomach churning, she turned away from him and hurried toward the exit, hoping she wasn't too late to catch

Liam. She cleared the building in time to see him folding himself into a sleek silver Mercedes coupé. He was on the far side of the carpark. She called out to him, but he'd already closed the door. A few seconds later, the roar of an engine drowned everything else out. She took a few steps toward him, but there was no way he could see her in the dark. Then, with a spin of his wheels, he exited the carpark.

Her shoulders slumped. Her emotions were in freefall. She'd made such a hash of things. Who knew what damage she'd done to her relationship with Nathan. As for Liam, she couldn't bear the thought she'd done irreparable harm.

What if he doesn't forgive me?

She was weighed down with guilt and dejection, but as she made her way over to her car, she was also overcome with resignation. As much as she'd wanted to set things straight with Liam, it was probably for the best that he'd left. He was angry, upset, and hurting. She was also a mess. Better to take time to get a grip on her emotions, to get to a point where she could think clearly again. It also wouldn't hurt to give Liam a chance to cool down.

She had to hope and pray that was still possible.

Vaughan Barrington gunned the engine of his motorcycle. The bike responded like it had been designed to do. It leaped forward, the thrumming between his legs as exhilarating as the wind that ruffled his hair. He'd been living in Bali for nearly nine months. Way longer than he'd ever imagined when he'd tossed things into a suitcase, focused on nothing more than getting the hell out of Sydney.

Bali had been good for him. The sunshine, the surf, the people. Their relaxed attitude toward life and their perpetual hopefulness, even in the face of many challenges, had rubbed off on him and reignited in him a sense of gratitude for the life he'd left behind.

After discovering his biological mother was none other than the Craigdon family matriarch, Elizabeth, he'd been equal parts furious and shattered. His only thought had been to leave. All those months ago, he'd hopped on a plane without a word to anyone. He still felt a little guilty about that.

Away from everyone and everything familiar, he'd been busy working through the stages of grief. He'd passed through denial and was well on the path to anger when he met Ruby Ashworth. She'd changed everything; made him feel whole. It didn't matter that everything he'd thought true about his past was a lie. He had Ruby. He was head-over-heels in love with her. Lucky for him, she felt the same way.

He'd recently found the courage to propose to her. He'd been bowled over with happiness when she'd said yes. It didn't matter that they'd only known each other a matter of months. So what if there was still plenty they didn't know about each other? So what if he hadn't told her he was wealthy? He'd wanted her to love him for who he was. And she did. He was certain of that.

She didn't care about wealth and privilege and status. She didn't care his father was one of the richest men in Australia. She didn't even know about those things. All she cared about was *him*. What they felt for each other transcended time and place. It was special and unique. They both felt that way. He couldn't wait to make things official.

But Ruby wanted to wait until they returned to Australia to get married. All her family lived in Sydney. So did most of his. None of them were in Bali. None of them even knew she existed. Not that he needed his family's blessing. They'd love Ruby as much as he did. But it was because he loved her so much that he'd acceded to her wishes. Now he couldn't wait to return home and make her his wife.

The thought made him smile. Not so long ago, the thought of returning to Sydney and having to deal with the fact the woman he'd always thought had given birth to him wasn't that woman at all would have been enough to keep him away indefinitely. Now he had all the reason in the world to return home. That would mean having to deal with Elizabeth Craigdon and reveal secrets that had remained hidden for more than forty years, but that was a sacrifice he was prepared to make for the woman he loved with all his heart.

Ruby. My woman. My soul mate. The love of my life.

Vaughan was still smiling as he rounded a tight corner. Too late, he spied a farm truck right in front of him, on the wrong side of the road. He swerved to miss, but there was no escape. The truck bore down on him. Horn blasting, brakes squealing and then nothing but pain.

Oh, God. Please, no. Not now. Not like this...

Chapter Fourteen

R uby Ashworth ran like her life depended on it. And maybe it did. One of the housemaids who worked at the same hotel where Vaughan was employed had just given her word that Vaughan had been taken to the hospital. An accident. He'd been hit by a truck. She dodged traffic, skipping in and out of mopeds, cars, and other obstacles. Horns blasted, people shouted, and yet she remained oblivious.

Her sole focus was on the hospital a few hundred yards up the street. Her heart pounded. Her chest was so tight she could barely breathe. And still she ran, desperate for news. No one could tell her how he was. All she knew was that any collision involving a truck and a motorbike didn't bode well for the rider of the bike.

Refusing to dwell on the tortuous images such knowledge conjured, she burst into the emergency department of the hospital and raced straight up to the front desk.

"Vaughan Barrington," she gasped. "Please. Tell me how he is."

The Balinese nurse behind the counter gave her a confused stare. "What's the name again?"

"Vaughan. Vaughan Barrington." She spelled it out.

The nurse tapped on her keyboard and then nodded. "Right. I'm afraid he's been taken to the theater. They're operating on him now."

Ruby's stomach clenched with fear. "S-surgery? Oh, God. How badly is he hurt?"

The nurse shook her head. "I'm sorry. That's all I know. Are you family?"

Ruby opened her mouth to say no and then stopped. She was the closest thing Vaughan had to family here in Bali. If she told the truth, they might not let her in to see him, nor keep her informed of his condition.

Oh, why was I so insistent we get married in Sydney? We could already be husband and wife if I hadn't been so stubborn.

On the heels of that thought came another: *You know why...*

She looked the nurse in the eye and responded. "Yes. I'm his wife."

"Very well. Take a seat. When I know more, I'll come and get you."

There was nothing more Ruby could do. Turning away, she stumbled toward the row of plastic seats that lined one wall of the emergency department. She collapsed onto one of them and buried her face in her hands, overwhelmed by the stress that had held her in its grip from the instant she'd heard the news.

Oh, God. Why didn't I tell him the truth? Now I might never get the chance...

Ruby didn't know how much time had passed, but from the crick in her neck and the numbness in her butt, it had been several hours. She woke abruptly as someone shook her lightly. She opened her eyes and blinked to clear her vision. The nurse from behind the front counter stood beside her, looking grim.

"W-what is it?" Ruby stammered, still half-asleep.

"You said you were Vaughan Barrington's wife?"

At the mention of Vaughan's name, Ruby came instantly awake. She sat up straight and stared at the nurse.

"Yes. Please, how is he?"

The woman seemed to take a lifetime to answer. The whole time, Ruby's heart pounded like she'd run a marathon. An icy ball of dread formed in her stomach.

"He's out of surgery," the nurse said. "The good thing is, he's still alive. But he's been gravely injured. The doctor will be along shortly to tell you more."

"Can I see him?"

"Not yet. He's been taken to the ICU. He's still unconscious."

Ruby gasped in alarm. She grabbed the nurse by the arm. "Please... How... How bad is it?"

The nurse merely shook her head. "I'm sorry. You need to wait for the doctor. He'll be able to answer your questions."

Before Ruby could implore her further, the nurse walked away. She tried to breathe, but the tightness in her chest made that difficult. Vaughan was badly injured. Unconscious. In the ICU.

He might even die...

"Oh, God." The words came out in an anguished moan. She leaned forward, with her elbows on her knees and rocked back and forth, trying desperately not to give in to the panic that threatened to overwhelm her.

She needed to notify his family. They had a right to know. As much as she didn't want their idyllic time together in Bali to be over, there was nothing else to do. She needed to get Vaughan back to Sydney where he could get the most up-to-date medical care. As much as she loved the Balinese people, Vaughan needed to be around the best doctors, the best surgeons, the best technology. She owed him that much.

She dreaded the thought of what would happen when he discovered she'd lied to him—or at the very least, deceived him. She'd thought she'd have more time to tell him the truth, to explain. There had never seemed to be the right time. Now it seemed that decision had been taken out of her hands.

She might not be in love with him, but she refused to let him die in Bali. She'd contact his family and ask for their help. They had the means to get him back to Sydney as a matter of urgency. She'd deal with the rest afterward. When Vaughan was well and truly out of danger, they could pick up the pieces of their life and move forward. That was all she could hope.

It had been three days since Hannah had last seen Liam. Three days since that awful Friday night at the bar. He'd been on the mine site since early that morning, but she'd deliberately stayed away from him. Though she'd begun to attend the start-up meetings at the beginning of each shift in an effort to try and ascertain where things were going wrong, the rest of the time she'd been hiding out in her office, hoping like hell he didn't ask to speak with her. She hated herself for being a coward. She'd never backed away from a challenge. But this was different. She wasn't yet ready to face him.

She was angry at herself for using Nathan, but she was also angry at Liam for making her want him as much as she did and for making her want more from him than a one-night stand. This was all new territory for her, and she was finding it hard to adjust. She'd never wanted any man for more than sheer physical pleasure. She took and she gave, and it was all a bit of fun. Both parties walked away happy.

It perturbed her to discover she wanted to spend time with Liam outside of the bedroom. She wanted to get to know him better. She wanted to discuss all sorts of things that had nothing to do with sex. Why? It was like a compulsion for which she had no explanation.

They shared a history of attending the same school at the same time and yet they'd never met. She was intrigued by his confession that he'd been in love with her in high school, along with his best mate, Ned, whom she'd met briefly under awkward circumstances. Then there was his fierce loyalty to Ned. That told her a lot about Liam's character.

She wanted to learn more about him, but she readily acknowledged she'd sabotaged any opportunity to do so when she'd aborted their dinner plans for a few minutes of mind-blowing pleasure and then walked away. She was mad at herself for wanting more and that wasn't a good thing. Not when she had no intention of getting serious about the man. Right?

Things were also tense with Nathan. Despite her apology, he was still annoyed that she'd come onto him and then changed her mind. Of course, that was her prerogative, but she'd given him every indication he was going to get laid. He'd been rude and petulant ever since, openly questioning her decisions in front of other employees.

Her turning up at the start-up meetings had also put his nose out of joint. He'd accused her of undermining him, of not trusting him to do his job. That wasn't her intention, but she didn't seem to be able to convince him of that. He'd grown increasingly disrespectful. The situation was growing intolerable. And she only had herself to blame.

She could talk to her father about it, but the topic was just too embarrassing. She couldn't imagine how he'd react if she told him what had preempted Nathan's attitude. No, she'd brought this on herself. She needed to fix it herself.

He was her open cut examiner. She relied on him to be her eyes and ears in the pit. He knew the day-to-day running of the mine as well as she did. Maybe even better. He definitely had a closer relationship with their employees. Mainly because he spent more time with them. That was another reason why she'd started to attend the start-of-shift meetings.

She sighed. Building a relationship of trust with the workers would take time. She needed to mend bridges with Nathan. But she also needed to find out why he hadn't done his job in finding out the reason for why two men had failed to give positive communications which would have prevented that collision and why there had been an outdated safety manual on the site. In fact, the more she thought about it, his whole attitude toward the accidents had been curiously casual for an OCE.

Perhaps if I apologize to him again? No, scratch that. I need to move forward and take a professional approach and demand professionalism from him. I also need to raise my concern with him about his performance—or lack thereof.

Frank Barrington scrolled through the mountain of emails that clogged his inbox and silently cursed his second son. He and Evelyn might have adopted Vaughan when he was eleven, but Frank had long since stopped thinking of him like that. As far as he was concerned, Vaughan was as much his child as all of his other offspring.

Before Vaughan had opted out of his life in Sydney, he'd worked with Frank in Barrington Mining as his right-hand man. While Frank still held the position of CEO and retained majority voting rights, Vaughan had been promoted to a senior executive position and had overseen a lot of the day-to-day running of their vast mining operations.

But now Vaughan was gone. Living the high life in Bali, or some such thing. Whatever he was doing over there, it wasn't helping Frank. His son had been gone nearly nine months. That was a long time to take to find himself—if that's what Vaughan was doing. Nobody knew for sure. He'd sent sporadic emails over the time he'd been away, mainly to let them know he was okay. The messages had contained very little information and certainly no indication when Vaughan intended to return. It was doing Frank's head in.

"What the hell are you doing in Bali, Vaughan? We need you here," he mumbled to himself.

The door to his home office opened and his wife of more than thirty years appeared in the opening. She smiled as she made her way into the room.

"Who were you talking to?" Evelyn Barrington said. "Careful. People will think you've gone dotty." She softened her words with another smile and pressed a kiss against his cheek.

He reached out for her hand and squeezed it. "I was thinking about Vaughan. Wondering what he's up to. Why he's stayed away so long. I miss him."

Evelyn's eyes teared up. "I miss him, too."

Frank made an impatient sound in the back of his throat and released his wife's hand. "I mean, I get that he might have freaked out about turning forty. It's a significant birthday and with no wife or family or even a significant other in his life... Perhaps he felt the need to disappear for a while. But it's been the better part of nine months! How long does he intend to stay away?"

Evelyn compressed her lips and nodded. She shifted away and perched on one corner of his desk. "I agree. I wish we could talk to him. Apart from sending an email and not knowing when he's going to respond, we have no way of contacting him. I hate that."

"I hate that, too," Frank admitted quietly. "What do you say, we take a trip to Bali?"

She blinked in surprise. "Really? But how would we know where he is?"

Frank shrugged. "We know he's been working in a bar on a beach. Knowing Vaughan, it wouldn't just be any bar. He's always had expensive tastes and an eye for the ladies. I'm betting he got a job at one of those fancy places in Nusa Dua. Remember when we stayed at the Ritz-Carlton that time, right there on the beach?"

Evelyn nodded. "Yes, I remember. And you're right. There were bars all along the beach that catered to the hotel guests and other tourists."

"I think we should take a little holiday. It can't be that hard to find him."

Her eyes lit up with interest. "That sounds like a good idea. Who knows? We might manage to convince him to come home."

Frank sighed. "That would be a start."

Turning back to his computer, he continued to scan his emails. And then his heart jumped. One of the emails was from Vaughan.

Speak of the devil...

He looked at Evelyn. "You're not going to believe this, but I've just received another email from Vaughan."

She gasped in surprise and leaned in closer to the screen. Frank opened the email and began to read.

"What does it say?" she asked impatiently.

He frowned. "It's not from Vaughan."

Evelyn sighed with disappointment. "I thought you said—"

"It's been sent from Vaughan's email address, but it's from a woman by the name of Ruby Ashworth."

Evelyn's brow furrowed with confusion. "Ruby Ashworth? Who's that?"

Frank continued to read. "It says here she's his...fiancée." He looked at his wife. Her expression reflected the shock he felt.

"His *fiancée?*" she repeated.

Frank nodded. "Yes." He kept reading. His stomach sank. Icy dread filled his veins. "Oh, no. Oh, please God, no."

Concern flooded Evelyn's face. She stood, looking shaky. Her eyes went wide. "What is it, Frank? Please, tell me what's wrong."

Frank closed his eyes against a surge of panic. "It says here he was hit by a truck. He's sustained a serious head injury. They've operated on him in Bali, but he's still unconscious. It's touch and go. They're not sure if he's sustained any permanent brain damage."

Evelyn gasped. Her eyes were filled with fear. She was so pale; Frank was concerned she might faint.

"I need to fly to Bali right away," he rasped, trying desperately to come to terms with what had happened.

"I'm coming with you."

Frank knew better than to argue. Instead, he nodded briefly and pushed away from his desk. Together, they strode toward the exit. He was already on the phone to his executive assistant, Casey, before they cleared the room. The first thing he asked her to do was to book two business class plane tickets to Denpasar.

Hannah had spent the past hour staring blindly at her computer screen and trying out various apologies to Nathan in her head. She had to tread carefully. If she did too much damage to his ego, he might hand in his resignation. Not only would she have to explain that to her father, she'd also be without her right-hand man. On the other hand, she wanted to make it clear there was no future for them, at least not in the romantic sense. It was a challenge, for sure.

The sound of her phone ringing provided a timely distraction. Swallowing a sigh of relief, she checked the screen and then smiled wryly.

Daddy.

"What a coincidence! I was just thinking about you," she said by way of greeting. "How are things?"

"Hi, Hannah."

Her father's somber tone registered. She frowned. "What is it? Is something wrong?"

His heavy sigh only served to further fuel her anxiety. Her stomach clenched reflexively. "Daddy? What's happened? Is it Mom?"

"No, honey. Nothing like that. Your mother's fine. So am I."

The panic in her chest eased. "Okay. Then what is it?"

"It's your brother. Vaughan. I'm afraid there's been an accident. It's bad."

A buzzing sounded in Hannah's ears. She strained to hear what her father was saying, but she only caught snatches of words. She was able to gather that Vaughan had been hit by a truck and that he was seriously injured.

"Your mother and I are flying out on the first plane to Denpasar," her father continued. "We're going to bring him home. Say some prayers for him. It sounds like he's going to need them."

Hannah shook her head in bewilderment. At the same time, she struggled to breathe. So many questions clamored to be asked, but the overriding feeling was fear. "Is he... Is he going to be all right?" Her voice was a ragged whisper. She fought to hold back tears.

"We don't know," her father said solemnly. "He's alive. That's all we know for sure."

"How... How did you find out?"

"I'm sorry, Hannah. I have to go. Molly's calling me. I'll talk to you when we arrive in Bali and I have more to report."

He ended the call. She stared down at the phone and started trembling. A delayed reaction to the shock. All she could think of was Vaughan. He must have been hurt pretty badly for her parents to be rushing over there to bring him back.

Oh, God. Please let him be okay...

Knowing her brother was so seriously injured—maybe even fighting for his life—put her problems with Liam and Nathan into perspective. They were nothing compared to the fact her brother was gravely injured, and in a developing country, to boot. That only made it even more serious. She understood the urgency driving her parents. She felt the same.

Please bring him home safely... Please let him be all right...

The silent prayers kept circling in her head.

Chapter Fifteen

Liam grabbed a key pass from Hannah's receptionist and headed into the pit. The sooner he got enough evidence to support his growing theory that someone was deliberately causing safety incidents at the Strathwaylin mine, the sooner he could close his investigations and get as far away from Hannah as possible. He'd already checked the rosters with Colin Hume, the principal of Hume Earthmoving who was contracted to the mine and who employed the men who'd either witnessed or been involved in the latest two accidents. The contractor had confirmed that all three men were on site that day.

The contractor had cleared out a makeshift office and invited Liam to conduct his interviews there.

"The walls aren't exactly soundproof," Colin explained, "but you'll have a little more privacy than you'd have out in the workshop."

"Thank you. I appreciate that. Do you mind sending Paul Hammond in?"

"He's right outside. I'll let him know you're ready for him."

Paul Hammond looked like a typical coal miner. He wore the standard-issue high-visibility work clothes, along with steel-toed boots. He carried a hard hat and sauntered into the room like he owned it. The same confident swagger and smirk that had been in evidence the first time Liam had interviewed the man. It seemed being reinterviewed by an investigator from the Resources Regulator didn't cause him concern.

Liam stood and introduced himself again. Hammond briefly shook his hand and then dropped into the seat opposite Liam.

"What can I do for you, Mr Hennessy?"

The man's sardonic tone rubbed Liam the wrong way, but he ignored the irritation and got straight to the point.

"You were involved in both accidents that occurred a few weeks ago."

"Yep. We've already been over that."

"Tell me again how you came to be operating a machine one day and rostered in the workshop a week later? I find that highly unusual. I would have thought an experienced operator like yourself would have been kept on a machine."

Hammond shrugged and gave Liam a challenging look. "What can I say? I'm an all-rounder. Some days I drive machinery, other times I give the fitters a hand in the shed."

"Who told you to drive the excavator that day?"

"Nobody"

Liam frowned. "Nobody?"

"I'm the supervisor of this crew. I get to choose what I drive."

"I see. What about your boss, Colin? Does he get a say?"

"Colin's not always here."

"So, was it also your decision to be in the workshop the following week?"

Hammond looked at him defiantly. "Yep."

"Are you friendly with Nathan Garcia? He's the OCE for the mine."

"I know who he is. And yes, we get on all right."

"Would you say you were mates?"

"I guess so."

"Do you ever socialize together? Go out for a drink after work?"

"Yeah, sometimes. So what?"

"No reason." Liam made some notes on the paper in front of him. At least the man hadn't lied about that. No doubt he knew how easy it was to look someone up on social media.

Liam glanced up at him again. "How long have you worked at Strathwaylin?"

"Three years."

"And you've worked for Hume Earthmoving all that time?"

"No. I used to work for Rodriguez Contracting."

Liam frowned. "You mean Joseph Rodriguez?"

"Yep."

There was that name again. Joseph Rodriguez. Nathan Garcia's uncle. Liam decided to play dumb.

"Why did you leave Rodriguez?"

Hammond shrugged and looked away. "He lost the mine contract and had to move on. So, I got a job with the contractor who replaced him."

"Fair enough." Liam made a few more notes and then looked back at Hammond. "You know what? I've been thinking about that collision between the dozer and the excavator. You were driving the excavator, right?"

Hammond's expression remained neutral. "Right."

"And Scott Stonewall was on the dozer?"

"Yep."

"You see, I just don't understand why neither of you used positive communications prior to the dozer coming into your swing radius. I mean, that's safety 101 and is standard procedure. An operator with your standing and experience must know that."

Hammond merely shrugged, but his gaze slid away. "I thought I had."

Liam eyeballed him. "No, you didn't. Neither did Stonewall. And I can't help but wonder why."

Hammond shifted in his seat but remained silent. Liam tried harder to shake the man's tree.

"You know, I've operated heavy machinery in a mine. Dozers, scrapers, diggers. I can't imagine ever coming anywhere near one of those machines without notifying any operator in the vicinity of my presence. The potential for a serious injury, even death, is too huge. Who'd put their life at risk like that? Stonewall was lucky he wasn't killed. In fact, looking at the damage sustained to that dozer, I find it hard to believe he escaped unharmed."

Liam eyeballed the man again. The more he'd studied the photographs of the dozer, the more he was convinced Scott hadn't been in the cab when it had been struck. There was no way the man could have walked away from that accident. And yet he had. Liam had a theory of how the collision had gone down and it didn't bode well for either man.

But he wasn't prepared to show his hand just yet. So, with a tight smile, he glanced back at Hammond. "I think we're done here. Thank you for your time."

"All good," Hammond muttered as he pushed away from the desk and got to his feet.

"Can you send Rodney Valentine in, please?"

"Sure."

A few moments later, Rodney walked into the room. His gaze darted every which way. He barely glanced at Liam. Unlike Hammond, Valentine was nervous.

Once again, Liam stood and introduced himself and offered his hand to the man. Valentine mumbled a response, shook his hand, and sat.

"Do you know why I'm here?" Liam asked.

Valentine shrugged and stared at the floor. "About those accidents, I guess."

"That's right. I have a few more questions."

Valentine remained silent.

"Where were you when the excavator and the dozer collided?"

"I was in a dump truck on the haul road."

"So, you had a clear view of what happened?"

"Yep."

"Who do you think was at fault?"

"I can't say."

Liam eyeballed him. "Can't, or won't?"

Valentine shifted in his seat but didn't respond.

"How long have you worked here, Mr Valentine?"

"Eighteen months."

"And you've worked for Hume Contracting all that time?"

"No."

Liam blinked. "No? Who else have you worked for?"

"I used to work for Joseph Rodriguez. Until he got sacked."

Liam kept his gaze steady on the man. "You know he got sacked?"

"Yep. Everyone does."

"Do you know why?"

"Because Frank Barrington hated his guts."

Liam stilled. "How do you know that?"

"Nathan told us. He's Joe's nephew. He was also one of Joe's supervisors. If anyone knows the truth about what happened, it's Nathan."

"I see," Liam said. He was onto something here. He could feel it. Taking his time, he asked another question.

"So, Nathan worked for his uncle?"

"Yeah."

"And now he works for Barrington Mining?"

"You already know that. He's the OCE."

"How well do you know Nathan?"

Valentine shrugged. "Pretty well."

"How often does he come down to the pit?"

"All the time."

"Does he spend time with the men, with you?"

"Yeah. Sometimes."

"Do you see each other outside of work?"

"Yeah. Sometimes. We go for a drink every now and then."

"Would you consider Nathan a friend?"

Valentine nodded. "Yeah. I guess so."

"Are *you* related to Nathan or Mr Rodriguez?"

"Nah. I only worked for Joe. But he's a good bloke."

"Thank you for your time, Mr Valentine. I think we're done for now. Do you mind sending Mr Stonewall in?"

Valentine left quickly. Liam thought about what he'd learned. Both Hammond and Valentine had worked for Joseph Rodriguez. They were also both friendly with Garcia. Liam had a growing suspicion that not only was Garcia behind the incidents, but he'd also recruited some of his uncle's former employees to assist him. It would be interesting to see what the next man had to say.

A few moments later, Scott Stonewall appeared. With gray bushy hair and a full, long beard, he was at least a decade older than Hammond and Valentine.

"Take a seat," Liam offered after reintroducing himself. "Do you know why I'm here?"

"It's about those accidents, isn't it? That's what you wanted to talk about the last time."

"Yes, you're right."

"I dunno what you want with me. I already told you everything I know."

"Yes, and I'm grateful for your cooperation. I just have a few more questions."

Stonewall briefly nodded. Though his attitude wasn't belligerent like Hammond's, he was far from friendly. Liam cleared his throat.

"Have you always worked for Hume Earthmoving?" he asked.

A flash of surprise registered on the man's face. Liam wasn't sure what he'd expected to be asked, but it obviously wasn't that.

"No. I've only been with them seven months."

Liam's heart skipped a beat. "And who did you work for before that?"

"An outfit called Rodriguez Contracting."

"Was that out here, at Strathwaylin?"

"Yes."

"And why did you leave Rodriguez Contracting? Weren't they paying enough?" Liam joked.

The man's demeanor remained somber. "Nothing like that. Their contract with the mine was canceled." Stonewall turned his head to one side and spat on the concrete floor. Liam tried not to react.

"I see. Do you know why it was canceled?"

Stonewall's eyes flashed, but when he responded, his tone remained calm. "I'm not sure of the details. Something about a disagreement between the boss and Frank Barrington."

Liam switched tack. "Do you know Nathan Garcia?"

"Yeah. He's the OCE."

"How often do you see him here in the pit?"

"Every day. Sometimes several times a day. It's his job to know what's going on. Not like that princess who calls herself the group manager for WHST. She wouldn't know one end of the mine from another. What a joke."

"You mean Hannah Barrington?"

Another globule of phlegm was hawked up and deposited on the floor. "Yeah. Hannah Barrington."

"You don't think she's qualified for the job?"

Stonewall merely gave him a droll look. Liam moved on. "Do you socialize with Nathan Garcia outside of work?"

"Sometimes. We're all pretty tight around here. He's a good bloke."

"Do you know he's related to your former boss?"

"Yeah. He's Joe's nephew. Everyone knows that."

Well, not everyone. Liam was betting Hannah had no idea of the connection between her right-hand man and the contractor her father had sacked.

"You were driving the dozer that day of the collision, weren't you?"

"Yeah. I already told you that the last time we talked."

"I'm curious. Why did you fail to give positive communications before approaching the excavator which was being operated by Paul Hammond?"

"I didn't fail to do anything. I gave pos comms."

Liam glared at him, his patience wearing thin. "Quit wasting my time, Stonewall. We both know you didn't. What I want to know is, why? You could have sustained serious injuries, even death, in that accident and the whole thing could have been avoided if you'd just called up Hammond on the radio and requested permission to come inside his swing radius. It's standard operating procedure and the most basic of safety regulations and yet you failed to adhere to them, perhaps even at the risk of your life."

Stonewall's cheeks flushed. With anger or embarrassment, Liam couldn't tell.

"The thing is," Liam continued in a reasonable tone, "the reason you and Mr Hammond didn't bother with pos comms is because you'd already had this planned out. You'd planned the collision ahead of time and at the moment that digger bucket collided with the cab of your dozer, you were nowhere near the place."

Stonewall's cheeks flushed darker. He sat up in his seat and glared at Liam. "That's bullshit. You don't have a clue what went on."

Liam regarded him steadily. "Oh, but I do. See, there's no way you could have escaped that collision unharmed. The damage sustained to the cab of your dozer... Well, you've seen it. How do you explain how you escaped without so much as a graze?"

"I got lucky, I guess," Stonewall blustered.

Liam nodded. "Oh, yes. You got lucky all right. Lucky that Mr Hammond gave you enough time to climb out of the cab and get out of the way before he sent his bucket careening into it."

Stonewall narrowed his eyes at him. "You can't prove that."

Liam glared right back at him. "Oh, but I can." He reached into one of his files and withdrew a handful of colored 8 x 10 photographs of the dozer. The photo showed a graphic image of the incredible amount of damage sustained by the glass cab.

"How about you tell me, Mr Stonewall, how you managed to climb out of that without so much as a scratch? In fact, you explain to me how you managed to climb out that at all."

Stonewall stared down at the pictures and looked flustered. Both guilt and fear passed over his face. His mouth opened and closed several times, but no words came out.

"That's what I thought," Liam said.

Slowly, Liam collected the photographs into a pile and slipped them back into his file. He looked at Stonewall again. "I think we're done here, Mr Stonewall. Thank you for being so cooperative. I really appreciate your help."

The man mumbled an incoherent response, then stood and quickly left. Liam leaned back against his chair and stacked his hands behind his head. Though he'd gone out on a bit of a limb accusing Stonewall of colluding with Hammond to cause the collision, right down to the fact Stonewall had climbed out of the dozer prior to the accident, it was obvious his gut instinct about what had gone down was on the mark.

Stonewall hadn't been able to provide any explanation for how he'd managed to escape unharmed, or at all. Not that Liam would have believed him. There was only one explanation for how Scott Stonewall had gotten out of that collision unscathed and that was that he hadn't been inside the cab when it had been struck. Now all Liam had to determine was who else had been in on it. He'd almost put money on Garcia.

Joseph Rodriguez was the one thing that linked Hammond, Stonewall, and Valentine together and to Nathan Garcia. It was plausible Garcia had a vendetta against Barrington Mining after what had been done to his uncle. Another possibility was that Rodriguez and Garcia were in it together, with Garcia doing the dirty work on his uncle's behalf. It was also plausible Garcia had recruited his buddies to help him sabotage the mine.

So many possibilities and they all revolve around Garcia…

What Liam needed was more proof. A smoking gun. Something more than his gut instinct that told him Garcia was responsible.

The sound of the office door closing interrupted his thoughts. Liam looked across the room and saw another miner coming toward him. The man looked to be in his early fifties and from the way his gaze darted around the place and wouldn't meet Liam's eyes, it was obvious he was nervous.

Liam frowned. "I'm sorry. Is there something I can do for you?"

The man sent another furtive glance around the room before taking the vacant seat. "You're that guy from the Resources Regulator, right?"

"Yes. I'm Liam Hennessy. I've been investigating recent safety breaches."

"Yeah. I saw you when you were here before."

"Who are you?"

"Malcolm White. I'm the head foreman of the workshop."

"I thought that was Paul Hammond?"

White snorted in disgust. "He'd like to think so."

Liam sat forward. "It doesn't sound like you're a fan."

"You're right. He's an asshole. Almost as big an asshole as his buddy, Nathan Garcia."

Now the man had Liam's full attention. He dragged the writing pad closer and picked up his pen. "What do you know about Nathan Garcia?"

"I know he has no business being employed at this mine."

"Why do you say that?"

"He's a traitor."

Liam regarded the man steadily, refusing to allow any emotion to show on his face. "That's interesting. What's your beef against him?"

"He's Joseph Rodriguez's nephew and he's been sent in here for no other reason than to cause trouble. And boy, is he causing trouble. At least for the mine."

"You think he's involved in the recent accidents?"

The man leaned forward. "Of course, he's involved! Oh, he didn't get his hands dirty, but he's the mastermind."

"You think he somehow set those accidents up?"

"He set them up all right. He got together with his buddies, who all just happen to have worked for his uncle, by the way, and he came up with a plan to cause trouble. And what better way to cause trouble in a mine, than to cause an accident? A safety breach is the worst thing that can happen. The mine runs the risk of being closed. That costs everyone."

"How do you know this?" Liam asked.

"I overheard him talking to his mates—Stonewall, Valentine, and that prick, Hammond. Garcia was telling them about his plans. He's been doing it from almost the first day he arrived here."

"Why are you only now coming forward?"

Malcolm flushed and averted his gaze. "I'm sick and tired of having to fix the stuff that gets broken every time Nathan comes up with one of his schemes. It's not my money that's getting wasted, but I hate waste of any kind. And deliberately causing damage is mindless vandalism. There's no need for it and it's not fair to Colin Hume who has to keep paying for the breakages.

"Not only that, I'm concerned that it's only a matter of time before someone gets seriously injured. We got lucky with Harry. He only suffered a scratch. That could have been a lot worse. He could have lost an eye."

Malcolm drew in a deep breath and looked at Liam. "I was here when Evan Wilson was killed. That was before Garcia's time, but there's no way in the world you'll convince me his uncle didn't have a hand in that."

Liam managed not to react. "I understand Wilson's death was thoroughly investigated by several independent sources. They couldn't pin it on anyone. It was deemed an accident."

"Yeah. That's what they said."

Liam could tell from Malcolm's tone that he didn't believe him. Still, that investigation was long since closed. There was nothing Liam could do about it now.

"Are you prepared to make a formal statement about this?" he asked.

The man slowly nodded. "Yeah."

"Okay, then. Do you mind if I record our conversation? It'll make it easier for me to transcribe when I get back to the office."

"Sure. No problem."

Malcolm's earlier nervousness appeared to have eased. It was as if, now that he'd made the decision to expose what had been going on, he was on board all the way. Though Liam was ecstatic to finally have concrete proof of Garcia's involvement, he dreaded the thought of breaking the news to Hannah. Their relationship was on rocky ground. This might be the final blow that would destroy it forever.

Chapter Sixteen

L iam ran into Nathan Garcia on his way out of the workshop. It was as if Garcia knew he was there, and perhaps he did. Though Liam wanted nothing more than to throw the information Malcolm White had given him into the asshole's face, he wasn't ready yet to show his hand, and in particular, he wasn't ready to out his star witness.

If Garcia got even a hint of what White had told him, Garcia and his buddies would make the man's life hell. White's safety might also be at risk. Liam couldn't be responsible for that. No, best to bide his time and pounce when he had everything in a row and White's safety could be assured.

"Well, if it isn't our hardworking investigator. I guess I should be grateful you're down here and not up at the office sniffing around my woman." Nathan smirked.

Liam clenched his jaw and refused to be provoked. "Good to see you again, Garcia. I assume you're down here to ensure all proper safety procedures and protocols are being followed?"

The asshole smirked again and then shrugged. "I don't think the men need me to be looking over their shoulders. They do pretty well on their own."

Liam narrowed his eyes at him. For a man who was supposed to be responsible for ensuring mine safety, he had an incredibly lax attitude toward the fact there had been a large number of incidents over the time he'd been in charge. Any other safety officer having to lay claim to so many breaches of the rules would have been embarrassed, contrite, and would most definitely have offered reassurances that everything was being done to ensure the incidents didn't happen again. His arrogance was astounding. Then again, if Garcia was deliberately causing them, he probably wouldn't give a damn. He didn't even seem concerned that his job might be on the line.

Perhaps he knew Hannah wouldn't fire him. And maybe he was right to feel that level of confidence. After all, she'd kissed him, hadn't she? And not just a kiss, but a full-on pash that made it clear they were a couple. Or at the very least, involved in some kind of passionate affair. It was enough to get Liam's blood boiling all over again.

I was an idiot to think she might care for me! It was always only sex for her. No doubt that's all it is with Garcia, too.

Liam refused to feel sorry for the man. Let him work it out for himself. Besides, Garcia didn't look like the type who'd suffer from a broken heart. He was much too self-absorbed to know what being vulnerable felt like. He was also way too cocky.

Impatient and irritated now, Liam glared at him. "Cut the bullshit, Garcia. We both know exactly what's going on here."

As Garcia tried to bluster out a response, Liam continued to glare at him. Though he wasn't yet ready to disclose the existence of a witness that could go a long way to proving

Garcia's guilt, he did have something else up his sleeve that was bound to rattle the asshole's cage.

"You know, as soon as I found out you were Joseph Rodriguez's nephew, everything fell into place."

Garcia's eyes went wide with surprise. His mouth gaped momentarily before he seemed to check himself. He gave Liam another cool glance, but this time it was tempered with fear. "What does that have to do with anything?" he demanded.

Liam continued to glare at the man. "The fact you even have to ask that question just confirms how stupid you are."

Garcia lunged at Liam. Surprised the man would try to assault a government official, but perfectly capable of defending himself, Liam held his ground. He stared at Garcia, challenging him with his eyes. He'd almost welcome an excuse to plow his fist into the man's arrogant face.

After a few tense moments, Garcia chose the wiser course of action and relaxed his stance and stepped back. Liam eased out a breath. Tucking his paperwork under his arm, he spared one last glare in Garcia's direction before slowly turning his back on the man and heading to his car.

Liam had a head full of steam by the time he arrived back at the building that housed Hannah's site office. He kept seeing Garcia's knowing smirk that said it all: *She's mine*. And she was, at least for now. What made it even more galling was that Garcia didn't even know Liam had spotted them making out in the bar. The asshole's reaction was nothing more than instinctive; he knew Liam wanted her and he was going to rub in the fact that she was his woman. The prick.

It only made Liam more determined to tell Hannah who was behind the spate of incidents. He wasn't sure if she'd believe him because he was pointing the finger squarely at her boyfriend, but that wasn't Liam's problem. He'd done his job, and these were his findings. She could take them or leave them.

But surely even Hannah would realize keeping Garcia around was a liability for everyone. Safety was paramount. If he was deliberately causing accidents, she needed to send him packing that very day. Either that or risk more incidents. Though Liam didn't intend to close the mine down over these two accidents, he might not feel the same way about the next one.

I guess that's Hannah's call... We'll see how much she cares about the mine... And how much she's attached to Garcia...

He scowled at the last thought and was still scowling when he strode down the corridor to Hannah's office. Knocking briskly on the door, he opened it without waiting for an invitation to enter. He found her behind her desk, staring off into space. Her eyes were wide and unfocused. Her cheeks were pale. She didn't even appear to register he was there.

He hated that his gut immediately somersaulted with concern. In three quick strides, he was leaning over her desk.

"Hannah? What's wrong?"

He repeated her name and then she blinked, slowly returning to awareness. She frowned up at him.

"Liam? What are you doing here?"

"I've been on site all morning, reinterviewing witnesses, but that's not important right now. What's going on with you?"

She looked like she was on the verge of tears. Her lower lip trembled. She bit down on it. Moisture filled her eyes.

His concern ratcheted up another notch. "Hannah? Please, talk to me. What's wrong?"

She drew in a shaky breath. "It's... It's my brother. Vaughan. He's... He's been in an accident. It's bad."

In halting sentences, she filled him in on what she knew. He didn't want to feel sorry for her, but he couldn't help it. Despite the fact she'd thrown him over for Garcia, he cared for her. A lot. He couldn't stand by and watch her distress and not do something to comfort her. As the tears that threatened started to spill down her cheeks and she made a hiccuppy little sob, he cursed under his breath and walked around her side of the desk. He tugged her upright. With another sob, she fell into his arms and clung to him, breathing fast.

"Oh, Liam! What if he doesn't pull through?"

Her words were filled with panic and fear, but there was nothing he could say to reassure her. He didn't know what condition her brother was in, but from what she'd told him, things weren't looking so good for Vaughan. Rather than give her false hope or say things he didn't know were true, he remained silent except for quiet murmurings of wordless comfort against her hair.

Her breath came in quick and shallow pants. Her body trembled with her distress. He stroked her back and held her close while she slowly fell apart.

"*Shh*, Hannah. Slow it down. Big, slow breaths or you'll hyperventilate. That's it. Slow, deep breaths."

"What if he never wakes up? What if he's like that forever? It's already been five days. Five days! And he's in Bali! A developing country. God knows what the medical facilities are like. Do they even have doctors over there?"

Her increasingly panicked questions were muffled against his shirt. He tightened his arms around her and continued to stroke her back.

"Of course they have doctors over there," he chided gently. "You can't think like that. I'm sure they're doing everything they can."

As if suddenly realizing where she was, Hannah pulled out of his arms and stepped away. She swiped at the tears on her cheeks and dragged in a deep breath and then began to pace.

"Thank God, Daddy's bringing him home. Oh, God. I can't bear the waiting. I want to do something to help, but what can I do? I'm useless. As useless as I am at preventing accidents at this mine."

Liam hated that she was blaming herself and second-guessing her capabilities as the safety manager. Okay, so there had been a number of incidents, but most were not serious and no one could deny she'd increased production. And then there was the matter of Nathan Garcia and Liam's certainty the man was behind many of the most recent accidents. Of course, Hannah didn't know that yet. It was unfortunate he was there to bring her more bad news.

Still, before he did that, he wanted to make sure she was all right. She'd had a terrible shock about Vaughan. Liam needed to reassure himself she was okay before he gave her another shock.

He reached out and touched her arm. Her skin was warm beneath his. She sucked in a breath, but she didn't move. His gaze fixed on her luscious mouth before shifting upward.

"Are you okay?"

Her tongue stole out to dampen her lips. It was all he could do not to groan. She stared at him, their gazes locked, as if she were also aware of the sudden tension in the room. The silence stretched between them. All Liam could hear was the thumping of his heart. Flashes of memory of their night together filled his mind. The heat of her mouth. The silky softness of her skin. The way her legs clung to his hips. Driving forward on a surge of need. Her little cries of fulfilment...

As if she could read his thoughts, her eyes darkened with desire. Her lips parted. His heart pumped. His blood surged. Looking dazed, she took a step toward him. He could tell she was about to kiss him. He tensed in anticipation, his body as hard as stone. At the last moment, he remembered she was with Garcia. Biting off a curse, he lowered his gaze and reluctantly stepped away.

He saw the flash of hurt in Hannah's eyes before she quickly concealed it behind a blank mask. He hated himself for it because all he wanted to do was to kiss her and never stop. But that wasn't the smartest thing to do right now for so many reasons. She was so vulnerable right now and he was also the bearer of bad news. Worse still, she'd chosen Garcia over him. He'd best remember that.

Taking a few steps away from her, he half-turned away from her and deliberately put some distance between them. When he glanced at her again, his heart sank. Her cobalt eyes had turned to ice. The raw passion of just a few moments ago had been replaced by a cold mask of anger and embarrassment. Drawing in a ragged breath, he eased it out on a weary sigh and cast around for the courage to give her the news he'd come there to deliver.

Hannah's face flamed with embarrassment.

How could I be so stupid? Am I a masochist? Why would I set myself up for rejection again? He's already made it clear our sleeping together had been a mistake. What did I expect? Especially after he saw me with Nathan...

She swallowed a groan and took refuge behind her desk. Keeping her face averted, she fought to regain her composure. When she felt sufficiently able, she looked up at him and glared. "What are you doing here, Liam?"

He held her gaze. Several emotions chased themselves across his face. Finally, it appeared resignation won out. In a low voice that was free from inflection, he replied.

"Like I said, I've been down at the pit, reinterviewing witnesses."

Her eyes narrowed. "Why would you do that? Didn't you talk to them already?"

He nodded. "Yes. But here's the thing, something wasn't adding up."

She looked at him, interested in spite of herself. She wanted to get to the bottom of what was happening as much as anyone. "What wasn't adding up?"

"I kept hearing from everyone, including your OCE, that what happened were simple accidents. Nobody to blame. Could have happened to anyone. Nothing anyone could have done to prevent it. But you and I know very well that's bullshit. There's always a reason why an accident happens and it's always someone's fault. Someone wasn't paying attention; they weren't following regulations—whatever. Accidents don't just happen. They're always a result of something else. You know that. I know that. And so does Nathan Garcia."

He stopped. Dread stirred in her belly.

"What are you saying?" she asked, hardly daring to put the question to him.

Liam's expression turned hard. "What I'm saying is that I believe Nathan Garcia's been causing the accidents."

Shock ricocheted through her. She'd already started to shake her head in denial when Liam spoke again.

"I'm sure you find it hard to believe your lover has been sabotaging your business from the inside, but that's what's been happening. I'm almost certain he's had a hand in every single incident since he arrived here."

"He's not my lover," she said faintly, her mind spinning.

Liam waved her words away. "Whatever. He's definitely responsible for what happened on the last two occasions. And before you ask, yes, I have proof."

She stared at him in disbelief, her thoughts still going a mile a minute. Nathan was sabotaging her business? How could that be? But Liam said he had proof. Unless he was lying...

"I'm not sure if you're aware," Liam continued, "but Nathan Garcia used to be a supervisor for Joseph Rodriguez. He's also his nephew."

These fresh revelations were just as shocking as the first. Hannah gasped. Her heart pounded. Before she could respond, Liam spoke again.

"I'm sure I don't need to remind you of the way Rodriguez left this mine site. Your father fired him for continuous safety breaches. So, this is my theory: Rodriguez didn't go quietly. He might have left the mine site, but he had no choice in that. Instead, he made sure his nephew wangled his way into your employ and then started white-anting you from the inside." He gave her a hard look. "You were the one to employ him, weren't you?"

She nodded distantly. She remembered sitting on the interview panel. Nathan's resumé had been exemplary. He had glowing references from several past employers. He was also sexy beyond measure. She might not have had any intention of getting into a romantic relationship with him, but she'd been aware of him from the moment he'd stepped into that room.

Then anger stirred inside her. While Liam had told her he was certain Nathan was behind the breaches, so far he'd provided her with no proof. How did she know this wasn't more about the fact he was upset with her for kissing Nathan?

"How do I know you're telling the truth?" she fired back at him.

He held her gaze without flinching. "Like I said. I have proof. I can't force you to believe me, but I wouldn't lie to you. Rodriguez asked Garcia to do his dirty work. He's been trying to discredit the mine and get it closed. There's no other explanation. Of course, he had a few accomplices—all former employees of Rodriguez, by the way—Paul Hammond, Rodney Valentine, Scott Stonewall. They're all in on it."

He paused. "Didn't you ever look at the damage caused to that dozer cab and wonder how Stonewall survived that accident? Not only survived, but escaped without a scratch?"

Hannah stared at him. She hated that she recalled thinking exactly that. Before she could respond, Liam spoke again.

"I don't know how so many of Rodriguez's former employees ended up working here again." He gave her a pointed look. "You might know more about that."

"I don't know either. Anyone who's ever worked on this mine site is recorded on our system," Hannah said weakly, still trying to sort out how she felt about the bombshells Liam had just dropped and whether or not she could believe him. Unfortunately, they made a horrible kind of sense.

Liam stared at her. "Then how come Nathan wasn't aware that those men had been employed by Joseph Rodriguez?"

Hannah compressed her lips. The dread in her belly morphed into a cold, hard lump. "He must have known."

Liam nodded briefly, his expression grim. "Just so you know, bringing you this news gives me no pleasure."

Hannah's lips tightened. She still didn't know what to think. He'd put her in an impossible position. If she believed him, she'd have no choice but to fire Nathan and all of his cronies. There'd be no other course of action open to her. If she chose not to believe Liam and kept Nathan on and the accidents kept happening... That would be untenable.

Then again, Liam had been investigating those incidents for weeks. Was it only just coincidence that a couple of days after he'd spied her making out with her OCE, he'd come to her with serious accusations against that very same man? Was that all this was? A simple act of petty revenge?

Maybe his anger at her also had something to do with Ned. Though Liam appeared to have accepted her explanation about the truth of what happened all those years ago and had apologized to her, was it possible that had only been for show? Her mind veered away from remembering what had happened later that night; the way they'd come together in an explosion of desire and red-hot passion and how she'd wanted to repeat the experience; had even considered entering into a relationship with him.

Ha! What a joke!

Feeling buffeted from all sides, she did the only thing she could: raised the walls. She needed time to think; to sort through Liam's revelations; to come to terms with what very well could be a betrayal of the highest order by Nathan. She couldn't do any of those things with Liam there.

"I'd like you to leave," she said quietly.

Liam's eyes flashed with anger. "Not before you tell me you believe me."

She made an impatient sound in the back of her throat. "I don't know what to believe!"

His gaze grew intense. "Yes. You do. It's just a matter of whether you're willing to set aside your pride and admit it." He drew in a quick breath and continued.

"All I did was follow the evidence. I ferreted out Nathan because I'm damn good at my job. Just so you know, I have a higher success rate than any of my colleagues in solving workplace incidents and I'm damned proud of that. Every time I make formal findings and recommendations at a mine, it makes that workplace safer for everyone. And that's all I care about. Keeping people safe."

She stood by and watched him in silence. His breath came fast. His color remained high. She opened her mouth to respond, but he wasn't finished yet.

"When I do my job well, workers get to go home to their families. They get to have dinner with their wives. Kiss their kids goodnight. Live to see another day."

He glared at her. "You once told me you also believed that was a good thing." He shook his head slowly back and forth. "I'm not sure I believe you. But whatever you think, that's your business. What you need to know is that I won't shy away from doing whatever needs to be done to make sure that happens."

Hannah was secretly impressed with Liam's passion for his job and the safety of the workers. It was obvious he felt very strongly about that. Even so, she needed some time alone to think.

"I'd like you to leave," she said again.

"But I haven't told you about the proof I—"

She held up a hand to cut him off. "No more. I've heard enough. Now leave. Please."

Her tone was no-nonsense. She followed it through with a narrow-eyed look. Though she was putting on a strong front, inside she was shaking. She felt like she'd been put through a wringer and was barely hanging on. She was sure her tenuous grip on the situation must be clear for him to see.

She glanced at him from beneath her lashes. She expected to see him gloating. After all, he'd just dropped a bombshell about her most trusted colleague and, despite her bluff and bluster, it had rocked her to the core. Instead, he looked sad and resigned. Slowly, and without another word, he turned and left.

With adrenaline still surging through her veins, she strode across the room and shut the door firmly behind him. Then she leaned against it with a weary sigh. She drew in some deep breaths. Her pulse rate slowly returned to normal. She walked back to her desk and sat down. Her thoughts were in turmoil. First the shock about Vaughan. Now, this.

Not so long ago, she would have immediately denied Nathan could ever want to do anything to damage the mine and its operations, but lately, she hadn't been so certain. Keeping the safety manuals current was his job. An outdated manual should never have been in the hands of a contractor, or anyone for that matter, and yet Nathan had provided no explanation for that.

Then there was the fact he would have known ex-employees of Rodriguez had applied to come back on site, under the employ of another contractor. If Hannah had been made aware of that, there was no way she'd have agreed to it. There was a reason her father had sacked Rodriguez and issued a blanket ban on all his employees, and Hannah was in full agreement with it.

Then there was the fact he'd concealed his relationship with Rodriguez. She would never have considered him for the job as her open cut examiner if she'd known of those close blood ties. And yet he'd remained silent about that. Rodriguez had been fired before Nathan had started at the mine, but he darn well knew about it. If he had nothing to hide, surely he would have disclosed his relationship to the man, if for no other reason than to ensure Hannah was okay with having Joseph Rodriguez's nephew in her employ and in such a position of trust, to boot.

To point the finger at Liam and accuse him of being hellbent on revenge was immature and petulant and she was ashamed of herself for even thinking along those lines, even momentarily. She'd also refused to listen to his proof. No matter that they'd butted heads on more than one occasion, she respected Liam's professionalism and he'd done nothing in his professional capacity to make her question his motives now.

That didn't mean she couldn't do a little digging of her own. Starting now.

Chapter Seventeen

Liam dragged his heels as he left Hannah's office, feeling worse than he had for a long time. He was weighed down by a hard knot of disappointment. He'd known from the outset there was a risk Hannah wouldn't believe him, but he'd been hoping to convince her anyway.

She hadn't come right out and accused him of lying, but neither had she reassured him she believed his every word. She hadn't given him a chance to tell her about Malcolm White's revelations, but the fact Garcia was related to Joseph Rodriguez should have been enough to give her pause. It was obvious she hadn't known about Garcia's connection to the man her father had sacked. Though Liam hadn't been privy to that conversation, the contract Frank Barrington had terminated without notice had been worth millions. That alone provided serious motivation for some payback.

Unfortunately, it appeared she didn't see it that way, and there was nothing he could do to change her mind. It just went to show how important Nathan Garcia was to her; that she'd take his side over Liam's. He'd known how risky it was to take a chance on Hannah Barrington. He'd had his heart broken by her once and she hadn't even been aware of it. Okay, so he now accepted what he'd felt for her was more a teenage crush rather than true love, but that didn't mean the feelings of loss and disappointment hadn't been real. He'd known how dangerous it was to be around her, to let himself become vulnerable. He'd thought he could handle it. He was wrong.

Along with the disappointment was an ache of loss so deep he didn't know if he'd ever get over it. But he only had himself to blame. Hannah had never made any promises. They'd had mind-blowing sex, but that's all it had been for her. A passionate encounter between two consenting adults who'd walked away afterward without a backward glance. At least, that's how it had been for her. He hated that it hurt so much.

Still, there was nothing he could do about it now except finalize his report, submit it to his superior along with his recommendations, and then go somewhere to hide out and lick his wounds. One thing was clear: he couldn't continue working in the Hunter Valley and risk running into Hannah again. He was tough, but he wasn't made of stone. He couldn't bear the thought of coming into her orbit and being reminded all over again that he meant nothing to her.

I'll put in for a transfer... Maybe I can convince Jacqueline to move? After all, that's why I came here in the first place. To be closer to her. My original motivation had nothing whatsoever to do with Hannah Barrington...

He'd had no idea Hannah even lived in the area, let alone that she'd come back into his life. As much as he wanted to despise her, he was more upset at himself for how things had gone down. Though he no longer blamed her for Ned's death and accepted that she wasn't the selfish and self-absorbed woman he'd thought she was, that still didn't change the fact he was nothing more to her than a warm body. He was a fool for thinking—hoping—for a breathless moment that they might have had something special between them. He should have known better.

The next couple of days passed in a blur for Hannah. Though she kept up the pretense of seeking out Nathan for advice and relying on him to ensure safety protocols were being followed at all times, she'd also taken to visiting the pit without notice, in addition to regularly attending start-up meetings, and touring the workshop and other areas of the mine. So far, she hadn't found anything out of order, but the reactions from some of the staff had surprised her.

They ranged in attitude from mild curiosity over her presence to downright hostility. Paul Hammond, in particular, seemed to resent her intrusion, no matter that she was the safety manager and able to go wherever she darn well pleased. She blamed it on his misogynistic attitude. He'd never been willing to accept she was the boss. In Paul Hammond's world, women had no place on a mine site. His sexist attitude only served to fire her up and make her all the more determined to show them she was up to the job, but it was also a little depressing that in the twenty-first century there were still men who felt that way.

"God help his wife or girlfriend," she muttered under her breath as she drew her keyboard toward her and started typing.

"What's that?" Nathan asked from his position opposite her desk.

They'd been going through the day's reports, including the daily production targets. It was coming up to Christmas and her father had advised he'd be closing the mine for Christmas Day so that everyone could spend the day with their families. It was an incredibly generous gesture and would cost the mine a small fortune in lost production time. The good news was, they were well on track to meet their targets. She glanced at Nathan and smiled.

"I was talking about Paul Hammond. I swear, that man's stuck in the 1800s."

"What do you mean?"

Hannah looked at him. "Don't tell me you haven't noticed? The way he talks to me? The way he thinks about women? If he had his way, we'd all still be stuck at home raising children, cleaning the house, and cooking meals. That's about all he thinks we're good for."

Nathan smirked. "I think that's a bit harsh."

"No, it's not!" Hannah protested. "You've seen the way he looks at me, the way he speaks. He has no respect for me, or my position and I know darn well that's because I'm a woman. There's no way he'd speak to a male manager like that."

To her annoyance, Nathan merely shrugged. "I think you're being a bit sensitive. Paul's a good guy."

"Yeah, except when he's causing accidents," she mumbled.

Nathan's eyes flashed. He sat up straighter. "What do you mean by that? Those accidents weren't Paul's fault."

Hannah stubbornly held his gaze. "So you say. But you can't deny he was involved in both of them."

"So, he was there. So were some of the other men. Don't tell me you think they all had a hand in them?"

His sarcastic tone stung, along with the disrespect she saw in his eyes. Her anger stirred. Nathan might need a reminder about which one of them was the boss.

As if aware of the direction of her thoughts, he spoke again. "Where's this coming from, Hannah?" he asked in a mollified tone. "Don't tell me that asshole from the Resources Regulator has gotten into your head."

Hannah flushed, but once again held Nathan's gaze. "Don't be ridiculous. As if I'd pay any attention to what a government investigator says." She paused. "I was down in the pit this morning, checking up on things. Paul Hammond was there. He was rude and obnoxious and disrespectful. If he wasn't such a good operator as you claim, I'd fire him."

"You can't just fire him!" Nathan exclaimed.

Hannah was taken aback by the passion in Nathan's voice. Here was another man telling her how to do her job. Anger settled like ice in her veins.

"Yes, I can," she said coldly. "I'm the safety manager. Have you forgotten that?"

"Of course not," Nathan mumbled, averting his gaze. Then he glanced at her. "The thing is, Hammond isn't employed by the mine. He's come through a labor hire company and is employed by a contractor. You have no authority to fire him."

Hannah continued to regard him steadily. "We both know there are ways and means of getting rid of people." She shook her head. "I must admit, I'm surprised by your reaction, Nathan. Hammond wouldn't be the first operator we've dismissed. Why's he so important to you?" She paused and then added, "Is it because he's a former employee of your uncle?"

Nathan's face turned to chalk. For a moment, he stared at her in shock and disbelief. Then he rearranged his expression to one of mild interest.

"How would I know who my uncle employed? We've never worked here at the same time."

"So, you don't deny Joseph Rodriguez is your uncle?"

His tone remained mild. "Why would I deny that?"

Hannah stared at him. "It would have been nice to know before I hired you."

"Why?" Nathan shot back. "You can't discriminate against someone because of their family."

"It would have still been useful information to know," Hannah insisted. "And I'm curious why you didn't know Paul Hammond was a former Rodriguez employee? That information would have been available to you through the HR department. And apparently, Hammond isn't the only ex-Rodriguez employee on this site."

Her eyes narrowed. "It's your job to know who's on this mine site. How do I know we're not hiring people who've been dismissed for good reason if you're not keeping an eye on that sort of thing? We keep a register of everyone's employment record for a reason. So we can keep tabs on who's here and so we don't have people here who've proved they're a potential threat to the mine. And yet, you seemed to have overlooked that very important procedure. Why, Nathan? Why would you do that?"

He averted his eyes, but not before she caught the anger that glittered in his gaze. He wasn't happy about having her question his decisions, but she wasn't happy, either. She had a sneaking suspicion that at least some of what Liam had said was true. It might not be Nathan behind the accidents, but with at least three former employees of Joseph Rodriguez working there, it wasn't beyond the realm of possibility that some of them were doing their utmost to cause trouble.

She was surprised when Nathan went on the offensive. "If you don't think I'm doing a good enough job, Hannah, why don't you fire me? You're throwing around all sorts of accusations, but you don't have a clue what you're talking about."

He pushed away from his desk and began to pace, his agitation evident. "I spend every hour of every day making sure things run smoothly. I meet with the men. I talk to them. I'm constantly in the pit, keeping an eye on things, making sure people are doing as they're told. Being *safe*. Okay, so I don't get that right all the time, but accidents happen. You know that better than most. You spend the first part of every day going through the reports on safety incidents that have occurred in mines around the world. Accidents happen. That doesn't mean I'm not doing my job."

Her gaze remained steady on his. "Did you know there were former Rodriguez employees working on this mine site?"

Nathan threw up his hands in a sign of frustration. "No, okay? That must have slipped by me. What do you want me to say? I'm sorry. I'm not perfect."

Hannah eyeballed him, not completely satisfied with his answer. She'd never demanded perfection, but she'd expected him to be on top of something like that. She was disappointed he hadn't given it the priority she believed it deserved. She made a mental note to review the current record of every employee on the site.

"I want you to ask anyone who used to be employed by Rodriguez to leave. They're no longer needed at this mine. I'm prepared to give them references, but I want them gone."

Nathan gaped. "You can't just ask someone to leave, Hannah."

"It's a euphemism, okay. You know what I mean. Find a way to get rid of them. I no longer want them working on this mine site. They should never have gotten through the door in the first place." She glared at him, her patience at an end. "Do you understand?"

Nathan's mouth tightened. There was tension around his eyes. She could tell he wanted to argue further, but he wisely chose to remain silent. A moment later, he muttered something about needing to go to the pit and took his leave.

Hannah breathed out a sigh of relief, pleased to have the office to herself. Ever since Liam had put the thought into her head that Nathan was behind the safety incidents, she'd been more impatient with him than usual. She'd also been more observant of his reactions and what he said. She should just come right out and ask him if he was involved, but something held her back. It wasn't fear. She wasn't frightened of anyone. But neither did she want to accuse Nathan of something without having definite proof.

Being related to a disgruntled contractor wasn't proof of anything and unfortunately, she'd refused to let Liam share what proof he'd purported to have. Given the way they'd left things between them, she wasn't inclined to call him and ask.

No, the best thing to do was to investigate herself. She was the boss, after all. It was ultimately her responsibility to know what was going on. She'd already been down to the pit several times. That had gotten her nowhere. The men didn't trust her enough to open up. She'd have to try other means of getting the answers. Starting with Nathan's emails.

She didn't think he'd be stupid enough to keep a record of his involvement (if he was, in fact, involved), but it was worth taking a peek. As a group manager, she had access to the Internet server where all the data was stored, including emails. Decision made, she typed in the necessary commands.

Nervous anticipation swirled in her stomach as she waited for the page to load. She located Nathan's email data and opened the file into another page. She groaned aloud at the sheer volume of material. It would be like searching for a needle in a haystack. An impossible task. Still, she'd come this far. She might as well open a few random emails and see what she could find.

First, she narrowed the data down to emails sent or received by Nathan and Paul Hammond. To her surprise, there were a lot. She clicked on a few and opened them. They mostly contained social invitations: to the local bar, a fishing trip, a night out in the city. She blinked in surprise. She'd had no idea the two men were such good friends.

She refined her search further by adding the name "Joseph" and "Rodriguez". A fresh page of hits began to load. As she clicked on the first one and started reading, her heart began to pound. The email had been sent by Nathan to Paul Hammond and talked about making things difficult for Frank Barrington.

With increasing dread and disbelief, Hannah opened more and more emails between the two men. The more she read, the more she realized it was just as Liam had said. Nathan had been actively sabotaging the safety at the mine. With the help of his mate, Paul Hammond, and a few other workers loyal to the cause, they'd manufactured one incident after another, all of them in breach of safety regulations.

Then her attention was caught by an email that detailed the incident involving the collision between the dozer and the excavator. She read the contents with increasing anger and disbelief.

"That plan worked a treat," Nathan had written.

"Yeah. Lucky for Scott, he got out before I swung the bucket," Paul Hammond responded.

"It had nothing to do with luck. I told Scott where to pull up and to get well out of the way so you could do your thing," Nathan wrote.

"Yeah, well I did my thing all right. That cab was crushed."

"At least a hundred grand's worth of damage, not to mention the down time," Nathan responded.

The worst of it was the gloating between the two men afterward. The way they congratulated each other on getting away with it. The way they were certain it was only a matter of time before the Resources Regulator shut down the mine. Then she saw her name mentioned and stared closely at the screen.

"That bitch, Hannah Barrington. She thinks she knows it all. Ha! What a joke! She came and looked at the dozer and didn't even question how Paul had managed to escape such a damaged cab unharmed. What a stupid bitch," Nathan had written.

Paul Hammond had responded with an equally derogatory reply.

Hannah's chest went tight with suppressed anger. Her hands clenched into fists. Her breath came fast as she fought to gain control and think, rather than react. She forced herself to read through every email sent between the two men. The more she read, the more it became clear they'd been in on it from the very beginning.

Nathan had applied for the job of open cut examiner. He'd doctored his resumé with fake information to ensure he was more than qualified. Coupled with his natural charisma, he'd been a shoe-in. Then he'd set about getting Rodriguez's former employees on site. His little posse of men were hellbent on revenge and boy, did they go about seeking it.

From the first few weeks of Nathan's employment at Strathwaylin, he'd set about doing all he could to cause accidents. He'd made sure to keep his hands clean, but it was obvious from the back and forth between him and Hammond via email that he was the mastermind behind the plan to destroy Barrington Mining.

Liam was right...

Feeling sick, Hannah cursed aloud. She couldn't believe this had been going on right under her nose and she'd been oblivious.

What kind of safety manager am I that I didn't even know? This happened on my watch, by a man I employed, and I didn't have a clue. I got caught up in his good looks and charm and couldn't see past that...

She made a sound of disgust in the back of her throat. How could she have been so blind? Then she thought about how she'd used Nathan to try and make Liam jealous. Her face flamed with embarrassment.

Oh, God. How stupid and immature I've been. I don't deserve to be the boss. Daddy's faith in me has been misplaced. I should never have taken on this job...

As she methodically set about transferring a copy of all of the incriminating data to an external drive, along with printing a hard copy of every email, she thought of how difficult it would be to tell her father and own up to what had occurred on her watch. She also owed Liam an apology. With her elbows propped up on her desk, she dropped her head into her hands and sighed. She didn't know which call she dreaded making the most.

Liam stalked into Jacqueline's house after work and made a beeline for the fridge. He'd been in a sour mood ever since he'd left the Strathwaylin mine site. No matter that a couple of days had passed and his supervisor had given him high praise over his report. His mood hadn't improved and that had everything to do with Hannah Barrington. He pulled out a beer and twisted the top off. He chugged down half the contents without drawing a breath.

"Someone's thirsty," his sister said from her position on the couch.

He started in surprise. The house was quiet and still. He hadn't expected her to be home at this hour. She'd told him the night before she was on an evening shift that day. Then he noticed the bandage wrapped around her ankle and frowned.

"What happened?" he asked, drawing closer.

Jacqueline grimaced. "I slipped on a spill at work. Twisted my ankle."

Liam perched himself on the edge of the couch. "Are you okay?"

"Yeah. I'm fine. I already took some painkillers. Now it's a matter of resting it and waiting for the swelling to go down."

"Are you sure it isn't broken?"

"Yes. One of the doctors looked at it. Nothing broken. Just a sprain. I'll be fine in a day or two."

He winked. "Thank God for subscription TV services."

She laughed. "You bet. This will give me time to catch up on "Suits." I'm up to season four."

Liam rolled his eyes. As much as his sister loved watching TV dramas, he preferred to read a book. He chugged down the rest of his beer. Already he could feel his tension easing. Jacqueline tilted her head and sent him a curious look.

"What's up with you?"

He pretended ignorance. "What do you mean?"

She shook her head on a wry grin. "Don't give me that nonsense, Liam. You've been stomping around here for days. Something's got you riled up." She paused and then a look of speculation filled her eyes. "Or should I say, *someone*."

He flushed and looked away. Jacqueline pounced.

"I *knew* it! It's Hannah Barrington, isn't it?"

He feigned innocence. "Why would you think that?"

Jacqueline straightened on the couch. "Because you've been out of sorts ever since you discovered she was here. Then there was that date that went to hell and—"

"It wasn't a *date*," Liam got out through clenched teeth.

Jacqueline waved away his words as if they were of no consequence. "Whatever. The fact is, you're in love with Hannah Barrington and always have been and she's not interested. That's why you're all worked up. Am I right?"

Liam stood and turned his back on her, heading for the fridge again. He set his empty bottle on the kitchen counter and reached for another before returning to the living room. He swallowed two gulps before responding.

"For your information," he said in an exaggeratedly calm tone, "I'm not worked up about anything. I'm perfectly fine. Couldn't feel better, in fact. I just finished two serious workplace investigations, and my boss applauded my diligence, conscientiousness, and overall commitment to my job. So, there. What do you think about that?" he finished triumphantly.

Jacqueline merely grinned. "I'm thrilled that everything's working out so well for you at the Resources Regulator, but you can deny it all you like, that doesn't change anything. You're angry and you've been that way ever since Hannah Barrington came back into your life. She's at the root of your bad mood. You'll never convince me otherwise," she said smugly.

Liam groaned in surrender and threw himself down in the armchair opposite. He took another swig from his beer and tossed his sister a disgruntled look. "I hate that you know me so well," he grumbled.

She smiled sweetly. "Of course, I do. You're my only sibling. Mom and Dad worked so hard outside the home, it seemed like we only had each other growing up." Her expression softened. "No matter what you think, I love you very much, Liam. I hate to see you upset."

He blew out his breath on a weary sigh. "You're right. It's Hannah. She's got me so twisted up in knots. I was determined to ignore her. Do my job and stay the hell away from her. Unfortunately, things didn't work out like that."

"You went out with her twice. She must have given you some encouragement for you to go back. What happened?"

He gulped down the rest of what was left of his beer and set the empty bottle aside. He wasn't usually much of a beer drinker. He much preferred wine. Already he had a nice buzz going, enough that he blurted out everything that had been going on. When he finished, Jacqueline regarded him with a mixture of sympathy and understanding.

"I'm sorry that happened to you, Liam. But you were a dick to tell her your night together was a mistake."

He tensed in surprise, then got annoyed. "What the hell? Why are you taking her side?"

"I'm not taking anyone's side. But when a woman has no-holds-barred sex with you and the first thing you tell her the next morning is thanks, but no thanks, how do you think she's going to feel?"

Liam shook his head in confusion. "I had no choice. I was in the middle of an investigation into Hannah's mine. Being involved with her, sleeping with her... It was a conflict of interest. It shouldn't have happened."

Jacqueline shot him a sour look. "You could have decided that before you slept with her."

Liam leaped off the couch, unable to sit there a moment longer. He dragged his hands through his hair, still perplexed by his sister's attitude.

"What about what she did to *me*? The sheets were hardly cold, and I found her making out with Nathan Garcia. It was like what we'd done meant nothing."

Jacqueline regarded him calmly. "I thought you told me you came across them after you'd told her your night together was a mistake."

Liam stared at her, frustration welling up inside him. "Yes. So?"

Jacqueline rolled her eyes and groaned. "Oh, little brother. Sometimes I wonder how someone so smart can be so dumb."

Her words irritated. They also pricked him with guilt. The truth was, he *had* told Hannah what they'd done was a mistake and that it wouldn't be repeated. It was only after that conversation that he'd seen her with Garcia. How was she to know he still had feelings for her? That it had felt like a kick in the guts to see her locking lips with her OCE? As far as she knew, their night together had been a one-off that wouldn't happen again.

"When a woman gets told by the man she's just slept with that it was a mistake, she's going to feel rejected. Then she's going to get mad. She might even want to get back at the man who's made her feel like that." Jacqueline stared at him pointedly. "Just saying."

Liam frowned. "Do you mean, Hannah might have deliberately sought out Garcia? That she kissed him in front of me out of revenge?"

Jacqueline waved away his words. "Hey, I don't know her well enough to know what was going on in her head. But you treated her poorly, brother. You bruised her pride and made her feel cheap and worthless. Nothing justifies that. As far as I'm concerned, you deserve all the flak you get."

Liam's head spun. He hadn't once considered how his words and actions had affected Hannah. After all, she was the one who'd up and left straight after. But maybe Jac was onto something. When he'd told her their night together was a mistake, maybe he'd hurt her feelings. Maybe that's why she'd reacted that way. His sister seemed to think so.

Before he could respond, his phone rang. He pulled it out of his pocket and checked the screen.

His gut clenched. He looked at Jacqueline and grimaced. "It's Hannah."

"Then answer it!" she said impatiently.

"What am I going to say? The last time we were together, she basically called me a liar and told me to leave."

Jacqueline looked dubious. "Did she really call you a liar?"

Liam shrugged and looked away. "Okay, so maybe not in so many words, but that's what she meant. She didn't believe me when I told her about Garcia."

The phone continued to ring. "For goodness' sake, just answer it!"

He sighed and tapped the screen. "Hannah. What is it?" he asked, his voice terse.

From the corner of his eye, he saw Jacqueline roll her eyes again. Mollifying his tone only slightly, he spoke again.

"I'm sorry. What can I do for you?"

"Liam. I... I owe you an apology. You were right. I've done some digging. Nathan's behind the safety breaches. He has been right from the beginning."

Liam tensed in surprise and then drew in a quick breath. Though it gave him no pleasure to know that his investigations had been proven correct, he was relieved just the same.

"How did you find out?" he asked, curious.

She sighed. "That doesn't matter right now. What matters is that you were right, and I should have believed you. I'm sorry."

He compressed his lips. "You had your reasons."

"I guess, but that still doesn't excuse my rudeness. I should have known you weren't just playing stupid games."

He frowned. "What are you talking about?"

She sighed again. "I'd rather not get into it over the phone. Is there any chance you're free to meet me for a drink? My shout."

His first instinct was to refuse. He'd been there before. Things hadn't ended well. "I'm sorry, but I'm kind of busy tonight."

Jacqueline frowned with annoyance and began shaking her head. She glared at him and whispered, "What are you doing?"

Liam waved her away, but his sister was having none of it. "Liam Hennessy. Quit this stupid nonsense right now. Tell the woman you'll meet her."

Liam's face flamed. Jacqueline had spoken so loudly, he was sure Hannah had heard every word.

"Where are you?" she asked.

"I'm at home. At my sister's place."

"Is she there with you?"

He squeezed his eyes shut for a moment on a silent groan. "Yes."

"Oh, okay. I'm sorry for disturbing your evening. I guess we'll try and make it another time."

Once again, Jacqueline made frantic motions with her hand and tried to speak to him with her eyes. Swallowing a sigh, he gave into her demands.

"On second thoughts, I've changed my mind. Where would you like to meet?"

When he ended the call, Jacqueline clapped her hands in delight. Liam glared at her. "It's on you if this doesn't work out."

Jacqueline merely smiled.

Chapter Eighteen

Hannah put on the finishing touches to her makeup and stood back from the mirror to survey the results. Just like the last two times she'd met Liam after hours, she'd gone out of her way to knock his socks off. But this time it wasn't a business meeting. Nor was it a meeting between two friends. She wanted to show him what he was really missing out on and perhaps to persuade him to give them another go.

He'd told her that being with her was a conflict of interest; that he refused to jeopardize his job. But that had been before. Now his investigation was over. Okay, so he was still the investigator for her mine, but who cared about such minor details? She hoped that this time at least she'd convince him that it would be worth his while if he was prepared to take a chance.

She looked good in the stretch-knit, crimson sheath that fit her like a glove. It set off her dark hair and olive skin tone beautifully. She'd teamed it with a matching red lipstick that drew attention to her full mouth. She knew from experience how much men liked that color on her. Not that she cared about other men. Not now. It was only Liam she sought to impress.

A wave of nervousness went through her. She wasn't sure what kind of reception to expect. They hadn't exactly parted as friends. Then again, he'd accepted her invitation. She hoped that meant he was at least prepared to be civil. That would be a start.

Her phone rang, interrupting her thoughts. She padded back into her bedroom and picked it up from where she'd tossed it on her bed. She glanced at the screen and was flooded with guilt.

Daddy.

She'd forgotten to call him. No, not forgotten. She'd been putting it off. Instead, she'd called Liam and she'd been so relieved that he'd agreed to go out for a drink, she'd decided not to mar the moment with a less-than-pleasant conversation with her dad. But now he was calling. She only hoped he hadn't already gotten wind of the debacle with Nathan.

Forcing a smile, she answered the call. "Hi, Daddy. How are things?"

"Hannah. I just thought I'd check in. I know it's not easy with me and your mother in Bali, but I wanted to see how everything is."

"Of course, Daddy. But first, tell me about Vaughan. How is he?"

"He's still unconscious. And right now, the doctors are telling us he's too unstable to move. We'll be in Bali a bit longer than I expected. I hope you're okay with that?"

"Yes, Daddy," she quickly agreed. "Vaughan's your priority right now. There's no need to worry about anything else."

I won't tell him about Nathan. At least, not right now. He has enough on his plate with Vaughan...

"What's going on at the mine? Anything I should know about?"

Hannah bit her lip. She didn't want to burden him with any more worries. Then again, this thing with Nathan was big. She hadn't yet worked out how she was going to deal with it, but there was no question she'd have to fire Nathan and all his cohorts. The only reason she hadn't done so already was because she was still trying to formulate a plan of action and she'd also wanted to speak with her father before she did anything. Now was her chance.

She sighed quietly and sat down on the edge of the bed. "Actually, Daddy. There's something you should know."

After she finished filling him in on what had happened, she was met with silence on the other end of the phone. Then Frank cleared his throat.

"Don't beat yourself up about it, Hannah. It could have happened to anyone. I didn't suspect Nathan, either."

Hannah eased out her breath. "Thank you for saying that, Daddy. But I was the one who employed him. I should have contacted every single one of his referees, checked them out thoroughly. Ran his name through some search engines. At least I would have learned about his connection to Rodriguez. Instead, I only called the first referee on his list. He must have been betting on that. The rest of his resumé was nonsense. Apparently, the only company he's ever worked for is Rodriguez Contracting."

"You couldn't have known that, Hannah, unless you'd gone looking. And neither could you have known he was related to that asshole I fired more than a year ago. How did you find out, by the way?"

Hannah sighed again. "Remember that investigator I told you about? Liam Hennessy?"

"The one from the Resources Regulator?"

"Yes. Well, he stumbled across the information in the course of his investigation. He said he had proof that Nathan was behind the accidents. At first, I didn't know whether to believe him."

"Why not?" Frank asked, too astute by half.

Hannah blushed. "It's complicated, Daddy."

"Oh, I see."

The knowing tone in his voice had her blushing again. She was grateful this was a phone call and not face-to-face.

"So, this Liam. He turned into a good guy, right?" her father continued.

Hannah reluctantly agreed. "Yes, Daddy. I think he's a good guy."

Except that he'd had sex with her and then dismissed it as if it were nothing; had even told her it was a mistake...

But her father didn't have to know that.

"Did you ever find out his history? Why you thought he knew the family?" Frank asked.

"Yes. As a matter of fact, we went to high school together in Broken. He was a couple of years ahead of me. That's why I didn't know him. But he remembered me."

"I see. Well, if you need help giving Nathan and the others their marching orders, let me know. I suggest you phone our lawyer and make sure everything's above board before you do anything. The last thing we want is an unfair dismissal claim."

"Sure, Daddy. I'll do that."

"Good girl. Well, honey. I must go. It's been good talking to you."

"You, too. Give Vaughan a hug and kiss for me. I hope you can bring him home soon."

"You bet. Love you."

"I love you too, Daddy."

With that, she ended the call. Glancing at the time, she realized she needed to get a move on, or she'd be late. Quickly, she pulled on her stilettos and then tossed her lipstick, credit card, condoms, and keys into her clutch. With a final check of her appearance, she headed out.

Liam sipped from his wine glass and surveyed his surroundings. He was relieved Hannah had suggested they meet in a different bar than the one he'd found her in with Garcia. He wasn't sure he was up for that kind of deja vu so soon. He hadn't been to this place before, but it was nice and classy in an understated way. The long bar that ran most of the length of the room had been made from a large hunk of Tasmanian Huon Pine. The knots and other minor imperfections had been left in situ, giving the wood a more authentic, rustic look. It complemented the rest of the décor in the room.

Hand-carved wooden booths with forest-green vinyl seats lined the opposite wall. In the middle of the room there were tables and chairs grouped together in twos and threes. The lighting came from wrought iron chandeliers that hung from large wooden beams in the ceiling and was dim enough to create an intimate ambiance that no doubt appealed to anyone seeking to escape and hide out for a while.

Country music blared from a jukebox in one corner. A handful of patrons filled some of the tables around the room. One couple had taken to the dance floor and were moving slowly to the music, wrapped in each other's arms.

He couldn't help but wonder if Hannah's invitation had been extended merely as further affirmation of her apology, or if she truly wanted to spend time with him. He deliberately tried not to read too much into it. In fact, if it wasn't for his sister, he probably wouldn't be there at all. He'd put his heart on the line before and had gotten burned. He wasn't so keen to do that again. No, he'd play it cool this time; let Hannah call the shots and see where things led.

As if his thoughts had conjured her up, in that moment she appeared before him. He almost gaped at the sight of her. Dressed in a form-fitting crimson dress that clung to every luscious curve, she looked like she'd just stepped off a Paris catwalk. The low V cut of the neckline displayed her generous cleavage to perfection. His fingers tingled as he vividly remembered how her breasts felt.

Her bright, lush lipstick was the exact same shade of her dress. The shiny gloss expertly traced the fullness of her lips. He wanted so badly to kiss her, but with a concerted effort, he controlled himself and offered her a smile in greeting instead.

"Hi," he said. "You look lovely."

She leaned in as if to kiss him, but at the last moment pulled back. Her cheeks turned as crimson as her dress. She fiddled with the catch on her clutch purse, looking adorably flustered. He took her nerves as a good sign. That meant she was concerned about the outcome of their get-together.

"Thanks for coming," she said, flicking a quick glance in his direction.

"My pleasure," he said. "Can I get you a drink?"

"Thank you, yes. A glass of house red would be great."

Liam caught the attention of the barman and put in a request for Hannah's drink. Her gaze kept darting around the room as if she expected him to start haranguing her at any moment. Taking pity on her, he covered her hand with his.

"Relax, Hannah. I come in peace."

She looked startled and then her face broke into a relieved smile. "That's funny. Really. Thank you. Do you mean it? Are we friends again?"

He grimaced. "I don't think we've ever been friends, have we? To tell you the truth, I'm not sure how you'd classify our relationship. It's changed so often; I haven't been able to keep up."

Her cheeks turned a rosy hue, but a smile still hovered around her lips. She looked at him with a wry grin.

"You're right. I must take my share of the blame for that."

He winked. "Apologizing again?"

She nodded. "Yep. I'm trying to wipe the slate clean in the hope that we might be able to start again." She stuck out her hand. "Hi. I'm Hannah Barrington. It's nice to meet you."

He laughed and shook her hand, happy to play along. "Liam Hennessy."

The barman arrived with Hannah's wine. Liam pulled out his wallet and paid for it.

"Hey, I thought I invited *you* for a drink," she protested.

"That doesn't mean you have to pay." He shrugged. "Blame it on my parents. I was raised with old-fashioned manners. Just be gracious and accept my generosity"

He softened his words with another wink and handed her the glass. She smiled and murmured her thanks.

"Here's cheers," he said, raising his glass and clinking it with hers. They both sipped their drinks.

"In all seriousness," Hannah said, looking at him once again, "I want to apologize for kissing Nathan."

"That's not necessary," Liam said. "You're a free agent. You can date anyone you like."

"But that's the thing," she said, looking earnest. "I'm not dating him. I asked him out once and things didn't work out well. I'm not interested in him that way."

Liam frowned. "I don't understand. If you're not interested in him, why were you kissing him like your life depended on it?"

She sighed and took refuge in her drink, as if seeking the courage to finish what she'd started.

"See, the thing is, I invited Nathan out for a drink because I wanted to get you out of my head. We'd had mind-blowing sex and then you rejected me, and I was feeling a little put out. Let's just say my ego needed a boost. So, I called Nathan. Right away, it became obvious it had been a bad idea. I was about to tell him I was leaving when you walked in."

She peeked at him, as if gauging his reaction. He was doing his best to remain unaffected, but it wasn't easy. He wanted to tell her he hadn't rejected her, but he also wanted to let her finish her explanation. So, he remained silent.

She drew in a breath and blew it out on a sigh. "I'm not proud of what happened next, but in the spirit of wiping the slate clean, here goes."

She cleared her throat and squared her shoulders and looked him straight in the eye. "The moment I saw you walk into that bar, I was overcome with a desire to hurt you, like you'd hurt me. Like I said, I'm not proud of that, but it's the truth. I grabbed hold of Nathan and started kissing him, knowing you'd see us and draw your own conclusions. And you did. I ran out after you, wanting to explain, but you were already driving out of the carpark." She drew in another deep breath and shrugged. "And that's that."

Liam's stomach churned with emotions. It was so hard for him to stay silent while Hannah spoke about how she'd deliberately tried to hurt him in the same way he'd hurt her. It was exactly like his sister had told him and until she'd pointed that out, he'd been completely and utterly oblivious. He'd even doubted Jacqueline's take on it. Now he couldn't help but believe her.

Hannah watched him with a wary expression, as if she wasn't quite sure how he'd react. Her uncertainty tore at him. She was fearless, a warrior. He hated that he was the cause of her insecurity and doubt.

"I'm sorry, Hannah. I'm so sorry. When I called and told you our night together had been a mistake, it was because of several things. Firstly, I was upset that you'd gotten up, showered, and left without so much as a fare thee well. I'd just experienced the most amazing night of my life but it felt like for you, the magic we'd made together meant nothing. So, yes. I was hurting and that probably factored into what happened next.

"I got thinking about other stuff, like how I was investigating your mine site for serious safety breaches and how being involved with you was such a bad idea. I was putting myself in a difficult position. Anyone would conclude the two of us together was a conflict of interest. How could I do my job objectively if I was sleeping with one of the mine bosses?"

She opened her mouth, as if to speak, but he held up his hand to hold her off. "Please, I need to finish."

"So, I called you that morning and told you it was a mistake, but what I didn't tell you was that I'd just had the best night of my life. Like you, I was hurting and like you, I guess I wanted to strike back. But I was equally concerned about how our relationship—if it ever got off the ground—would be perceived by the outside world, and more importantly, by my supervisor."

He kept his gaze steady on hers, needing her to understand. "I love my job. It's what I was born to do. The potential for a conflict of interest weighed heavily on my mind. While I very much wanted to spend time with you on a personal level, there was no getting away from the fact that professionally we were on opposing sides." He slowly shook his head. "I didn't see any way out of that, other than breaking things off with you before they had a chance to start."

He drew in a ragged breath. "Despite all that, I'm sorry for hurting you. That was never my intention. Well, not really. The truth is, I didn't give any consideration to how you'd feel when I told you that our sleeping together had been a mistake. I merely reacted, based on all the things I've mentioned. I'm not excusing my behavior, just trying to offer an explanation. I hope it helps."

Hannah regarded him solemnly. "Thank you for explaining your reasons and for apologizing. You did hurt me, but I'm in no position to throw stones. I hope you believe me when I tell you Nathan means nothing to me."

"I do."

"There's something else. I lied when I agreed with you that the sex between us meant nothing. In fact, it was beyond anything I could have imagined. Magical. I only said that because I wanted to protect my pride. Stupid, yes. Immature, you bet. But that's the truth."

A growing warmth spread through him. She'd just admitted their night together had been something special. Unable to help himself, he reached out and squeezed her hand. She responded with a luminous smile. His heart swelled. He opened his mouth to confess that he was in love with her; had always been enamored of her...

But something held him back. It was early days. He still didn't really know how she felt. He didn't want to get hurt again. No, better to take things slowly and see where they ended up. In the meantime, he could enjoy his evening spent in the company of a beautiful woman who made his heart smile.

Chapter Nineteen

Hannah sat in her office the next day and stared blindly out the window. Though she still needed to speak with the lawyers about a plan of action regarding Nathan, she couldn't focus on anything other than Liam. The night before, after leaving the bar, he'd left her at the front door of her cottage with no more than a brief kiss on the lips.

She respected his unspoken decision to take things slowly, but that didn't mean she wasn't tense with the need to tear his clothes off and have her way with him. She'd spent the rest of the night tossing and turning and trying to get him out of her mind. By the time the sun peeked its face over the horizon, she was finally willing to accept she had strong feelings for him. Even more surprising, the thought of giving up her free-spirited approach to relationships and becoming exclusive with him didn't cause her to break out in hives.

She grinned ruefully. *I must really like this guy...*

If only things weren't so complicated. It would be foolhardy to get involved with a man whose job it was to investigate her business, and always with a view to shutting it down. Liam was right. If they were to get into a relationship, any objective observer would identify the conflict of interest. She acknowledged it herself. The simple fact was, they couldn't be together while he was an investigator for the Resources Regulator.

Her shoulders slumped on a sigh. Now that she'd found the courage to acknowledge her feelings for him, she wanted to move forward, make things happen, and get naked with him again. But even if she left the mine, it was still owned by her family. The conflict would still exist, albeit slightly removed.

The only way they could be together was if Liam changed careers. She immediately rebelled at the idea. There was no way she could ask that of him. He'd already told her how much he loved his job; that it was what he'd been born to do. It left her wondering if there was any future for them at all.

Liam leaned back against his office chair and sipped from his cup of coffee. He'd been at work for more than an hour and had yet to switch on his computer. It wasn't like him to be so slack. The problem was Hannah. She was all he could think about. After having a few drinks together, he'd shared a cab with her and had dropped her off outside her house. He'd instructed the driver to wait while he walked her to the front door. He'd placed a chaste kiss on her lips before leaving.

This was what it meant to take things slowly. Though he hadn't said anything to her, they owed it to each other to get to know each other better before they hopped into bed again. He hoped they could get to know each other quickly, because he was desperate to get naked with her again.

Of course, no matter how much he got to know her, that didn't remove the problem of the conflict with his work. The truth was, he wasn't sure what he was going to do about that. For the time being, the investigations into her mine were over. That meant he had some time to work out how he intended to deal with the issue. He very much wanted a relationship with Hannah, but he also valued his job.

Stacking his hands behind his head, he sighed. Right now, he couldn't find a workable solution, but he refused to give up hope. He was generally a glass half-full kind of guy. He refused to give up just yet. He wondered what she'd done about Garcia. No doubt he'd been fired by now. He was also curious about what evidence she'd found against him that had made her change her mind about his guilt. He decided to call her and find out. Besides, he wanted to hear her voice again. It had been way too long already since they'd last spoken.

By mid-morning, Hannah had finally shaken herself out of obsessing over Liam and had phoned the law firm Barrington Mining retained on their payroll. She'd relayed the situation with Nathan and his cronies and had received advice on the best way to go about securing their dismissal. The main point the lawyer made was to ensure she had airtight evidence of serious wrongdoing. If that were the case, she was within her rights to fire them.

She wasn't sure if the emails were enough. A good lawyer could argue that anyone could have written them, especially if Nathan had left his password unsecured. No, she needed more. She needed him to admit it. Her stomach churned at the thought of confronting him with what she'd found. It wasn't that she was afraid of him, but she sure as hell wasn't looking forward to it. She just hoped he didn't make a scene.

The sound of her phone ringing snagged her attention. She picked it up, grateful for the distraction. A glance at the screen told her it was Liam. She couldn't help but smile.

"Hi. How are you?" she asked.

"I'm great. How are you?"

"Not too bad. I'm supposed to be formulating a plan to fire Nathan Garcia and the others, but all I can think about is you."

She heard his sharp intake of breath and her smile widened. It was a bold statement. She was curious as to how he'd respond. She didn't have to wait long to find out.

"I see."

His voice was low and husky and sent ripples of desire down her spine. Two little words and yet they had the power to send warmth rushing to her core. She crossed her legs and shifted in her chair.

"Were you thinking about anything in particular?" he asked in that same low, sexy drawl.

"As a matter of fact, I was. I kept thinking about how much I wanted to tear your clothes off."

Once again, she caught his quiet gasp. Desire continued to flood her veins. She wished he was there in front of her so she could show him just how much she wanted to get naked with him.

"I see," he repeated. "I'd made a decision to take things slowly this time round, but maybe I could be persuaded to change my mind." He paused. "What are you wearing?"

It was her turn to gasp. A fresh surge of heat flooded her core. "The usual. A high-vis shirt and work pants. My steel-toed boots."

"I love those steel-toed boots. So sexy."

She shifted again on her seat in an effort to get more comfortable. She'd never had phone sex before, but she was fast warming to the idea.

"I'm pleased you think so."

"Oh, yeah. I think so. What are you wearing underneath?" he drawled.

Her heart stuttered and then took off. "A satin bra and matching panties."

"Ah. So silky and soft. I love the feel of satin. Almost as much as I love the feel of my cock inside you."

Oh, God. I'm going to combust...

Her face went hot. Her chest was so tight with need, she struggled to formulate a response. "You have such a big, fat cock," she murmured.

"Where are you?" he asked, his voice a strangled rasp.

"In my office."

"Are you alone?"

"Yes."

"Is the door closed?"

"Yes."

"I want you to touch yourself."

His husky words were so erotic, she could hardly breathe. She'd never done anything like this before. It was both exciting and a little nerve-wracking.

"Are you touching yourself?"

Feeling incredibly naughty, Hannah undid the button on her pants and slid the zipper down. Then she slid her hand beneath the waistband of her panties and stroked her slick flesh. She moaned softly.

"Are you touching yourself?" he asked again.

"Yes," she breathed.

"How does it feel?"

"Good. It feels good."

"You're already wet, aren't you?"

"Yes."

She increased the pressure of her hand and rode a wave of pleasure. She moaned.

"Slip two fingers inside yourself."

Hannah heard the growing need in Liam's voice. His breath was harsh in her ear. She did as he asked and her breath caught.

"Stroke yourself, Hannah. Just like I stroked you with my cock. I'm stroking my cock right now. My big, fat cock. Do you want my cock, Hannah?"

With her fingers working double time and almost overcome with desire, she cried out. "Yes! I want your cock."

"Do you want me to fuck you?"

His crudeness only served to catapult her desire to a fever pitch. She continued to work her fingers as her climax began to build.

"Do you want me to fuck you, Hannah?" he asked again.

"Yes!" she gasped. "Yes."

"Yes, what?"

"Yes, Liam. I want you to fuck me."

She'd never talked dirty before, not even when she'd been up close and personal with a lover. It was both shocking and exhilarating and only fueled the need that now gripped her like a vice.

"I'm sliding my cock inside you, Hannah. Can you feel it?"

"Yes! Oh, God, yes!" Her fingers stroked faster. Her pulse raced.

"I'm fucking you, Hannah. God, you feel so wet."

His words tipped her over the edge. She gasped aloud as she reached her climax and collapsed against her chair. Liam's breath came faster, rasping in her ear. And then he was at the pinnacle too.

"Oh, God, Hannah. I'm going to come."

His cry of pleasure and release made her smile with contentment. It was the most erotic experience Hannah had ever had. She was weak and deliciously exhausted. If she weren't in her office, she might even curl up somewhere comfortable and take a nap. She'd had no idea phone sex could be so good. Or maybe it was just because she'd done it with Liam...

She heard him draw in a deep breath and blow it out. "Wow. That was...so good."

"Yes," she agreed, ducking her head as she was overcome with a sudden bout of shyness.

"I want to see you," Liam said in a low tone, his voice still husky.

"I want to see you, too."

"Too bad you're so busy."

She nodded. "Yes. Too bad." Then she had an idea. "Maybe you could come over and help me with the Nathan problem?"

"How so?"

"I don't know. I spoke to one of our lawyers about the best way to go about firing Nathan and his cronies. I need to make sure I have watertight evidence of serious misconduct."

"What evidence do you have?"

She told him about the emails. When she finished, Liam whistled under his breath.

"Wow. That's even better than what I found."

"You mean the fact Nathan's related to Joseph Rodriguez?"

"Yes, there's that. But I also spoke to a whistleblower who provided me with plenty of ammunition. That's what sealed Garcia's guilt for me."

Hannah sat up straighter. "A whistleblower? Someone who works at the mine?"

"Yes. Malcolm White. He's the head foreman of the workshop."

Hannah frowned. "That name's not familiar."

"Probably because he's employed by a contractor. Colin Hume. The same contractor who employs Paul Hammond and his mates."

"I see. Wow. You said he had dirt on Nathan?"

"Yes. He told me he was present on a number of occasions when Garcia hatched a plan to cause an incident. Apparently, Garcia was so confident he had everyone's support, he didn't even try to keep it secret."

Hannah gasped in shock. It was still difficult for her to believe her once-trusted open cut examiner had been actively working against her all this time. She shook her head in disbelief. "Why didn't he come forward and say anything?"

"I asked him that. He said he wanted to mind his own business, stay out of it. When I started hanging around and asking questions, he came clean. He also told me he'd had enough of witnessing avoidable accidents that caused unnecessary damage to the machines."

"Do you think he'd talk to me?" she asked.

"I think so. Especially since he's already opened his mouth to me." Liam paused. "I have an idea."

"Go ahead."

"What if we set Garcia up?"

"How do you mean?"

"I mean, we can use Malcolm White to engage Garcia in conversation, get him talking about the next incident he has planned. We can be somewhere in the vicinity, out of sight. I could record the whole thing. That would give you irrefutable evidence. Better than the emails. Garcia could just claim he was hacked. That the emails weren't from him. Same thing with White's evidence. It's hearsay. It's good enough for the purposes of my investigation, but it might not hold up in court."

Hannah's mind whirred. Getting Nathan to admit to setting up "accidents" might very well provide her with the airtight evidence she needed. And if Malcolm White was willing to play along, it might just work.

"I like it," she said slowly. "Can you set it up with White?"

"Sure. I'll call him and fill him in on the plan. There's no love lost between him and Garcia."

"Let's hope that's true and he's willing to help us."

"Leave it with me. I'll get back to you as soon as I've spoken with him."

"Great. I'll also talk to security. I want to make sure we have some extra hands on standby when this goes down. Not only to escort Nathan and his cronies off the mine site, but just in case things get nasty between Nathan and Malcolm. We have a responsibility to keep him safe. He's shown great courage in coming forward. The least we can do is offer him protection."

"I agree. The last thing we want to do is expose him to danger and who knows how Garcia's going to react when he realizes the game's up."

Hannah drew in a deep breath and blew it out. In such a short time, she'd been on a rollercoaster of emotions. Still, she wanted to put the whole nasty period of Nathan Garica behind her, and this might be the best way to achieve that. After thanking Liam, she ended the call, her stomach alive with anticipation and a few nerves thrown in for good measure.

Liam arrived at the mine the next morning and was directed straight to Hannah's office. He knocked briefly on her closed door and then opened it and stepped inside. Her face lit up at the sight of him. His heart turned over with love.

Oh, hell. I'm so gone.

She pushed away from her desk and came toward him. They met in the middle of the room. He took her in his arms and kissed her. It seemed like the most natural thing to do. Her lips were warm and willing. She kissed him back with as much passion as he gave her. It felt so nice, so *right*. He longed to do more, especially when his mind was filled with images of her masturbating behind her desk, but taking things to the next level would have to wait.

"Good morning," Hannah said a little breathlessly when they finally pulled apart.

Liam grinned. "Good morning."

"Have you spoken to Malcolm White?"

"Yes. He's agreed to be part of the plan. He's been rostered on this morning. Is Garcia on site?"

"Yes. He was here about twenty minutes ago. He told me he was headed for the pit."

Liam nodded. "Good. What about the additional security?"

"All organized. They've agreed to hang out at the workshop and remain close by in case we need them."

Liam compressed his lips, his gaze steady on hers. "Are you ready to do this?"

Hannah wiped her hands on her workpants, looking nervous. "Can we go over it again?"

"Sure. White's agreed to get Garcia talking about the next "accident" he has planned. In fact, he's actually going to have a go at Garcia for all the damage he's causing. White's sick to death of having to keep fixing the machines. This won't be the first time he's complained to Garcia about it, so it shouldn't raise Garcia's suspicions."

Hannah nodded. "Okay, so where do I come in?"

"You and I are going to hide in one of the offices adjacent to the workshop. I've instructed White to keep Garcia within hearing range. I'll record their conversation on my phone. Even if that isn't admissible as evidence in court, knowing we have it will make Garcia sweat and we can always provide oral evidence of what we heard. Provided Garcia falls for it, we'll have him."

Liam grinned. Satisfaction surged through him. Though he didn't consider himself a vindictive man, he'd be glad to see Nathan Garcia go down. It was nothing less than the asshole deserved.

Hannah licked her lips, still looking nervous. Liam reached for her hand and gave it a squeeze.

"It's going to be okay. The worst that can happen is that Garcia gets wind of what we're doing and refuses to cooperate. If that happens, we'll regroup and come up with another plan."

She drew in a deep breath and slowly nodded. "Okay. Let's do it."

Chapter Twenty

Hannah couldn't remember the last time she'd felt so nervous. No, scratch that. The last time was when she'd met with Liam after her disastrous attempt to make him jealous. In the long run, that hadn't turned out so bad. She hoped they'd have the same luck this time round but without the delay in satisfaction.

She and Liam had snuck into the workshop and concealed themselves in a makeshift office. Hannah had checked in by telephone with the extra security guards she'd stationed in that area and they confirmed they were nearby. Nathan and Malcolm were in the adjoining room. As far as the two men knew, they were alone. Liam pressed the record button and held the phone as close to the wall as he could. Hannah could hear Malcolm talking.

"You have to cut out this bullshit, Nathan. I'm sick and tired of having to fix the gear."

"What are you talking about?" Nathan replied.

Hannah's heart sank. She looked at Liam, but he was focused on the conversation taking place on the other side of the wall.

"Don't give me that bullshit. You know exactly what I'm talking about," Malcolm replied. "I'm well aware that you're the mastermind behind all these accidents. You're just damn lucky you haven't killed someone."

"Ha!" Nathan replied. "That's not going to happen. It's not about getting someone killed. I only want to cause enough trouble to close the mine down. Nobody said anything about anyone getting hurt."

"What about Evan Wilson?" Malcolm demanded. "That poor boy left here in a body bag and that wasn't any accident."

"Hey! Don't go pinning that one on me," Nathan replied. "I wasn't even working here when that happened."

"No, but your uncle was. Joseph Rodriguez caused that accident, didn't he? As payback for getting fired. Don't worry, I know all about it."

"Like I said, that was before my time. You'll have to ask my uncle about that."

Hannah silently fumed. Nathan couldn't have sounded less interested in the fact someone had lost their life and it was possible his uncle had been responsible. She bit down on her lip in an effort to contain her fury.

"Yeah, well your uncle's not here now and I know exactly who's responsible for what's been happening around here. Just so you know, I've had enough."

"Why are you so worked up about a little damage? It's not like the mine can't afford it."

"That's not the point," Malcolm bit out. "It's mindless vandalism, done for no other reason than to make trouble.

Don't you understand? If this mine closes, we're all out of a job."

Nathan laughed. "That's a risk I'm willing to take."

"Yeah, well it's all right for you. I have a wife and three kids to feed. I need this job."

"Calm down, Whitey. You're not going to lose your job."

"Says the man who's going out of his way to bring the Resources Regulator down on our heads. Haven't you seen that investigator sniffing around? He was back here again the other day, asking a lot of questions."

Nathan laughed again. "Don't you worry about him. He's nothing but a big pussy."

Hannah saw Liam tense and his jaw clenched, but his focus remained on the conversation.

"Yeah, you won't be saying that if he discovers it's you who's behind all these safety breaches. That you've gone out of your way to set them up and you've brought your mates along for the ride."

"That pussy's not going to discover anything of the sort. I've been doing this for the best part of twelve months, and I haven't been caught yet. Hannah Barrington doesn't have a clue. In fact, she can't get enough of me. We went out for drinks the other night. She kissed me! She doesn't have a clue I've been white-anting her all these months. Talk about dumb."

It was Hannah's turn to freeze in shock and anger. It was all she could do not to march out there and give Nathan a piece of her mind. As if privy to her thoughts, Liam shook his head briefly. She sucked in a breath and forced her anger down.

How much longer are we going to have to stand here and listen to this insulting drivel? Surely, we have enough by now?

"So, you're finally admitting to being the culprit. You prick," Malcolm said.

"Hey, what can I say? They fired my uncle for no reason. That contract was worth millions! Do you think he was going to take that lying down?"

"The way I heard it, your uncle had caused plenty of safety breaches before old man Barrington fired him. As far as I'm concerned, he had it coming. None of us want to put our lives on the line if we don't have to. We're all entitled to go home to our families each night."

"Yeah, yeah, yeah. Whatever you say, Whitey. I don't know why you're so worked up about it all. Your safety was never in jeopardy."

"That doesn't mean I don't care about the safety of all the others. What you're doing isn't fair, Garcia. I want it to stop."

"Oh, you want it to stop, do you? Who died and made you the boss? No one tells me what to do. No one. If I want to blow this whole fucking place up, no one's going to stop me. I'll quit causing accidents the day I get this mine closed for good."

Liam's face was grim. He turned to Hannah. "I think we've heard enough."

She nodded, relieved. "What do we do now?"

"You stay here. I'm going to confront him."

But Hannah was having none of it. "This is my mine. I'm the boss. I want to be the one to confront him. That jerk. To think how he played me…" She clenched her fists and held back groan of frustration and anger.

Liam regarded her steadily. "Are you sure? It could get ugly."

Determination surged through her. "Oh, I'm sure. Bring it on. But first, just let me text the security guards. No sense being stupid about this. Besides, I'll need them to escort Nathan and the others off the mine site."

After sending a text and receiving confirmation the security officers were ready to act, she and Liam stepped out of the office and walked straight into the adjoining room. Nathan blanched at the sight of them, but quickly recovered his usual aplomb. He smiled at her, all charm.

"Hannah. This is a surprise. What brings you down here?"

Hannah glared at him. "Oh, yes. This is a surprise all right. Too bad the surprise is on you."

A flicker of fear flashed in Nathan's eyes but was quickly concealed behind another insouciant grin. His bark of laughter fell flat.

"I'm sorry. I don't have a clue what you're talking about," he said.

Liam waggled his phone in the air. "The game's up, Garcia. We heard every word."

As Liam's words registered, the fear on Nathan's face returned and stayed there. His lips tightened. His fists clenched. Hannah watched closely and could almost see the conscious effort he made to continue to try and bluff them.

"Like I said, I don't have a clue what you're talking about."

Hannah had heard enough. She glowered at the man she'd once trusted above everything, angrier than she'd ever been in her life.

"How dare you! I trusted you! I thought you had my back. Ha! What a joke! You've betrayed me in the worst way possible. From the very first day you stepped foot on this mine site, you've been hellbent on destroying me and my family and everything we stand for. It's because of you that people have been injured. It's because of you we've suffered significant financial losses, not only in the thousands of dollars we've had to spend on repairs to damaged machinery, but the countless millions that have been stolen from us in lost production. You're responsible for every single accident that's occurred at this mine since you started working here. You disgust me."

"Steady on, Hannah. That's a bit rich. You don't know—"

"Oh, but I do know," she cut him off. "Like Liam said, we heard everything, and every single word you said was recorded on Liam's phone. Then there are all the emails between you and Paul Hammond. So don't tell me what I do and don't know."

Her tone was filled with scorn. The narrow-eyed look she shot at him was filled with abject disgust. Anger flooded Nathan's face. His body tensed.

"You fucking privileged, spoiled bitch. You wouldn't even be here if your daddy didn't own the mine and every fucking person here knows it."

Hannah stood frozen in shock. Nathan advanced upon her as vitriol continued to spew from his lips.

"You think you fucking know everything. Let me tell you, you know shit! You wouldn't even know the difference between an excavator and a dump truck. Do you know how hard it was for me to keep a straight face during all those morning briefings?

The way you'd talk about safety issues like you had a clue what they meant? Please! Give me a fucking break. You would have fallen on your face in your first few weeks if it hadn't been for me and you fucking know it."

Hannah did her best to withstand the verbal blows. The extent of Nathan's malice continued to send shockwaves through her, but she refused to let him see how much his words affected her.

Liam looked furious. "Shut your fucking mouth, Garcia."

Hannah dragged in a deep breath and glared at her former right-hand man. "Are you done? Good," she said, without waiting for him to answer. "Listen, and listen well, Nathan Garcia. You're done here. Finished. And if I have my way, you'll never be employed at a mine in this country again. Now, pack up your things and get the hell off this mine site and if you ever come back, I'll have you arrested for trespassing."

Pulling out her phone, she called security. Moments later, two burly men appeared. "Gentlemen. I'd like you to escort Mr Garcia off this mine site, along with Paul Hammond, Rodney Valentine, and Scott Stonewall. If any of these men attempt to step foot here again, I want to be notified immediately. From this moment on, those men are banned from this mine site."

The security guards nodded in acknowledgement of her words. They each took one of Nathan's arms and walked him out of the workshop. All the time, Nathan continued to spew hate. Doing her best to ignore it, she turned to Malcolm White.

"Thank you for coming forward. We owe you a great debt of gratitude."

The man looked at the ground and blushed. "I wish I'd done it sooner," he mumbled.

"No matter. You've done it now and I speak on behalf of everyone at Barrington Mining when I say how much we appreciate your courage. I've taken steps to ensure your safety in case there's a backlash from anyone sympathetic to Joseph Rodriguez and his accomplices, but please, let me know if anyone's giving you trouble. They'll go the same way as those men."

Liam held out his hand toward Malcolm. "You were great. Thanks again for doing that."

Malcolm nodded. "I hope it's enough."

A gleam of satisfaction shone in Liam's eyes. "We're going to nail these bastards. You have my word."

Hannah still trembled with adrenaline and delayed shock fifteen minutes later when she and Liam stepped back into her office. She threw herself down in her chair and groaned. Though Liam had warned her things could get ugly, she hadn't expected it to get as hideous as that. In silence, he took the seat opposite her. His eyes shone with pride.

"You were magnificent," he said quietly. "A fearless warrior. I'm so proud of you. No wonder your father had such faith in you. I'm in awe of your courage."

Hannah smiled faintly. His words helped to ease the residual anxiety and tension inside her and filled her with warmth.

"Thank you," she said. "That means a lot. And thank you for all that you did to ferret out that rat. I still can't believe how he duped me. I owe you a lot."

Liam shook his head and got to his feet. He walked around to her side of the desk and tugged her by the hand until she stood.

"You owe me nothing. I was only doing my job."

She looked up at him and smiled. "That might be so, but I'm still grateful for everything you've done."

Unable to resist, Liam took her in his arms and kissed her. Her lips were warm and willing and within moments passion ignited between them. On a groan, he deepened the kiss, plunging his tongue into her mouth, seeking out her secret places, her sweet warmth. When the fire between them raged almost to the point of no return, Liam reluctantly pulled back. Both of them were breathless.

"We should stop," he gasped.

Though Hannah looked disappointed, she nodded. "Yes."

By unspoken consent, they returned to their seats. Liam cast around for something to say to distract him from the hard-on that still pressed insistently against his pants.

"How's Vaughan?" he asked, latching onto the first thing that came into his mind.

Hannah drew in a deep breath and sighed. "He's still in a coma. My parents are over there trying to arrange to bring him back to Australia, but the doctors are advising against transporting him anywhere right now."

"I'm sorry," Liam said. "That sucks."

"Yep. It sure does."

They were silent for a moment. Liam tried to think of something to lighten the mood. "What are you doing for Christmas?"

Hannah gave him a soft smile. "Christmas. Wow. I'd forgotten all about it. There's been so much going on with the issues at the mine and now with Vaughan."

"Will you head over to Bali?" Liam asked.

Hannah shook his head. "I don't think so. Daddy's hoping to have Vaughan home by then. Besides, from what I can tell, there's nothing I can do for Vaughan over there. I'm more use to my family if I stay here and make sure things continue to run smoothly at the mine."

Liam nodded. "Now that you've ousted Garcia and his mates, things should look up for you."

"Yes. I've prepared written notices of dismissal for all of them. Anyone who had anything to do with Nathan's machinations will be permanently removed from this site."

"Good on you. If you need my help with anything, please let me know."

"Thank you. I really appreciate that." She paused. "What about you? Do you have any plans for Christmas?"

Liam shrugged. "Well, there's only me and my sister. I guess we'll spend the day together. Or maybe not. She's a nurse. I haven't even asked her if she's rostered on for Christmas Day."

Hannah looked at him in horror. "You can't spend Christmas Day alone!"

Liam shrugged again. "It wouldn't be the first time."

Hannah's eyes widened again. "Really? You poor thing! I couldn't imagine not celebrating Christmas surrounded by my family. Maybe not all of them every year, but whoever can make it. My mom does an amazing Christmas Day feast."

Liam nodded. "I remember you telling me she's a good cook."

"Absolutely. I learned from the best. If your sister's working, maybe you could come and celebrate the day with us? Even if Mom and Dad are still in Bali, there'll still be plenty of us around."

Liam's heart swelled. "That would be lovely."

"If Jacqueline's not working, you could both come over. We'd love to have you."

"Haven't you already got like a million brothers and sisters?"

"Eight, yes. And most of them have significant others and there's also a few kids, too. So?"

"Are you sure your family won't mind if you invite a couple more?"

"No, of course not! We always say, the more the merrier."

Liam thought about it. He could think of nothing better than to celebrate Christmas with Hannah's family. He was sure he could convince Jacqueline to join him.

"My brother, Zac, is getting married in four days, right before Christmas. He and his fiancée, Emily, talked about postponing it, given the uncertainty with Vaughan, but Mom and Dad assured them that Vaughan wouldn't want them to do that. Apparently, Dad told Vaughan about my brother, Christopher's, wedding well ahead of time. We celebrated it last month. Vaughan didn't feel the need to come home for it.

"Dad says there's every chance Vaughan would feel the same way about Zac's wedding. It's not that he doesn't love his family, but whatever has been keeping him in Bali was more important. That's all there is to it. Of course, things are different now with Vaughan being in a coma. I'm not sure that he even knows about Zac's wedding. But we're all hoping he'll be awake and home by then and he can decide what he wants to do."

"Tell me about Zac's fiancée," Liam asked. "Do you like her?"

Hannah smiled. "Absolutely. Emily's a treasure. You won't believe it, but they actually dated in high school."

Liam's eyes widened in surprise. "That's right. I remember them now. They were in the year below me. A cute couple."

"Yes. They're still a cute couple."

"Have they been together all this time?"

"No. They went their separate ways after graduation. Evan's death didn't help matters. They only got back together earlier this year."

Liam frowned. "Evan?"

"Yes. Emily's brother. Evan Wilson."

Liam blinked in surprise. "You mean the man who was killed in the mine accident just over a year ago?"

She grimaced. "Yes. It was a terrible tragedy."

"Didn't your father suspect Joseph Rodriguez?"

Hannah nodded. "Yes. It's curious that Nathan alluded to that today. Daddy hired private investigators to look into what happened. We were also investigated by the Resources Regulator. No one could definitively lay the blame at anyone's feet. I guess we'll just have to accept that. Fortunately, Emily and her family no longer have any hard feelings for the Barringtons. We're all very happy for the couple."

She paused and then looked at him. "Would you like to go with me?"

"To the wedding?"

"Yes."

She glanced away as she replied and he realized she was a little nervous about his response.

"Would you like me to?" he asked, wanting to be sure.

"I'd love you to!" she exclaimed. And then she blushed. "I mean, it would be great to have you there. The Barringtons know how to throw a good party. I'm sure you'll have a good time."

Liam smiled, setting her at ease. "Anywhere you are, is where I want to be. I'd love to come to the wedding with you."

She smiled back, her cheeks pink with pleasure.

Careful. I don't know how she feels about me. She likes me, she finds me attractive. But is that all this is?

For his own self-preservation, he needed to tread carefully. He sure as hell didn't want to suffer another broken heart.

He cleared his throat and changed the subject. "At least we have enough now to put Rodriguez's nephew behind bars."

She appeared momentarily confused at the abrupt change in subject, but quickly recovered. "You're right. And that reminds me, I need to call the police and hand over everything we have on Nathan and the others."

"Tell them they can have my files, too."

Her eyes filled with warmth and tenderness. Liam felt it all the way to his gut.

"Thank you, Liam. You've been such a rock. I can't thank you enough for everything you've done."

"Hey, we've been over this," he said gruffly. "No thanks necessary. And by the way, I've submitted my report. No penalties for those breaches this time. I'm satisfied you've done everything you need to ensure those accidents won't happen again."

And though his recommendations had been completely divorced from the way he felt about her and their growing relationship, her answering smile was a balm to his heart.

Chapter Twenty-One

In an effort to distract herself from the nerves that held her stomach taut, Elizabeth Craigdon leaned forward and began to pour the tea. She'd invited her stepson, Christopher, and his wife, Lexi, and their nine children over to Craigdon Manor for afternoon tea. Though Christopher was the product of a relationship between her late husband, Henry Craigdon, and Christopher's mother, Evelyn Barrington, Elizabeth had always been close to him and had kept abreast of his life.

She'd been as pleased as anyone when he met Lexi. They were so in love. Together, they were raising a family and it was beautiful to behold. Even now, the sounds of the children squealing with laughter while they played a game on the back lawn filled her heart with joy. The most recent addition to their family, a six-month-old baby boy Christopher and Lexi were fostering, lay asleep in his pram in a quiet corner of the music room.

"Tea, Lexi?" she asked.

"Yes, thank you."

"What about you, Christopher?"

"Thanks, that would be great."

Once the tea was poured, Elizabeth handed around a plate of petit fours prepared by her faithful housekeeper, Amy. The woman had been with the family for more years than Elizabeth could remember and was a treasured member of the Craigdon clan.

"The place is looking good," Christopher commented as he glanced around him.

"Thank you," Elizabeth said. "Archie and I are very pleased with the renovations. I love the new blue color scheme."

Christopher nodded. "I see you've kept the piano in here."

Elizabeth smiled. "What's a music room without a piano?"

They sipped their tea in silence. The nerves swelled in Elizabeth's stomach. Her primary reason for inviting Christopher and his family over was to probe for information about Vaughan. Her son. Of course, nobody but Archie and Vaughan knew she was his mother. He'd been adopted by Frank and Evelyn Barrington when he was still a child. She'd kept her connection to him a secret for forty years. Then when she'd finally found the courage to break her silence, Vaughan had up and taken off for Bali. She hadn't heard from him since.

She had no idea how he felt about the revelation. Whether he was angry, sad, confused. Probably all three. It had been tearing her up inside all these nine long months that he'd been gone. She hoped Christopher might have an update about his half-brother. Setting aside her teacup, she plastered on a smile.

"So, what's been happening in the Barrington household, Christopher? There always seems to be something going on."

"You're right," Christopher said. "The latest excitement is around Zac and Emily's wedding."

Elizabeth's smile widened into something far more genuine. This was exactly the opening she'd hoped for.

"Another wedding? How wonderful. When will it be held?"

"The day before Christmas."

"Wow. That's...brave."

Christopher chuckled. "I'm not sure what you call it, but that's the date."

Elizabeth drew in a breath and strived for a casual tone. "Will Vaughan be there? I understand he's been living overseas for most of the year."

"Yes. In Bali." Then Christopher frowned. "You did hear about the accident, didn't you?"

Elizabeth's heart stopped. "Accident?"

"Yes. Poor Vaughan. He was riding a motorbike and was hit by a truck."

Elizabeth gasped. She pressed her hand against her heart, feeling faint. "Is he...all right?"

"I'm not really sure. He's still in a coma. Mom and Dad flew over there as soon as they heard. They're trying to get him transported back to a hospital in Australia."

Elizabeth's heart thumped so hard she thought it might beat right out of her chest. Once again, she strived to keep calm.

"Oh, dear. That's terrible. Your poor family."

Christopher looked grim. "Yeah. We're all praying he pulls through."

It was all Elizabeth could do not to run tearing from the room. She was shocked beyond measure and devastated she might never be given the opportunity to speak with Vaughan, to explain. To tell him how much she loved him. How she'd never stopped loving him.

Oh, God. Please bring him home to me. Please give me the chance to talk to him. I need to talk to him. I need to make him understand. I did what I did because I loved him. Please, I need to make him see.

Hannah turned this way and that in front of the tall mirror in her childhood bedroom and surveyed the results of the past few hours. The pale pink suit she'd chosen to wear to her brother's wedding fit her to perfection. The jacket was tailored and clung to her curves. The short skirt emphasized the length of her slim, tanned legs. She'd teamed it with a white silk blouse.

She'd also spent a good deal of time on her hair. Her hairdresser had offered to come to the house and had turned Hannah's usual straightforward do into something that was a wonder to behold. A mass of intricate, intertwining braids crisscrossed her head, interspersed with cream-colored pearls that had been scattered throughout. Hannah couldn't be more pleased with her look and hoped Liam appreciated the efforts she'd gone to for him.

Liam.

The very thought of him made her heart beat faster. She couldn't believe how quickly her feelings had developed from mere lust to something far more substantial. Something that felt like it could last forever. He'd been such a mountain of strength and support during the past week while she'd been dealing with the fallout after Nathan and his cronies had been sent packing. Unfortunately, they hadn't gone quietly.

She was grateful for the legal advice that had meant none of them had any recourse against Barrington Mining. She'd insisted on hand-delivering the dismissal notices to each of them and had been glad she'd taken Liam up on his offer to accompany her. While things hadn't gotten out of hand, Nathan had certainly made his anger known. While she was sure he wouldn't have attacked her, the vitriol that had spewed from his mouth while she'd been serving him his notice had been difficult to take. It was only Liam's silent and strong presence beside her that had gotten her through it. He'd been there for her when she needed him.

She'd always prided herself on being a strong and independent woman, but she'd come to realize it was okay to rely on someone when it was warranted. It was nice to know Liam was in her corner. That he had her back, no matter what. There was nothing in it for him to accompany her while she delivered the dismissal letters, but he'd wanted to come anyway, for no other reason because he cared for her and wanted to keep her safe.

Knowing that made her feel warm inside and went a long way toward easing her instinctive aversion for commitment. It wasn't that she'd ever been against that kind of thing. More that it hadn't suited her lifestyle or what she wanted out of life. Liam had given her a reason to reassess. To look at things from a different perspective. What she thought she wanted had lost its shine. Now she couldn't think of anything she wanted more than to spend each day with Liam by her side.

She shied away from thoughts about his job and the problem that represented. Today was a day for celebration. She wouldn't mar it with negative thoughts of issues that for now she had no solution.

Taking one final look at her appearance, she turned away from the mirror and headed across the room. She slipped on her stilettos and collected her clutch. She pulled the door to her bedroom closed behind her. The thought of seeing Liam again filled her heart with light, joy, and anticipation. She couldn't help but smile.

Liam fought a wave of nerves as he fumbled with the bow tie at his neck. He'd tried three times already to tie it properly, but it was like he was all thumbs. It was because he was about to meet an onslaught of Barringtons. He might have gone to school with a lot of them, but he'd left school seven years ago and he'd never actually been friends with any of them. They were always hanging around the popular group and that had never been Liam's scene.

He'd been eager to go as Hannah's date to the wedding because he wanted to spend as much time with her as he could, but now he was almost regretting that he'd accepted her invitation. They'd been taking things slowly over the past week, spending more and more time alone. Heavy petting, another round of phone sex, but that had been all. She hadn't invited him back to her place and he'd issued no such invitation, either. His self-imposed abstinence was slowly driving him mad, but he was determined to wait until he was certain of her feelings for him before giving his body to her again.

The good news was that Vaughan's condition had stabilized enough that he'd been transported back to Australia and was currently in the ICU at the Sydney Harbour Hospital. Though he was still in a coma, the doctors were quietly confident he'd regain consciousness soon. It meant he'd miss another Barrington wedding, but at least the rest of the family would be there and they could take comfort from the fact their son and brother was back on home soil.

The beep of a horn outside his window interrupted his thoughts.

That must be Hannah...

He'd opted to stay at a hotel in Broken, the small country town a few miles from the Barrington Estate where the wedding was being held. Hannah was spending the night at her family home, but she'd offered to come and collect him and take him to the wedding. He appreciated her thoughtfulness and the fact he got to spend a little more time with her alone.

Hurrying now, he finished with the bow tie, patted down his damp hair and gave himself a final glance before grabbing his suit jacket off the bed and slinging it over his shoulder. Pulling the door to his room closed, he strode down the corridor. A few moments later, he stepped out into the bright afternoon sunshine. He squinted against the light.

"Hey," he said, greeting Hannah with a smile. "Can you just give me a minute? I've forgotten my sunglasses."

She rolled her eyes and grinned. "Be quick about it. I don't want to be late."

He hurried back inside the hotel and quickly retrieved his sunglasses from his room. Slipping them on, he returned to the car and climbed in beside her. He gave her a slow and thorough once-over.

She looked beautiful in a designer linen suit of the softest shade of pale pink. The fitted skirt fell to just above her knees. Beneath the jacket, she wore a white silk blouse. He was sure it would feel as soft as it looked. His fingers itched to touch her.

Her hair was caught up in some kind of intricate braid that circled her head and gave her the look of a Greek goddess. Tiny tendrils of dark hair had escaped and curled enticingly around her ears.

She wore a shade of lipstick that matched the color of her suit. He was struck with the urge to kiss her, to taste those plump pillows of flesh, but now wasn't the time. She'd be mad if he messed up her makeup.

As if privy to his thoughts, she shot him a wry grin. "Don't even think about it."

He settled with leaning over and cupping her cheek. He stroked her soft skin with the pad of his thumb.

"You look beautiful."

She smiled, looking pleased. "You don't look half-bad yourself. I love that charcoal-gray color on you. It makes me want to get down and dirty with you."

His gut clenched with desire, but he forced the feeling aside. Instead, he grinned at her. "Don't even think about it."

Their shared laughter filled the inside of her BMW. She pulled out of the hotel parking lot and took a left out of town. Liam reached across and took her hand, threading his fingers through hers. His nerves of a short time ago dissipated. He was with the woman who'd stolen his heart. He was where he belonged.

He was quietly confident her feelings for him were growing and that one day soon she'd realize she was just as much in love with him as he was with her. Perhaps it would even happen during the day's celebrations. Weddings had a habit of opening people's hearts and spreading love around. He crossed his fingers and sent up a silent prayer of hope.

Hannah glanced at Liam as she negotiated the winding road that led to her parents' home. With Emily's family also coming from Broken, it had made sense for the wedding to be held locally. Hannah's mother had offered to host the celebration at the Barrington Estate and Zac and Emily had been only too happy to accept her offer. And why wouldn't they be?

Hannah's childhood home was grander than most. Though her parents remained modest and humble in their attitude and had raised their children to be grateful for what they had, the success her father had made in business was obvious to anyone who viewed the opulence of his home. The two-story Hamptons-inspired mansion was recessed into the side of a mountain. The paved driveway was lined with mature trees. Their branches swayed gently in the breeze.

Hannah drove to the top of the driveway where the road curved around. A cobblestone pavement met wide stone steps that led up to the grand front door. The grounds were immaculate, as usual. While her mother had two gardeners on hand to help her, she spent a lot of time working in the grounds and took pride in the way they looked. Right now, with Christmas only a matter of hours away, they were decorated in festive theme.

Huge gold baubles hung from the trees, interspersed with large, red velvet bows. Thousands of fairy lights strung between the house and other structures twinkled cheerily overhead. Wide swathes of perfectly manicured lawns were punctuated by neat, colorful flowerbeds. Shrubs and hedges were expertly pruned, all set against the stunning backdrop of the southern highlands. The warm summer breeze carried with it the scent of orange blossoms from a nearby murraya hedge. As Hannah parked the car and climbed out, she filled her lungs with the perfumed air.

"Oh, I just love that smell," she breathed.

Liam came around to her side and smiled. He slipped his arm around her waist and pulled her in close against him. He dipped his head and nuzzled the side of her neck, breathing deeply.

"I love the way *you* smell," he murmured.

His warm lips sent shivers of desire tingling along her spine. She wanted nothing more than to turn her head and kiss him with all the passion she felt inside, but now wasn't the time. They had a wedding to attend. She swallowed a sigh.

As they walked arm in arm up the wide stone steps, she glanced at him, gauging his reaction to her family home. If he were overawed, he didn't show it. Instead, he looked around with interest at his surroundings. He appeared comfortable and relaxed and that put Hannah at ease.

He'd always known she'd come from money, but having that confirmed in such a dramatic way as being confronted with a house that would put some of the homes in the Hollywood Hills to shame was another matter. She didn't want him to feel intimidated, or that he didn't somehow measure up. She didn't care that he came from modest means or that the house he shared with his sister was only rented. Hannah had grown up in a wealthy household, but her parents had been adamant in ensuring their children knew that money didn't trump good character, or what was in someone's heart. And Hannah truly believed that.

"It's a shame Jacqueline had to work this afternoon. She would have enjoyed seeing this," Liam murmured. "You have a beautiful home."

"Yes. My mother can take credit for that. With the help of an architect, she designed the original building and she's been in charge of all alterations and additions over the years, including the gardens."

"She's very talented," he replied, looking around him once again.

His words filled Hannah with relief. It was obvious he wasn't intimidated by his surroundings, and she was glad. As they entered the grand foyer and made their way through to the back of the house and passed a beautifully decorated Christmas tree, she began to relax.

They were still a few minutes early and Hannah took the chance to re-introduce Liam to her siblings. The first couple she ran into was Charlotte and Grayson.

"Hannah, you look lovely," Charlotte said, pecking her on the cheek.

Hannah smiled and returned the compliment. Charlotte was glowing in a pale blue halter neck dress that skimmed her figure, but clung in all the right places, including a bustline that seemed to have expanded since the last time Hannah had taken notice.

Charlotte saw how Hannah's eyes reflexively widened and smiled. "Before you ask, yes, Grayson and I are having a baby."

The loving look the couple exchanged melted Hannah's heart. "Oh, my goodness!" she exclaimed. "That's wonderful news. Congratulations! I'm so happy for you both."

Grayson beamed, looking as proud as he had a right to be. Charlotte smiled. "Thank you, Hannah. And we're happy for you, too. It's so very nice to see you again, Liam. It's been a while."

Liam chuckled, appearing completely at ease. "It sure has. High school feels like a lifetime ago."

"You have that right," Charlotte agreed. "Hannah tells me you're an investigator with the Resources Regulator."

Liam nodded. "I am. But don't tell your father."

Everyone laughed. Hannah linked her arm in Liam's and after promising to catch up with Charlotte and Grayson after the ceremony, steered him toward her sister, Molly, and her new fiancé, Shane.

"Hannah, great to see you!" Molly said. The two sisters embraced. Hannah introduced Liam.

"It's nice to see you again, Liam," Molly said.

"Likewise," Liam replied.

"It's so lovely to be here to celebrate Zac and Emily's wedding, don't you think?" Molly asked.

"Absolutely," Liam agreed. "What's not to like about witnessing two people celebrating their love."

Molly glanced at Hannah and grinned. Hannah could tell her sister approved of Liam and that filled her with warmth. Her family's acceptance of him was important to her. She didn't think it would be a deal breaker if they didn't, but it certainly made things easier.

Does this mean I'm finally willing to admit I'm in love with him?

Molly pulled her to one side. "I'm not sure I remember Liam from high school, but he seems nice. Just so you know, I approve." She winked.

Hannah laughed. "Thanks, sis. In case I haven't told you, I approve of your choice, too. And I'm so proud of you for finally finding the courage to make a commitment to someone, to take a risk and put your heart on the line. I hope you're not suffering from any regrets?"

Molly beamed. "Of course not!" She waggled her ring finger. A huge solitaire diamond flashed brilliantly in the sunlight. "I said yes, didn't I? Not only that, Shane and I have moved in together."

"Oh, Molly! I'm so pleased! And how's it going? Any teething pains?"

"No, we haven't had a single argument. Not even when I took over most of his wardrobe space."

The sisters laughed. Hannah glanced at Liam and was filled with a yearning so swift and sharp it snatched her breath.

Is that what I want with Liam? Commitment, togetherness, everlasting love. Sharing wardrobe space?

She had a sneaking suspicion she wanted all of that. Maybe it was time to set aside her free-spirited, easy come, easy go ways and accept that Liam was her guy. Now and forever.

But what about his job?

There it was again. That problem hadn't gone away. Unless he requested a transfer out of the Hunter Valley... But that would mean a long-distance relationship and she wasn't sure she was cut out for one of those. Hell, until recently, she hadn't done relationships at all. She could see now that the four months she'd spent with Chad, she hadn't been invested in him at all. Not like she was with Liam. Nothing compared to the way he made her feel, but she still wasn't sure how a relationship with him was going to work.

As the priest called for the guests to take their seats, Hannah swallowed a sigh. She was determined to set aside her worries for now and embrace the joy and excitement of her brother's wedding. There would be plenty of time later to make decisions about her future. Right now, she'd make the most of every moment she had by Liam's side.

Chapter Twenty-Two

With the wedding vows spoken and the official paperwork signed, Liam took Hannah by the hand and tugged her to her feet. He'd watched her while she'd been immersed in the wedding celebration and had taken heart from the love and tenderness that filled her face. It was obvious she believed in true love and the sacrament of marriage and that gave him hope for their future.

Way back in high school, he could never have imagined Hannah Barrington might have feelings for him, no matter how much he'd hoped and prayed she would. But from her soft touches and the tender glances she kept sending his way, he was filled with quiet optimism. Especially when she heard his news. He had yet to make it official. He'd wanted to be sure of Hannah's feelings before he went public, but something told him he'd made the right decision. Sometime soon, he'd share it with her. Maybe even tonight...

He was suddenly filled with nerves.

What if she doesn't love me? What if I've been reading this all wrong? What if she laughs in my face?

No, he was being ridiculous. Paranoid. It was a throwback to their time in high school when she hadn't given him the time of day. But they'd been over that. She hadn't been interested in boys. It wasn't a personal affront. And he was no longer an insecure teenager, unsure of his place in the world, second-guessing every word, every look. Desperately wanting her from afar, knowing she'd never be his.

Those years were behind him. She was with him now, standing proudly beside him. That's what he needed to focus on. He couldn't change the past, but he could leave it where it belonged. Behind them.

As Hannah gazed up at him, her forehead creased in a frown. "Liam? What is it?"

He forced a smile and banished the memories. "Nothing. I'm fine. How could I not be? I'm here with the woman of my dreams, celebrating the coming together of two people who are madly in love. Does it get any better than that?"

Her eyes darkened to a shade of cobalt. "Is that what I am? The woman of your dreams?"

Tired of sidestepping the issue, Liam simply nodded. "Yes."

His heart was in his throat as he waited for her to respond. Neither had said the "L" word yet. This was as close as he'd come to admitting he was in love with her. He prayed desperately she wouldn't crush his heart a second time.

She shifted closer and cupped his cheek. She stared into his eyes. Her expression grew intense.

"That's the nicest thing anyone's ever said to me," she whispered huskily.

Liam's heart leaped with hope.

Yes! She loves me! There's no way she can look at me like that and not be in love with me. I can feel it!

But instead of saying the words he longed to hear, she merely smiled and took his hand. "Come on. Let's go and offer our congratulations to the bride and groom and say hello to the rest of my family."

Hannah's heart thumped with a tumult of emotion. Telling Liam she'd fallen in love with him had been on the tip of her tongue and then her courage had failed her. She'd never been in this position. Had never had to contemplate the enormity of committing herself to just one man. It was both nerve-wracking and overwhelming and at the last moment, she'd gotten scared.

What if these feelings don't last? What if I change my mind? After all, I thought I was in love with Chad. I gave him four months of my life.

No, that wasn't fair. What she'd felt for Chad couldn't compare to what she felt for Liam. With Chad, her physical needs had been assuaged, but he'd never come close to stealing her heart. She'd been fond of him and they'd had some fun times, but he'd never once made her think of forever.

And that's what frightened her the most about being around Liam.

The thought of him seeing other women, sleeping with them, filled her with wretched hurt and disappointment, along with a decent slice of jealousy. She didn't want to think about him with someone else. That told her just how much he meant to her. In only a month, she'd come to know him and now she couldn't imagine a future without him. No matter that they still had some hurdles to cross, that's the way she felt.

She risked a glance in his direction. He looked disappointed. Her heart sank. She was responsible for putting that expression there. The last thing she wanted to do was to hurt him with her cowardice. She opened her mouth to offer him reassurances, but before she could speak, she was engulfed by her older brother, Trace, in an enthusiastic bear hug.

"Hannah! Looking good, sis. How are you?"

She laughed. "Put me down! You're crushing my suit."

Trace chuckled and did as she asked. His fiancée, Cassie, stood beside him, smiling indulgently. Hannah introduced them to Liam. They all shook hands.

"It was a lovely ceremony, wasn't it," Hannah said.

"Yes. Very romantic," Cassie agreed. She looked at Trace. The love in her eyes was obvious to everyone. And then she smiled. "Are you going to tell them, or shall I?"

Hannah looked from one to the other. "Oh, no. Don't tell me you're having a baby, too?"

Trace looked momentarily confused. "A baby? Who's having a baby?"

Belatedly realizing she might have just broken Charlotte's confidence, Hannah hastily waved the comment away.

"No one. Nothing. Forget I said anything." She reached for Cassie's hands and squeezed them. "I'm dying to hear your news."

Cassie's smile widened. Once again, she glanced at Trace before returning her gaze to Hannah.

"Trace and I have set a date."

Hannah whooped. "Congratulations! That's fantastic news! When?"

"The first week in March. The weather should still be warm, but not too hot. It'll be perfect," Cassie said.

"Of course, it will," Hannah agreed. "I'm so thrilled for you both. Mom's going to be busy making more wedding plans."

Trace laughed. "We both know how much she loves it."

"That's true. Have you told her yet?"

"Yes," Trace said. "We gave Mom and Dad the happy news last night."

Hannah nodded. "I'm glad they have something to look forward to. Things have been tough with all they've gone through with Vaughan."

Her mention of Vaughan dimmed everyone's mood. Then Hannah forced a smile. "Let's not think about Vaughan's challenges right now. He wouldn't want that."

"You're right," Trace agreed, draping his arm around Hannah's shoulders. "He'd want us to sing and dance and get roaring drunk and have a whopping good time."

Hannah grinned. "Then let's get to it. In honor of Vaughan."

The speeches had been delivered and the cake had been cut by the time Hannah brought Liam over to meet her parents. He'd read so much about Frank Barrington and the mark the man had made in the Australian mining industry; he was a pioneer in his field. Liam couldn't help but feel nervous. As they approached, Hannah squeezed his hand, as if she could sense his hesitation. He smiled down at her, glad for the silent reassurance.

"You'll be fine," she whispered.

"Does he know what I do for a living?"

"Of course. Don't worry, he won't hold that against you." She winked. "I don't. At least, not anymore."

She chuckled to let him know she was teasing. It only worked marginally to set his nerves at ease. He drew in a surreptitious breath and tried to slow his pulse and then fixed a smile on his face.

"Dad. Mom. This is Liam Hennessy," Hannah said.

Liam stuck out his hand toward Frank. The man eyed him up and down and then shook his hand, his grip firm.

"Nice to meet you, Liam. I hear you've been spending a lot of time out at the Strathwaylin mine."

Liam flushed. Then Frank smiled. "Relax. I'm just giving you a hard time. In fact, I want to thank you for all you did in bringing that traitor, Garcia, to justice. He'd been doing that right under our noses for the better part of a year and no one else had noticed."

Liam nodded, pleased. "I only did my job."

"Yes, but I'm grateful all the same," Frank replied. He eyed Liam shrewdly. "My daughter also tells me you've been a great deal of support to her since the fallout with Garcia and Rodriguez's men. I'm sure you know as well as I do how capable Hannah is, but we can all do with someone in our corner, and the way she tells it, you've been a rock. So, thank you again. I appreciate everything you've done. Not only for me and my business, but for Hannah. She's a wonderful daughter and I'm very proud of her." His gaze narrowed. "You take care of her, okay?"

Liam nodded once again and breathed a silent sigh of relief. So far, so good. He turned to Evelyn. He held out his hand toward her. She shook it firmly and smiled.

"It's lovely to meet you, Liam. I hope you're having a good time."

He nodded. "Thank you for inviting me. You have a beautiful home and the grounds... They're spectacular. The rose garden and the lavender hedge. It's obvious they've been given a lot of love and care."

Evelyn flushed under his admiration. Hannah snorted. "It's okay, Liam. You don't have to lay it on too thick."

"Hey! I mean every word!" he protested.

She smiled indulgently. "I know. That's why I I—like you so much."

Once again, Hannah stopped short of telling him she loved him. She still couldn't say why. It wasn't that she hadn't accepted that she'd fallen for him. It was more that, now she'd come to that position, she felt a little shy about coming out and saying it. She definitely wasn't going to say it for the first time in front of her parents. No, she'd wait for the right time. Let it happen naturally. When they were alone, and she could properly gauge his reaction.

Hopefully he'd be happy about her declaration of love. It wasn't as though he'd made one to her. He'd told her he'd once been in love with her in high school, but did that still count? After all, he'd been a teenager and hadn't even known the real her. It would be nice to know how he felt now.

Her only clues that he might feel the same were in the way he kissed her, touched her, sought her out. Called her for no reason. Spent time with her. Made out. He certainly found her desirable. There was no question about that. But was that all it was? Physical desire? Her intuition told her it wasn't.

The thought that he might be in love with her made her dizzy with anticipation. A surge of happiness washed over her and she couldn't prevent a wide grin.

"What is it?" Liam asked, smiling.

She laughed softly. "I love weddings. Don't you?"

He nodded and pulled her close. He pressed a gentle kiss on her lips. "I do."

The look of intensity in his eyes caused her chest to tighten with emotion. Once again, the words were on the tip of her tongue and once again, she let them die there. Instead, she took him by the hand and led him to the makeshift dance floor. The band was playing a popular, upbeat song that everyone knew the words to, including Liam. As he sang and danced, her love and admiration grew. She loved that he was secure enough to dance and sing and have a good time in front of everyone.

Then the music changed to something slow and sultry. Liam gave her a look so hot it ignited a fire in her veins. He took her by the hand and drew her close. She curled her hand around his neck. Her head came naturally to rest on his shoulder. He held her pressed against him with his hand firmly on her waist. She felt safe and protected and loved.

Some of her siblings had also taken to the dance floor. She looked up and saw her brother, Lincoln, and his girlfriend, Zoe. Hannah had never seen him looking so happy. She was so glad after the terrible time he'd had adjusting to life after surviving three tours of duty of Afghanistan war. Her brother, Wade, and his girlfriend, Alice, also looked loved up as they danced cheek to cheek. She wouldn't be surprised if there were more engagement announcements in the future.

She returned her attention to Liam. He smiled down at her with a look so tender, it melted her heart. Reaching up, she brought his head down to hers and kissed him. It was meant to be a chaste kiss filled with love and devotion, but passion soon ignited between them. She opened her mouth and Liam's tongue boldly stole inside. She slanted her mouth and deepened the kiss and clung to him with a need so great she wasn't sure it could ever be extinguished.

And then slowly, slowly the pressure from Liam's mouth eased and he lifted his head. Her heart pounded. Her breath came fast. She wasn't even aware they'd stopped moving until she opened her eyes.

"Liam..." she breathed.

He smiled and then traced her mouth with the pad of his thumb. "You're so beautiful."

Hannah was gone. There was no dispute. She was in head-over-heels in love with him and the knowledge filled her with wonder, awe, and joy. She couldn't wait to tell him. But not here. Somewhere private. She had a sudden idea.

"Come upstairs with me," she murmured, her voice low and husky with need.

Liam's eyes flared bright with desire. He nodded and took her hand.

"Follow me," she said and led the way back into the house, leaving the wedding celebrations behind them.

"Where are we going?" Liam asked as he followed her down a long corridor and then upstairs.

Hannah gave him a sultry look. "To my old room."

Without waiting for him to respond, she turned away and continued up the stairs. She swung right at the landing and strode all the way to the end. She came to a halt outside a closed door and shot Liam another teasing look.

"Are you ready for this?"

He gave her an inscrutable look. "I've been ready all my life."

Her heart leaped into her chest and her pulse took off at a gallop. She opened the door and stepped inside. Liam followed behind her. She barely had time to register that the room looked the same way it always had, including the Keith Urban, Carrie Underwood, and Taylor Swift posters on the wall.

Kicking off her heels, she pulled off her jacket and flung it over her shoulder. Then she started on the buttons of her blouse. Not to be outdone, Liam's jacket went the same way of hers and then his bow tie quickly joined the growing pile of discarded clothing. His hands went to the buttons of his shirt. In short order, it was on the carpet.

Hannah's fingers stilled. She stared at the perfect musculature of Liam's bare chest. The one and only time she'd seen him naked, she'd been in too big a hurry to jump his bones to take the time to appreciate his sheer male beauty.

His nipples were little brown nubs peeking out from a scattering of darker hair. Her gaze moved lower, over the washboard stomach, tracing the thin trail of hair that tracked all the way into the waistband of his suit pants before it disappeared. As desire burned a path to her core, she licked her suddenly dry lips and refocused on getting naked.

Similarly driven, Liam sat on the bed and pulled off his boots and socks and then stood and shucked out of his pants. His blue satin boxers cupped his impressive erection. She ached to wrap her lips around it; to feel him driving his cock inside her. Unable to help herself, she drew closer and pressed herself against him, deliberately rubbing herself against him.

His eyes glittered with desire. His hands came up and rested on her shoulders, drawing her even closer. She tilted her head upward, expecting that he'd kiss her. Instead, his expression grew somber and he stepped slightly away.

She frowned in confusion. "Liam? What is it?"

He was silent for a moment and then, as if coming to a decision, he spoke. "There's no secret that I want you. I'm so hard right now, I could explode. You're a beautiful woman, inside and out and…I'm madly, hopelessly in love with you."

Hannah gaped. She could hardly believe what she'd just heard.

He loves me! He loves me! He loves me!

Liam's expression remained somber. She realized belatedly she hadn't yet responded. She threw her arms around him and hugged him tightly. "Oh, Liam! You're in love with me?"

"Yes," he said, still looking grim. Then he averted his gaze.

It was obvious she wasn't doing much of a job convincing him she was happy with the idea. Taking hold of his hands, she squeezed them reassuringly.

"Liam," she said softly. "Look at me."

He did, albeit reluctantly.

"It took me a long time to realize this," she said quietly, "but I got there in the end. I love you, too. I know that complicates everything for us because of your job, but I can't deny it any longer. I love you and I want to spend every minute of every day with you. Does that frighten you?"

The longer she spoke, the brighter his expression became. By the end of her speech, he was shaking his head and smiling and laughing all at once.

"You love me?" he asked. His voice was filled with hope.

Hannah laughed elatedly. "I do! I truly do!"

With a *whoop* of joy, Liam took her in his arms and swung her off her feet. He spun her around and they laughed together and it flooded her heart with light. When he finally set her back on her feet, both of them were gasping.

"I love you, I love you, I love you," she chanted.

He grinned. "I love you, too."

Their lips met in a passionate kiss and then they slowly drew apart. Hannah looked up at him, loving the feel of him in her arms.

"There's something else I haven't told you," he said.

Her heart hitched. For an instant, she thought he might have bad news. She braced herself for what was to come.

"I've resigned from the Resources Regulator," Liam said.

Hannah's jaw dropped. She stared at him in shock. "You *what?*"

"I resigned my position with the Resources Regulator. That means there's no longer a conflict of interest."

"But... You love your job. You told me you were born to do it!"

"Yes. I said that. And yes, I do love my job, but I love you more. If it comes down to a choice between you and my job, I choose you."

Hannah was lost for words. She opened her mouth and closed it and then opened it again. And then she slowly shook her head back and forth.

"I don't believe it," she rasped. "You love me that much?"

He nodded. "I do."

"But... What will you do for work?"

Liam merely smiled. "I'm sure we'll think of something. I have some savings set aside that will see me through for a while until I can find another job, but to tell you the truth, I don't care. All I care about is you."

Chapter Twenty-Three

Hannah was overcome with so much emotion, it choked her up inside. She struggled to find the words that adequately conveyed to him how she felt, so she decided to show him instead. To the beat of the waltz that reached them through the open window, she framed his face with her hands and rained kisses all over him. When she reached his lips, he brought his arms around her and crushed her to him.

Locked together, they stumbled to the bed and toppled down on it. Frantic now for the feel of skin on skin, they tore off the rest of their clothes. Within seconds, they were naked. Hannah lay on her back with Liam full length on top of her. His hard cock pressed against her stomach, further fueling the white-hot need that burned inside her. She shifted restlessly beneath him, urging him silently onward.

"I want to take things slowly this time," he murmured, his voice husky with desire.

"No, not slowly. Please, not yet, I need to feel you inside me. Right now. It's been so long. Too long. Please."

The mindless words fell out of her mouth. She hardly knew what she was saying. All she knew was that she needed him to fill her and stretch her and stroke her until she reached her peak.

Hannah took the guttural sound Liam made in the back of his throat as agreement. He positioned himself between her thighs and then paused.

"Condom?" he rasped.

"In my clutch."

He leaned over and grabbed her purse from where she'd set it on the bedside table. Unsnapping the clasp, he pulled out a foil packet and then set the purse aside. Ripping the condom open with his teeth, he quickly sheathed himself and was soon back between her thighs. His cock nudged at her entrance. Her legs fell open, encouraging him all the way.

He stared down at her with hooded eyes. She held his gaze. "Fuck me."

On a groan of desire, Liam surged forward and filled her in one thrust. She gasped and clung to his shoulders as he stoked the fire inside her to the point where she thought she might combust. As he pounded inside her, the need grew until she dug her fingers into his skin. And then she was there and toppling over the edge, falling, falling, falling... And then collapsing in relief.

A few moments later, Liam tensed and cried out and then collapsed against her, his breath harsh in her ear. She held him close, loving the solid weight of him pressing against her. Then he rolled off her and onto his back and sighed and slowly caught his breath.

Hannah reached for Liam's hand and threaded her fingers with his. She'd never felt so relaxed, so sated...so loved. Music and muted conversation from the wedding celebration continued to drift in the through the open window. She idly wondered if anyone had missed them and then realized she didn't care. Though she couldn't wait to spend time exploring every inch of Liam's glorious body, for now, she was content to lie there beside him, surrounded by his love. As if privy to her thoughts, he pressed a kiss against her forehead.

"I love you so much," he said.

She turned on her side so she could look at him. "And here I thought you liked blondes and redheads," she teased.

He frowned in confusion. "What are you talking about?"

"Georgina Wakehurst?" she said, recalling the name of his date at the ABBA concert.

"Georgina Wakehurst? I only went out with her twice."

"What about the redhead?"

"Who? Sally Meredith?"

"I don't know her name."

"Hang on a minute. How do you know these women?" A knowing look filled his eyes. "Have you been checking up on me?"

She flushed with embarrassment and glanced away. "I might have put your name into a search engine once or twice."

"Might have?" Liam teased.

"Okay, so I did. I looked you up online."

"And you discovered I had a preference for blondes and redheads?"

She blushed again. "Maybe."

"I'm surprised you didn't add leggy models to the list."

Her face was on fire. She wished she hadn't said anything about the other women in his life. But the truth was, she was a tiny bit jealous. She looked at him again and forced herself to ask, "Do you have a preference for leggy models?"

He shifted and snagged an arm around her waist. He dragged her closer until she was pressed snugly against his side. He bent his head and started kissing his way across her stomach, skimming her ribcage, and then pausing to suckle her breast. Her heart thumped with renewed excitement. She breathed in his spicy scent. Finally, he made it to her lips and kissed her long and deeply.

"In answer to your question, yes, I have a preference for leggy models. Most especially those who not only look fabulous in little black dresses and crimson gowns, but those who look breathtakingly sexy in high-visibility work shirts and steel-toed boots. I love a woman who can carry off a hard hat as easily and with as much style as she can carry off a five-thousand-dollar suit and stilettos. But most of all, I love you, Hannah Barrington, every delicious, sweet, silky inch of you." He punctuated each word with another kiss.

She melted beneath him, basking in his every word. She could never have imagined she could feel so elated, so full of wonder, so overawed. Now she had some inkling as to what her siblings felt. No wonder they all looked so happy.

"I love you so much," she whispered, looking into his eyes.

Somewhere in the distance, a grandfather clock chimed out the hour. When it had finished, Hannah's eyes went wide.

"Twelve chimes! It must be midnight."

Liam grinned. "You know what that means, don't you?"

She chuckled. "What?"

"Merry Christmas!"

THE END

Get a free book when you sign up for Chris Taylor's newsletter at: http://www.christaylorauthor.com.au

If you enjoyed Hannah and Liam's story don't forget to leave a review at your favorite digital retailer. Every review is really appreciated and helps with visibility so that other readers can find and enjoy my books.

Broken Homes is the next and final book in the Barrington Family Series. Keep reading for a sneak peek at ***Broken Homes***.

CHAPTER ONE

There was an elephant on his chest. Or a ton of bricks. Something hard and immoveable. Something that made it impossible to breathe. He hurt all over. His chest was on fire. Every breath was an agony. White-hot knife points stabbed at his brain. The pain was beyond anything he'd ever imagined.

The agony in his head was the worst. He couldn't think past it.

Ruby...?

Oh, God. I can't stand it. Please, God. It hurt's too much. Please...

On a sigh of defeat, he prayed for death.

Ruby Ashworth clung to Vaughan Barrington's hand so tightly her fingers ached. She'd been a fixture beside his bed ever since he'd arrived at the Sydney Harbour Hospital. Frank Barrington had arranged for his son to be medevacked from Bali and Ruby was glad for his intervention, even if he'd ruffled a few feathers along the way, including hers. She'd never met Frank or his wife, Evelyn, until they'd landed in Denpasar. They'd come straight to the hospital.

From that moment, Frank had taken over. Though Ruby was grateful to have some support, it was like she no longer existed. Frank didn't care that she was Vaughan's fiancée. All he cared about was his son. For two weeks, Vaughan had been too unstable to move. Everyone had chafed at the delay. Frank's temper had grown shorter with every day that passed and Vaughan remained in the Denpasar hospital.

Ruby understood Frank's agitation. She was also keen to see Vaughan moved to Australia and to more sophisticated medical care. After all, she was the one who'd contacted

Vaughan's father. But she hadn't expected the man to stomp all over everyone – nurses, doctors, technicians, her. For Vaughan's sake, she'd set aside her irritation at Frank's overbearing ways and had fallen in with his plans, but now they were back in Australia, she was done with his arrogant and domineering attitude.

In response to Vaughan's serious condition, the hospital had limited his visitors. Only one person could be with him at a time. Right now, that was Ruby. As she stared down at the man she'd come to care for, her eyes filled with tears. She was riddled with guilt.

"Please, Vaughan. Please, wake up. I need to talk to you. I need to tell you how much you mean to me. How sorry I am for not telling you the truth…"

Her voice hitched on a sob. She swiped at her tears with her free hand and tightened her hold on Vaughan with the other. She brought his hand up to her lips and kissed his fingers, holding them close against her mouth. His skin was warm. He felt so alive. If only he'd open his eyes, smile at her, speak…

But he remained still and quiet, except for the rhythmic sound of the respirator that kept him alive, pumping air into his lungs. It was funny. If she overlooked the fading bruises on his face and the fact his beard had grown thicker and longer than she'd ever seen it, he looked like he was merely asleep. Like he'd wake up any moment and give her that heart-stopping grin that sent butterflies swirling through her stomach…

A nurse appeared by her side on silent, rubber-soled feet. Ruby started when she spoke.

"I'm sorry, Ruby. Your time's up. Vaughan's father has been waiting outside for nearly twenty minutes." The nurse grimaced. "He's growing impatient."

Ruby compressed her lips on a wave of anger. "Of course, he is."

"I'm sorry. I wish I could let you stay, but you know the rules," the nurse replied, not unkindly.

"Yes. The rules." Ruby glared at the nurse, even though her anger was for Frank. "Tell me, what does it matter to Vaughan how many visitors he has at one time? He's unconscious. He doesn't have a clue who's here."

The nurse held her ground. No doubt this wasn't the first time she'd had to deal with a difficult relative.

"There's a lot we don't understand about a patient's level of awareness while they're in a coma. There have been plenty of recounts from patients who recall hearing conversations around them while they've been unconscious." The nurse shrugged. "Who knows? But our priority is our patients, and we'll always err on the side of what's best for them. It's tiring for conscious patients to deal with a constant stream of visitors. We have to assume it's that way for coma patients too."

She gave Ruby another understanding look. "I know it's hard for you. For everyone. But patients who have suffered as much as Vaughan has need all the rest they can get so they can heal. Limiting his visitors is one way to do that. Surely that's what you want too?"

Ruby's cheeks heated with embarrassment at the nurse's pointed look. "Yes, of course," she mumbled.

Averting her gaze, she gathered up her jacket and handbag. Bending low, she gave Vaughan a peck on the cheek and turned away. Squaring her shoulders, she drew in a deep breath and prepared herself for another confrontation with Frank.

Hannah Barrington clung tightly to her boyfriend's hand as they waited with her father outside the ICU. She and Liam had stopped by to visit with her brother, Vaughan. He'd been transported to the Sydney Harbour Hospital from Denpasar two weeks earlier and though he was receiving the best of medical care, he was still in a coma and no one could tell them if or when he might regain consciousness. So far, the signs were positive that he hadn't suffered any permanent brain damage, but they wouldn't know for sure until he woke. *If* he woke.

No. I refuse to believe that. he's going to wake up. He's going to get better. He's going to be fine...

If she repeated the words often enough, they might come true. If only things worked like that.

The door to the ICU swung open and the woman who was apparently Vaughan's fiancée came out. Ruby Ashworth barely glanced in their direction. Her shoulders were slumped and her eyes were red. She headed toward the lifts without a word.

Sympathy flooded through Hannah. It must be so hard for Ruby to see Vaughan like that. They were all finding it difficult to comprehend the extent of his injuries, including the fact he might never wake up. His condition hadn't improved. On the other hand, it hadn't worsened either. She guessed they ought to be grateful for that.

"I'm going in," her father said, his voice gruff with emotion.

Hannah nodded. "Okay, Daddy. We'll wait for you here."

Frank disappeared inside the ICU. The double doors closed silently behind him. Hannah leaned her head on Liam's shoulder and sighed.

"I hate this," she murmured.

Liam reached for her hand and threaded their fingers together. "It's tough. The waiting."

"Not only that. It's the not knowing whether he's ever going to get better. I could stand the waiting if I knew there was an end to it."

Liam tightened his hold on her hand and pressed a kiss against her hair. She was grateful when he didn't offer any useless platitudes. Silence fell between them. The waiting room was quiet. Only the occasional muffled conversation from a nearby ward broke the stillness. She dropped her head to Liam's shoulder and drew in a deep breath, filling her lungs with the smell of his cologne. His presence brought her comfort. Made her feel safe. Loved.

Though they'd only been a couple a short time, it felt so right. She couldn't imagine wanting to spend her life with anyone else. She guessed that's what love was. She'd always thought love was overrated and had never felt the need to commit to anyone for longer than a week or two, let alone for life. But Liam had changed all that. Now the very thought of dating anyone else was anathema. It was funny how life turned out.

"What do you know about Ruby?" Liam asked quietly.

Hannah shrugged. "Not much. She met Vaughan in Bali several months ago. Now they're engaged. That's it. Why?"

"There's something about her that seems familiar. I can't put my finger on it, but it's been bugging me from the moment I first saw her. It's like I've seen her before."

"Well, apparently, she comes from Sydney, so I guess it's possible you might have seen her before. Although in a city of more than five million people, I'd hate to fathom the odds of that."

"It'll come to me, don't worry. I never forget a face."

She smiled tenderly and pressed a kiss against his lips. His arms came up around her and he pulled her close. She sighed softly. It felt so good to have his support, his love. Knowing he was in her corner and would be there for her, no matter what.

"Why did I spend so much time trying to avoid relationships?" she murmured against his shirtfront.

"Maybe it was because you were with the wrong guy. Not every relationship's a success. Not everyone finds their soul mate."

Her heart swelled with love. She pulled back slightly to stare up at him. "Is that what I am? Your soul mate?"

His gaze remained clear and steady on hers. "Yes."

Her heart stuttered. Happiness flooded her veins. She reached up and pulled his head down to hers and kissed him once again.

"I love you, Liam Hennessy."

He smiled, his eyes filled with love and tenderness. "I love you too, Hannah Barrington."Caught up in each other's eyes, they didn't notice Frank had returned until he cleared his throat.

"If you two lovebirds are done, let's get out of here."

Hannah blinked in surprise. "Daddy! You're finished?"

"Yes." Frank looked away and shuffled his feet. "I can't stand to see him that way."

Hannah's heart clenched at the raw pain in her father's eyes. She stood and went to him. "Oh, Daddy." She put her arms around him and hugged him. "He's going to be okay."

"You don't know that Hannah," her father said.

Hannah bit her lip against a rush of emotion, too choked up to respond. Liam stepped forward.

"Hey, let's go downstairs and grab a coffee."

Hannah shot him a look of gratitude. He reached for her hand and drew her in close beside him. They walked toward the lifts.

"How was he?" Hannah managed.

Frank looked grim. "Same as always."

Over coffee in the hospital café, Frank asked her for an update at the mine. Glad for the distraction, Hannah filled him in on what had been happening since they'd last talked.

"Have you met the new investigator yet?" her father asked.

Hannah glanced at Liam before responding. "No. Liam has a couple more days in the job before his resignation becomes effective. The Resources Regulator has started advertising for someone else. I guess we'll meet the successful candidate in due course."

"Let's hope they're a bit more amiable than the last one."

Frank's gruff tone belied the twinkle in his eyes. He looked at Liam and winked. Everyone laughed and sipped their coffee. Then a speculative look filled Frank's gaze.

"What are your plans after you leave the Resources Regulator?" he asked.

Liam set his coffee cup down before replying. "I've put out a few feelers with some private companies. Right now, it's a matter of waiting and seeing what comes up."

Frank eyed him steadily. "Would you be interested in working for Barrington Mining?"

Hannah started in surprise. "That's a great idea!" She glanced at Liam. "I mean, is that something you might be interested in?"

To her relief, Liam's expression remained open. He shrugged. "Maybe. I'd really like to stay in the Hunter Valley region if possible." He smiled at her and winked before turning back to face her father. "What did you have in mind?"

Hannah flushed. Her heart raced. Though she'd never given any thought to Liam coming to work for her father because of their past history, that didn't mean the idea didn't appeal to her.

"I was thinking you could come on board as one of our safety officers," Frank said. "You'd be working under Hannah, of course, but with your extensive background in safety, there's no denying you'd be a real asset to our team."

Liam grinned. "Despite the fact I used to work for the Resources Regulator?"

Frank chuckled. "*Because* of that."

Hannah laughed, along with Liam. She looked at him, her excitement at the thought of them working together too hard to contain.

"I'd love to work with you," she said.

Liam's grin widened. "I'd love to work with you, too."

"We'd make a great team," Hannah added.

Liam chuckled. "You won't get any argument from me."

"Then it's settled," Frank said, finishing the last of his coffee. He pushed away from the table and stood. "I have to get going. I'll see you later."

As her father left the café and headed toward the hospital exit, Hannah reached for Liam's hand and squeezed it.

"Do you really mean it? Do you really want to come and work for my dad?"

Liam leaned over and cupped her cheek. He pressed a soft kiss against her lips. "I love being with you, Hannah. The thought of working together fills me with joy."

She frowned. "You won't mind me being the boss?"

"You can boss me around all you like."

The look he gave her was so hot it scorched her. Heat flooded her veins and centered in her core. Even with her brother lying seriously ill in a hospital bed, she couldn't help but be filled with desire for the man who'd lit up her life and captured her heart.

She grinned back at him. "Careful what you wish for."

He leaned forward and kissed her. "Promise?"

It wasn't until after Hannah had been in to see Vaughan that Liam remembered where he'd seen Ruby Ashworth before.

"She's related to Joseph Rodriguez," he said.

Hannah frowned as they made their way out of the hospital and toward the carpark where they'd left Hannah's car.

"The earthmoving contractor Daddy fired?"

"Yes. She's he's daughter."

Hannah came to a sudden halt. She stared at Liam, her heart thumping. "Are you sure?" "Yes. They were at some function for mining executives. I remember seeing her in a photo with him, along with Nathan Garcia."

Hannah's lips twisted at the mention of the man who used to be her righthand man at the mine and who'd turned out to be Joseph Rodriguez's nephew. Nathan had betrayed her and the mine in the worst kind of way and she was still struggling to come to terms with what he'd done. No doubt everything would be stirred up once again when the case went to trial.

She shook her head, still bewildered by Liam's revelation. "That means Vaughan's fiancée is Nathan's cousin. What are the odds?"

Liam looked grim. "Exactly."

Something in his tone caught her attention. "What? You think there's more to this?"

Liam sighed and began walking again. Hannah hurried to keep up with him.

"Don't you think it's a bit too much of a coincidence?" Liam asked. "I mean, Joseph Rodriguez gets fired by your father for continuous safety breaches. He sends his nephew into the mine for the sole purpose of causing accidents—enough to get the mine closed—and about the same time, his daughter happens to meet your brother in Bali?"

The disbelief in Liam's tone filled Hannah with dread. "Oh, my God!" she whispered. "Do you think their meeting was planned? But for what purpose?" Then another thought occurred to her. She grabbed Liam's arm and gasped. "Don't tell me you think she had something to do with Vaughan's accident?"

Liam shook his head. "No. Of course not." He paused and then added, "I don't know what to think."

Hannah stared at him in shock. Her thoughts galloped a mile a minute. No, to think Ruby had anything to do with Vaughan's accident was ridiculous. Anyone could see how much she cared for him. She'd been practically glued to his side ever since he'd been hurt. Even her father had complained he couldn't get time alone with his son because of Ruby.

But still... She was Joseph Rodriguez's daughter. The same man who'd put into action a plan to get their mine closed. And he hadn't cared who'd gotten hurt in the process.

Could it be true? Could Ruby Ashworth have deliberately set out to hurt Vaughan at her father's request? Was she that cold? That callous? Was her apparent devotion to Hannah's brother all an act?

She was determined to find out.

Chapter Two

After spending most of the day at the hospital, Ruby was relieved to return home to her inner-city apartment and chill out for a little while. Keeping vigil was exhausting. So was her concern for Vaughan. Okay, so she might not be head-over-heels in love with him, but she'd come to care for him over the past months in Bali. Seeing him lying unconscious, so pale and quiet and still... It was confronting. It reminded her how fickle life could be and how it could be taken away in an instant. It also made her realize how much Vaughan had come to mean to her.

He was a good guy. He didn't deserve this. If anyone deserved to be punished, it was her. She was the one who'd deliberately set out to deceive him. The fact she had solid reasons for doing so didn't seem to matter anymore. She wished she'd told Vaughan the truth. She should have come clean as soon as she realized he was so good and decent and was nothing like his father. But she hadn't. Now she might never get the chance. The very real possibility of that was killing her.

So was having to put up with his family. In particular, Frank. She'd heard so much about the Barrington patriarch from her father. It was all she could do not to spit in Frank Barrington's face. But for now, she had to keep up the act of grieving fiancée. Not only for her sake, but for her father's. He was counting on her.

A fresh wave of guilt over her deception depressed her spirits. As she tossed her handbag on the hall table and toed off her sandals, she clung to the hope that Vaughan would wake. Despite everything, she wanted the chance to tell him the truth and beg his forgiveness. There was no guarantee that would be on offer, but she had to at least try. She also had to keep up the subterfuge of a loving fiancée. If his family got even a hint that her relationship with Vaughan wasn't legitimate, she'd be refused access to him at the hospital and that was something she couldn't bear.

Padding into the kitchen, she opened the fridge and pulled out the bottle of Sauvignon Blanc she'd uncorked the evening before. Pouring herself a glass, she plopped down on the leather sofa that took up most of the space in the adjoining living room. She reached for the remote and activated the TV and then distractedly surfed the channels. Nothing held her interest. All she could think about was Vaughan.

Blowing her breath out on a heavy sigh, she took a healthy sip of her wine. The crisp tartness exploded on her tongue. Halfway through the glass, she began to relax. The wine was just what she needed after another long day. Another long day of not knowing whether Vaughan would regain consciousness.

Another long day of not knowing if she'd ever be given the chance to explain and apologize.

The sound of a knock at the door interrupted her thoughts. Frowning, she set down her wineglass and padded down the hall toward the front door. She lived on the ninth floor of a high rise. Random visitors were an oddity, and she certainly wasn't expecting anyone. Peeking through the security hole, her stomach dropped on a gasp. Hannah Barrington stood on the other side. She didn't look happy.

Ruby's guilty conscience immediately jumped to conclusions. *She knows... Somehow, she's discovered the truth... She knows I'm a fraud...* With a gargantuan effort, Ruby reined in her wayward thoughts and took a deep breath. There's no way Hannah could know about Ruby's deception. She and her father were the only two in on that and there was no way her father had gone running to the Barringtons. She was being silly. Way too sensitive. Given the current circumstances and everything that had gone on recently, who could blame her.

But now wasn't the time to fall apart. It was more important than ever to maintain the façade. She was so close. So close to getting what she wanted; what her father wanted. Provided Vaughan woke up. She couldn't afford to blow it now. Squaring her shoulders, she drew in another deep breath and plastered a smile on her face. Then she opened the door.

"Hannah! Oh, my goodness! What are you doing here?"

Hannah pushed rudely past her and strode down the hall. Ruby's disquiet deepened, but she forced herself to remain calm.

"What are you doing here?" she asked again as Hannah came to a halt beside the kitchen counter.

Hannah rounded on her, eyes blazing. "Oh, no. You don't get to ask the questions, Ruby Ashworth. Or should I say, Ruby Rodriguez!"

Ruby's stomach dropped like a stone. She stared at Hannah and fought to remain calm.

She knows! She knows who I am! What else does she know? Oh, hell. What do I do now? Keep calm. Keep calm. Keep calm...

The steady mantra had the desired effect. Ruby held Hannah's gaze, grateful for her outward composure. At the same time, she curled her hands into fists to conceal their trembling. She forced an indifferent smile.

"You're right. My father's Joseph Rodriguez."

"The same Joseph Rodriguez who my father just happened to sack from one of his mines a year ago," Hannah said coldly.

Ruby shrugged nonchalantly. It was all she could do to maintain the veneer of disinterest. "If you say so. I wouldn't know. I don't get involved with my father's business dealings," she lied.

Hannah shook her head scornfully. "Oh, don't you go expecting me to believe you didn't know anything about it. The contract my father terminated was worth millions. There's no way your father didn't tell his family about it."

Once again, Ruby worked hard to maintain her façade of indifference. "Whatever. It's obvious to me you've already made up your mind about what I do and don't know. Why would I waste time trying to convince you otherwise?"

She advanced a couple of steps toward Hannah who held her ground. Though Hannah wore high heels, the two women stood eye to eye. Physically, they were equally matched, but Ruby had at least a decade on Hannah. And yet the younger woman didn't appear the least bit intimidated. Ruby couldn't help but feel reluctant admiration for the woman.

"My brother has no idea who you really are, does he?"

Something in her face must have given her away. Hannah pounced.

"Oh, my God! He doesn't know! He proposed to you, and he doesn't even know who you are! What did you do? Cast a spell on him? I don't believe this. How could you have been so deceitful?"

Ruby fought to keep her breathing even. "Your brother doesn't care about things like that. He loves me for who I am."

Hannah glared at her. "What are you playing at, Ruby Rodriguez? What the hell are you doing with my brother?"

It took all of Ruby's courage to maintain eye contact, but she managed it. "I'm not playing at anything. Your brother and I met by chance in Bali. We fell in love. He proposed. I accepted. Then he got hurt. That's it. End of story."

But Hannah wasn't buying it. "Vaughan didn't get to forty years of age and still be single by being reckless with his heart. I don't know how you got him to fall in love with you. What I do know is that my brother's lying in a coma, and no one can tell me who's responsible. Given your father's history of causing accidents for the Barringtons and the things they hold dear, I've got you firmly in my sights."

Ruby gasped, enraged. "How *dare* you say that about my father! He was innocent in all of that. Your father was the one in the wrong. He fired my father for no reason!"

Hannah's eyes gleamed with triumph. "Ha!" she pounced. "So you *do* know about that. Why did you lie? Or does dishonesty come so easily to you, you're not even aware you're doing it?"

Ruby clenched her jaw to prevent herself from saying something she'd later regret. It was hard to remain silent when fury pounded through her veins. She wanted nothing more than to grab Hannah and shake her until she saw sense. Instead, Ruby drew in a deep breath and fought for calm.

Hannah glared at her. "You owe me an explanation."

Ruby glared right back. "I owe you nothing."

"You know—"

"What I know is that my father was treated abominably by yours," she spat. "I don't expect you to believe that because that would mean you'd have to admit your father isn't the paragon of virtue you seem to think."

While Hannah sputtered with outrage, Ruby continued. "As for Vaughan, believe what you want. We're in love and we're getting married, just as soon as he's well enough. Come to the wedding, or not. That's your decision. It makes no difference to me."

Hannah's gaze turned icy. "We only have your word that Vaughan proposed. He never said anything to his family. Don't you think that's strange? Then again, perhaps your family isn't as close as ours. Whatever. Just be warned. I'm watching you."

With that, Hannah flung her long hair over her shoulder and stomped past Ruby, headed for the front door. With fury still burning through her veins, Ruby couldn't help one last parting shot.

"How did you know where I live?"

Hannah slowed and turned around. "I asked someone at the hospital to check your contact details. I wanted to make sure they had them right. You being Vaughan's fiancée and all."

Her smirk filled Ruby with fresh anger. With fists clenched, she strode toward her. "You had no right," she hissed.

Hannah merely shook her head. "Save it. If what I suspect is true, a so-called invasion of your privacy is the least of your worries." With that, Hannah pulled open the door and slammed it behind her.

The apartment fell silent. Ruby's shoulders slumped. She trembled all over, both shocked and shaken by the confrontation. She couldn't believe Hannah knew who she was. She couldn't help but wonder how many other Barringtons knew the truth. She was filled with a surge of panic.

I need to tell Vaughan. I need to tell him who I am before he finds out from someone else.

If only he'd wake up.

High above him, the sun shone brightly in the cloudless blue sky. It was the kind of perfect summer day Vaughan loved. He floated on his back in the warm salt water, utterly relaxed. Gentle waves broke over him. Their swaying movement lulled him half to sleep. In fact, if he closed his eyes, he'd almost certainly fall asleep.

It reminded him of the perfect days he'd spent with Ruby in Bali. Lazing on the beach. Swimming in the ocean. Kissing, making love. Falling asleep in each other's arms beneath a chandelier of stars, the air heavy with the scent of tropical flowers.

Ruby...

His heart clenched with love. He turned his head this way and that, hoping to see her. He was disappointed to discover he was alone. There was nothing but deep blue ocean as far as the eye could see. And then a different feeling took hold of him. Panic.

Where am I? What am I doing out in the middle of the ocean, alone? Where's Ruby?

"Ruby!"

The sound of his voice in the stillness frightened him. Croaky and rough, he barely recognized it as belonging to him. He tried to shout again, but it took too much effort. His voice was barely above a whisper. And then he felt a soft, cool hand press against his cheek. Slowly, he opened his eyes.

"Ruby...?" he croaked.

"Yes, it's me! Ruby! Oh, Vaughan! You're awake! Thank goodness you're awake!"

He heard the joy and relief in her voice and couldn't hold back a smile. "Ruby…"

She was there. Beside him. Holding tightly to his hand. Tears filled his eyes. His chest went tight. He was so in love with her.

"Ruby…"

He tried to move, to touch her. Pain, sharp and immediate, hammered through his head. He gasped. "Fuck."

"It's all right," Ruby soothed, brushing back the hair from his forehead. "Take it easy. Big deep breaths. It's going to be all right."

He frowned. "What…? What happened?"

Ruby's forehead creased. "You don't remember?"

"I remember the truck. I tried to swerve, but it was too late."

"Yes. You were hit. You've been unconscious for almost a month. You gave us all a big fright."

"Us?"

"Yes. Me. And your family. They've all been by to see you."

"In Bali?"

"No. You're in Sydney now. Your parents came over to Denpasar and arranged to fly you out of there."

Vaughan nodded slowly. "You met them?"

Ruby smiled. "Yes."

"Did you tell them about us?"

She held out her hand and waggled her fingers. The impressive solitaire diamond he'd given her flashed brilliantly beneath the light. "Of course."

He smiled. He wished he'd been awake to see it. Their engagement would have come as a surprise to his family, but he was certain they'd embrace Ruby wholeheartedly and welcome her into the fold. Once again, he reached out to touch her. The pain in his head wasn't quite as severe as the first time, but it was there all the same. In fact, everything was still foggy and thinking about anything other than how thrilled he was to be alive and to have Ruby by his side was beyond him.

With a sigh, he closed his eyes and gave in to the exhaustion that gripped him. He fell asleep with a smile on his face.

Ruby clung to Vaughan's hand, her heart pounding. She was so glad he was awake and had recognized her. His head injury wasn't as bad as she'd feared. The doctors had warned her there might be brain damage, memory loss—anything could happen with a brain injury as severe as his. But it appeared he was okay. He knew who she was and what they meant to each other. She could only hope he still felt that way after she told him who she was.

Now the moment was upon her, she cast around for courage. Her mouth went dry. Her palms grew damp. Her heart picked up its pace. She drew in a deep breath and opened her mouth. Vaughan's soft snores slowly infiltrated her awareness. She stared down at him. He'd fallen back asleep.

Her shoulders slumped with relief. She was immediately flooded with guilt. She needed to come clean. She owed him the truth. Now that he'd regained consciousness, the clock was ticking. She had to tell him before someone else did. There was no doubt he'd be shocked.

Hannah's reaction was testament to that. The Barringtons were sensitive about what had happened with her father. That was their problem, but she still owed Vaughan an apology and no matter how much she dreaded coming forward, it would be much better received if it came from her. But first, she had to call for the nurse and give her the good news.

Vaughan's awake!

Chapter Three

Hannah paced the length of her father's city office, unable to stand still. The morning sun poured through the floor-to-ceiling wall of glass that formed one side of the room. It was normally a view she enjoyed. The corner office overlooked the lush Botanical Gardens. In the distance was a glimpse of the sparkling blue Pacific Ocean. But today, Hannah was blind to the impressive view. Though it had been twelve hours since her confrontation with Ruby, she was still agitated.

"I can't believe she hasn't told Vaughan who she is!" she exclaimed, her voice reflecting her irritation.

Her father sat composed behind his carved walnut desk, his fingers steepled beneath his chin. He regarded her steadily.

"What makes you think knowing who her father was would have made any difference to Vaughan? We still don't have any proof Joseph Rodriguez was involved in Evan Wilson's death and Vaughan fled to Bali before the other mess with Nathan Garcia came to light. He knows nothing about the recent spate of accidents that almost got the mine closed. At the very most, he might be surprised at the coincidence of meeting Rodriguez's daughter overseas."

"But why would she keep her identity a secret?" Hannah exclaimed. "What's she got to hide? How did she even know who Vaughan was that she had to give him a false name?" Hannah folded her arms across her chest and narrowed her eyes. "There's something fishy going on."

Frank nodded. "I agree it gives me some cause for concern, but we don't know why Ruby Rodriguez was in Bali. She could have simply been there on holiday, like so many thousands of other young Australians who flock there every year, including Vaughan." He paused. "I'm not sure why you're so worked up about this. There could be any number of reasons their paths crossed and most of them aren't sinister."

"So, why wouldn't she offer me an explanation? You should have seen her, Daddy! She looked like she was going to die of shock when I told her I knew who she was. Why the subterfuge? She meets a cute guy in Bali, and she gives him a false name. Why would she do that?"

"Maybe she wanted to see how trustworthy he was before disclosing too much personal information," Frank said in a reasonable tone.

"Okay, but why not tell him the truth later? Apparently, they're engaged. Surely there was plenty of time to come clean about her real name."

Frank nodded. "You're right. If she got to the point of accepting a marriage proposal, she should have trusted him enough to disclose who she was."

Hannah pounced. "Exactly! And yet she didn't. I could tell from the look on her face that she hasn't told him."

"Did you ask her why?"

"Of course, I did, but she refused to answer my question."

Frank fell silent. After a few moments, he drew in a deep breath and let it out on a sigh. "You're right. It does seem a little strange. We need to get to the bottom of it. I can understand why she might not have said anything in the early days, but this is the man she's agreed to marry. It's not unreasonable to expect she'd be more forthright about her family."

"Especially since she knew you'd sacked her father, although she seems to have a different interpretation on the facts." Hannah grimaced.

"What do you mean?"

Hannah propped a hip against her father's desk. "She seems to think her father was treated poorly by the Barringtons; that we were the ones in the wrong. Who knows what she was told about all that. No doubt her father slanted the whole sordid incident in his favor," she muttered.

Frank nodded. "No doubt. It's too bad Vaughan can't shed any light on all of this."

Hannah sighed. "Let's hope he wakes up soon and can tell us everything himself. Then we won't be forced to take Ruby's word for it."

Frank's phone began to ring. He pulled it out of his pocket and checked the screen. He glanced back at Hannah, his expression tense.

Her heart skipped a beat. "Who is it?"

"The hospital."

Vaughan's head thumped. He was sore all over. Everything ached. But still, he was alive and from what Ruby had told him about the accident, he was thankful for that. He was also grateful that there appeared to be no lasting effects from the head injury, apart from the headache that put all other headaches to shame.

A bevy of doctors had been in attendance, called by a nurse as soon as Ruby had alerted them he was awake. They'd put him through a truckload of neurological tests. He'd passed them all with flying colors. He couldn't be more relieved. Or happier.

He looked at Ruby. She was perched on a chair that she'd pulled up to his bed and now clung tightly to his hand. They'd already shifted him out of the ICU and onto another ward, convinced he was on the mend. Things were looking up. He wondered why Ruby looked so uncomfortable and why she wouldn't meet his eye.

Please, God. Don't let it be over between us... I couldn't bear it if she's come to say goodbye... I love her so much...

"What's wrong?" he asked quietly, taking his courage in his hands. He was determined to face whatever was going on with her head on. No matter that she might be about to break his heart, life was too short for games.

The color left her cheeks, further fueling his sense of foreboding. She let go of his hand. He immediately felt bereft. She glanced at him and then looked away.

"There's something I have to tell you," she murmured.

His gut clenched. He fought to keep his breathing steady. "Okay. What is it?"

She blew her breath out on a heavy sigh. Her gaze skittered over his. "I... I told you my name's Ruby Ashworth," she said in a rush.

Vaughan frowned in confusion, not sure where this was headed. "Yes."

"The thing is... I—"

"Ruby Ashworth is Joseph Rodriguez's daughter," Hannah interrupted as she sailed unannounced into the room.

Vaughan's frown deepened. The pain in his head worsened. It still felt like he was plowing through mud whenever he tried to concentrate. "Joseph Rodriguez? Why does that name sound familiar?"

"He was one of the lead earthmoving contractors out at the Strathwaylin mine. Daddy fired him a year ago for numerous safety breaches. He was given his marching orders the very same day Evan Wilson died," Hannah said.

Vaughan gasped. *"What?"*

The past came back to him in a rush. His head thumped as blood flooded his brain. He turned and stared at Ruby. "Your father's Joseph Rodriguez?"

Her expression was one of overwhelming guilt. She hadn't even opened her mouth, but Vaughan already had his answer.

Confusion coursed through him. His fists clenched. "Why didn't you tell me?"

Ruby's gaze remained fixed to the floor. Her fingers twisted in the pleats of her skirt. She squirmed in her seat and then shifted as if she were about to leave.

Vaughan's belly filled with dread. Something was awfully wrong. Why would Ruby keep something like that from him? He'd never told her about his family; that his father was Frank Barrington, the mining magnate. He'd wanted her to love him for who he was. As far as she knew, he was just another fun-loving Aussie hanging out in Bali, having a good time.

She had no reason to suspect he had any idea about who her father was or that he'd been fired from Frank's mine. In fact, she had no reason to suspect anything at all. They were merely two tourists who'd hooked up on holiday and had fallen in love.

Unless...

In a sudden moment of clarity, Vaughan's eyes widened. "You knew who I was from the very beginning, didn't you?"

Ruby's cheeks turned crimson. She made a sound of distress in the back of her throat. Her hands came up to press against her mouth. When she finally met his gaze, the expression in her eyes was tortured.

"I'm sorry, Vaughan. Please, let me explain."

Shock ricocheted through him. He stared at her in disbelief. "Who are you and what the hell were you doing in Bali?"

"That's exactly what I asked her," Hannah said, coming further into the room. His father crowded in behind her and hurried over to his bed.

"Vaughan! It's so good to see you awake!" Frank said, reaching down and squeezing his arm. Tears shone in his eyes.

Vaughan swallowed past the lump in his throat. His joy at seeing his father again after so long temporarily overrode the shock he felt about Ruby's revelations. "Dad," he croaked.

"Oh, Vaughan," Frank said again, his voice thick with emotion.

"Where's Mom?" Vaughan rasped, still overcome at seeing his family again.

"She's on her way. Hannah and I were at my office in the city when the hospital called, so we got here faster. Your mother's driving in from Broken. She'll be here as soon as she can. We're all so thrilled you're awake! You can't believe how worried we've all been."

Vaughan compressed his lips against another wave of emotion. "Ruby said you and Mom traveled to Bali and arranged to have me brought home."

"Of course," Frank replied.

Vaughan looked at him. "Thank you," he rasped.

His father merely nodded, his lips tightly pressed together. Vaughan could see how hard he was struggling to maintain his composure. Vaughan had never felt so loved. Then his gaze drifted toward Ruby. She stood with her back to him, her arms wrapped around herself. Her shoulders were slumped in defeat.

Guilt stabbed through him, but he swiftly pushed it away. She was the one who'd tricked him. Their so-called chance meeting hadn't been so coincidental after all. She'd known all along who he was and had made it her business to introduce herself. Anger and hurt warred inside him.

He looked at his father and his sister. "Dad. Hannah. It's so good to see you, but if you don't mind, could I ask you both to step outside for a moment? I need a few minutes with Ruby. Alone."

Though Hannah looked like she was about to argue, when his father took her by the arm and led her toward the door, she didn't object. Once they were alone, he pushed through his hurt and anger and spoke.

"That was your plan all along, wasn't it? To snag a wealthy husband."

She spun around. Her eyes blazed. "No, I was there on a holiday, like I told you. Staying at the hotel on the beach. Our meeting that day was nothing more than a coincidence."

"So why did you give me a fake name?"

"Ashworth isn't a fake name," she said tightly. "It's my mother's maiden name. I use it sometimes when I'm traveling overseas." She paused and then rounded on him. "I'm not the only one who was deceptive. Why didn't you tell me who you were? Who your family was?"

Vaughan took his time in responding. "I've lived under the shadow of my family's success all my life. Everyone in Sydney knows the Barrington family name and what it represents. Before I left for Bali, I found out something that turned everything I'd once believed about myself on its head and by the time we met, I was still confused about so many things. On top of that, I wanted you to like me for myself. I wanted to be plain old Vaughan, an easy going guy who worked behind a bar on the beach."

He shook his head. A coldness settled in his heart. The smile he offered her was completely devoid of humor. "But the joke's on me, isn't it? All this time, I thought you'd fallen in love with a stranger. Me. Now I find that's all a lie. All this time, you've known exactly who I am."

"No, you're wrong! Yes, I knew who you were, but that's not why I fell in love with you."

Vaughan regarded her scornfully. "How am I supposed to believe that now?"

Her expression filled with panic. "Because I'm telling the truth!"

Impatience and irritation suddenly flooded through his veins. He'd been lied to so many times. Not only by Ruby, but by the woman who'd been supposed to love him unconditionally. Instead, she'd given him up for adoption at birth and he'd never heard from her again. Until now.

e still hadn't come to terms with the fact Elizabeth Craigdon was his biological mother. That was a battle for another day. He was exhausted, both physically and mentally. The truth was, he was done with it all.

He glared at Ruby. "Enough. I want you to leave."

She gaped. The panic in her eyes intensified. "Vaughan! No! Please, don't do this! I love you! You love me! We're getting married!" She flashed her ring finger in his face. "See! You picked this out yourself. You gave it to me. You told me you'd love me forever."

Her tone had risen to fever pitch in line with the fear and panic in her eyes. For once, her distress failed to move him. With an effort, he turned on his side away from her, without another word. He heard her gasp of shock and disbelief but maintained his position. It was only after the door to his room opened and closed behind her that he eased out his tortured breath and let the tears of anger and hurt escape.

Broken Homes will be released in January, 2023. It is available now for preorder from your favorite digital retailer.

Other books by Chris Taylor

The Munro Family Series
(in order)

The Profiler
The Investigator
The Predator
The Betrayal
The Deception
The Negotiator
The Christmas Vigil (A novella)
The Ransom
The Defendant
The Shooting
The Maker

The Sydney Harbour Hospital Series (in order)

The Perfect Husband

The Body Thief
The Baby Snatchers
The Final Bullet
The Debt Collector
The Lab Test
The Stolen Identity
The Cliff-top Killer
The Likeable Fraudster

The Sydney Legal Series (in order)

An Accidental Murderer
At the Hand of her Father
A Woman Scorned
Lies and Deception
Ordinary Evil
The Ties that Bind
The Perfect Crime
A Toxic Inheritance
Malicious Love

The Craigdon Family Series
(in order)

Callum
Joel
Isabella
Nicholas
Sophia

Flynn
Noah
Logan
Elizabeth

The Barrington Family Series
(in order)

Broken Lives
Broken Promises
Broken Bonds
Broken Spirits
Broken Minds
Broken Vows
Broken Hearts
Broken Dreams
Broken Homes

The Fairfax Family Series (in order)

A Cattleman in Disguise
A Cattleman's Quest
A Cattleman's Daughter
A Cattleman's Secret Baby
To Catch a Cattleman
The Doctor and the Cattleman
To Rescue a Cattleman
A Cattleman's Heart
For the Love of a Cattleman

Bachelors and Brides Series (in order)

Matilda
Austin
Farrah
Benjamin
Verity
Denver
Ebony
Tyrone
Willow

Books by Chris Taylor
Writing as
Bella
Christian

This Is Where It Ends Series
(in order)

Jessie's Story
Ryan's Story
Holly's Story
Sarah's Story
Veronica's Story

Love audiobooks? Check out Chris Taylor Books on audio
iTunes   Audible   Amazon

Join Chris Taylor's Facebook reader group/fan page and be among the first to receive news of book releases, read and review books prior to release and other amazing offers.

Join Now!

Acknowledgments

As usual, no book comes into being without a lot of help and support from my friends and family. A world of thanks must go to my editor, Nancy Cassidy. Thank you for everything that you do to make my stories even more amazing than I could ever dare to dream. To my son, Angus, thank you for your invaluable suggestions and for lending my story credibility. Any mistakes are wholly my own.

To Justin Mendez and all of the team at 100 Covers, thank you for the fantastic book cover. To my sister, Nicole Guihot and to my friend, Ally Thomson, thank you for your excellent editorial comments, proof reading skills and suggestions. I hope you like the final result.

To the fantastic writer organizations such as Romance Writers of Australia, Romance Writers of America and Romance Writers of New Zealand for all the help, support and encouragement they offer new and aspiring writers, including me.

To my readers, thank you for your support and love for my stories. Your encouragement and enjoyment make this journey all worthwhile.

And lastly, to my friends and family, especially my husband and children. Thank you for putting up with late dinners and even later conversations as I've emerged day after day from the sometimes scary but always enthralling world I've created on my computer.

About the Author

Chris Taylor grew up on a farm in north-west New South Wales, Australia. She always had a thirst for stories and recalls writing her first book at the ripe old age of eight. Always a lover of romance and happily-ever-afters, a career in criminal law sparked her interest in intrigue and suspense. For Chris to be able to combine romance with suspense in her books is a dream come true.

Chris is married to Linden and is the mother of five children. If not behind her computer, you can find her doing the school run, taxiing children to swimming lessons, football, ballet and cricket. In her spare time, Chris loves to read her favorite authors who include Richard North Patterson, Sandra Brown, Kathleen E Woodiwiss and Jude Devereaux.

You can find out more about Chris and get a free
book when you sign up for her newsletter at her
website:
http://www.christaylorauthor.com.au

Join Chris on Facebook at:
    https://www.facebook.com/christaylorauthor/